The Education of Aubrey McKee

The Education of Aubrey McKee

a novel by
Alex Pugsley

A John Metcalf Book
BIBLIOASIS
Windsor, Ontario

FIRST EDITION

10 9 8 7 6 5 4 3 2 1

Library and Archives Canada Cataloguing in Publication

Title: The education of Aubrey McKee / Alex Pugsley.
Names: Pugsley, Alex, author.
Identifiers: Canadiana (print) 20230573908 | Canadiana (ebook) 20230573916 |
    ISBN 9781771965835 (softcover) | ISBN 9781771965842 (EPUB)
Classification: LCC PS8631.U445 E38 2024 | DDC C813/.6—dc23

Edited by John Metcalf
Copyedited by John Sweet
Cover and text designed by Ingrid Paulson

Some of this material originally appeared in the following magazines: *The Antigonish Review*, *The New Quarterly*, *The Quarantine Review*, and the *Toronto Journal*.

Published with the generous assistance of the Canada Council for the Arts, which last year invested $153 million to bring the arts to Canadians throughout the country, and the financial support of the Government of Canada. Biblioasis also acknowledges the support of the Ontario Arts Council (OAC), an agency of the Government of Ontario, which last year funded 1,709 individual artists and 1,078 organizations in 204 communities across Ontario, for a total of $52.1 million, and the contribution of the Government of Ontario through the Ontario Book Publishing Tax Credit and Ontario Creates.

PRINTED AND BOUND IN CANADA

For my mother and father

Contents

WE ARRIVED IN THE CITY from places far flung—Halifax, Selkirk, Napanee—and settled somewhere between Kipling and Kennedy. "The city is always full of young worshipful beginners," writes E.B. White, "young actors, young aspiring poets, ballerinas, painters, reporters, singers—each depending on his own brand of tonic to stay alive, each with his own stable of giants." Calvin Dover, Gudrun Peel, Quincy Tynes, and I were several such worshipful beginners. We were all in exile. It was exhilarating. Everyone invented themselves. There was no history. No one seemed to have a family. We were beginning relationships with new mothers, Memory and Necessity, and everyone reconceived themselves as they wished. People named Sharon changed their name to Pagan or Jonathan or Fucknuts von Trapp. We began to create, ideate, interact. We auditioned. We interviewed. We catered, we waitered, we borrowed our rents. We designed buttons, gave readings, wrote screenplays on spec. Started zines, put on shows, delivered demos, amassed portfolios, rode bikes, crashed open mics, drank beer, stayed up too late. We were, as undergroundlings everywhere, a crew of newbies sort of hopeful, sort of faithful, and sort of making out with someone in a darkened alley. With various destinies available, just who would we become?

— 1 —

The Calvin Dover *Show*

CALVIN DOVER WAS WONDERFUL. I loved Calvin Dover. He was absurd and gruff and brilliant and responsible for a large part of my adult brain. I was one of the writers on his sketch comedy series *The Calvin Dover Show*, which ran for one under-the-radar season on a Canadian cable network. A year after the show was cancelled, and six months after stints at *Letterman* and *SNL*, Calvin went to Los Angeles for pilot season, got a starring role on a sitcom called *Oodles and Smidge*, and vanished into all things Hollywood. Communications since have been fitful. I hadn't heard from him in a year when out of the blue an email arrived. "Eekcm! Ima get on a plane and fly to da Big Smoke. See u Friday? Lub-blub. Nivlac."

He was in Toronto promoting the sitcom's third season, staying at the Sutton Place, and, as the curtain rises on this rainy evening, I am waiting for him sixteen streets away in what, for most of the year, is the parking lot of the Tranzac Club but which, during the Toronto Fringe Festival, is a licensed patio known as the Fringe tent. It's the first Friday of the festival and I sit at a picnic table festooned with flyers and postcards advertising some of the festival's hundred or so productions. A quick sampling includes *Throwing Up Skipper, Hamilcar Barcalounger, Twat Honkers, Prima Donna Ding-a-ling, Halfway to Fuck It,* and *Hail to Thee Drunk Moron.*

There is at Fringe festivals generally a spirit of randomness and adventure, everyone is looking for some kind of magic, and, as I see Calvin jump out of a stretch limousine on Brunswick Street, I realize I'm sort of looking for something from him, too, though what that is I couldn't tell you.

"Hey, McKee," he says, "you Fringe tent slut. How long does it take to get to the airport from here?"

"On Friday? An hour."

"My flight's at eleven-fifty. So—" Calvin checks the time on his cellphone. "I got to be done by nine."

He returns to the limousine, speaks to the driver, and takes from the passenger cabin a cellophane-wrapped gift basket and a bottle of Fiji water. With these in hand, he trots towards me. He has recently shaved his head—his skull and beard at a six-day stubble—and wears an inside-out T-shirt, torn jeans with a wallet chain, and scuffed brogues with no socks. All this slovenliness is a front, you should know, because Calvin is a truly quick person, his pale blue eyes alert to any change in his environment.

"So—" Calvin sets his items on the picnic table. "You want this gift basket? I can't take it on the plane."

I glance at its contents—a giant Toblerone bar, Asian pears, and Carr's Table Water Crackers, among other foodstuffs—and ask how it's going in LA.

"Great," says Calvin, sitting down. "Except for the occasional heart attack. Heart attacks and vaginal rejuvenation. That's what it's all about."

"And how's the wife? Is Annabel here?"

Calvin's wife had perfect brown hair, small hoop earrings, and seemed to me sleekly feminine. She used to watch the tapings with my ex-girlfriend in the green room, making sarcastic comments about everything, and for a moment I recall the thrill of writing for that comedy show, the different sketches and characters, and all that unsupervised creative excitement.

"Nah." Calvin speedily shakes his head. "She's in LA."

"Is she good?"

"She's good. Just got a promotion at work." Calvin looks around the patio. "So do we go inside to order?"

The server on the patio is a theatre piece in her own right. Her name is Emma Follows and I took an acting class with her when she was known as Trish Follows. At that time, she was dark-haired, faintly plump, and stalled in an unhappy relationship. Tonight, she has a platinum pixie cut, she's slim and vaguely single. She wears a sleeveless black frock with a daring side-slit and there's an elegance to her movement as if, at some time in her youth, she apprenticed with the National Ballet School and I half expect to see, as she checks on a far table, her fingers spread in an upflare. Emma Follows, as you may have gathered, is rather instantly noticeable, but, as she stands at our table in third position, Calvin seems scarcely aware of her presence.

"You need a drinks menu?" she asks. "Or do you know what you'd like?"

"I do know what I like," says Calvin, inspecting the flyer for *Throwing Up Skipper*. "I like tigers and dinosaurs and pictures of rainbows."

"Right," Emma says blandly. "You want a rainbow?"

"For every storm I suffer, maybe."

I raise a finger. "I'll have another ginger ale."

"What?" Calvin glares at me. "You can't *not* drink, motherfucker. How often am I in Toronto?"

"I'm sort of not drinking."

"Listen to you. 'I'm sort of not drinking.' I got two hours in this town. You're drinking." Calvin passes Emma a Gold Visa card. "He's drinking. Let's start with two Kilkenny."

Emma dips her head. "We don't have Kilkenny."

"Of course you have Kilkenny. I came here for Kilkenny. This is the Fringe tent sponsored by Kilkenny."

"Maybe ten years ago it was."

"What're you saying?" Calvin looks around, bewildered. "Everything's *changed* now?"

"We have Amsterdam Blonde, Amsterdam Nut Brown, Harp Lager—"

"Please—" Calvin lifts a hand in protest. "Don't say any more beer names. I don't want to hear word descriptions of any more beer names. Just two pints of whatever. Harp Lager."

Emma gives Calvin a you-might-be-more-interesting-than-I-thought glance, then neatly turns to her left and strides away.

"McKee," says Calvin, picking up the Fiji water, "our waitress has the most beautiful legs I've ever seen."

"Emma Follows."

"Does she?" Calvin opens the Fiji water and brings it to his mouth. "And how do you know Emma follows?"

"She's an actress from Montr—"

Calvin spit-takes the Fiji water. "An *actress?*" He wipes his lips. "Where the fuck have you brought me?"

"This is the Fringe tent. It's part of a theatre festival."

Calvin considers the other patrons. "Do you mean to say that *all* of these women—"

"And all of these men—"

"Are *actors?*" Calvin replaces the cap on the Fiji water. "Ah, yes, I remember now. Look there—" He nods at a woman three tables away. "Red hair, peasant blouse. She's a drama major open to life and looking for an agent." He examines another. "And there? Nose ring on the outside, anarchy on the inside? She's going to do Brecht any way she can. And everyone's got a show at the Fringe."

"After this, they go to Lee's Palace and dance in bare feet."

"Wow." Calvin sighs. "We're oldsters. We're middle-aged. It's not all keggers and random hookups anymore."

"Speak for yourself. I like keggers."

Calvin's cellphone rings. He pulls it from his pocket, checks the call display, and answers. He listens a few seconds then tells the person he'll call back.

"Annabel?" I ask.

"Paula," he says. "The publicist."

"How's Paula the publicist?"

"She wants to know how the day went."

"How'd the day go?"

"Fucking exhausting. I was up at five for a radio thing. It was one of those"—Calvin adopts an overexcited announcer voice—"'Bowser and the Bear!' morning shows. Then eTalk, Movie Television. Plus a bunch of phoners."

"But you're done?"

"Canada's done. Paula's trying to organize a day of American media. She's pitching 'Us Weekly' and 'InStyle.' But you have to have a nice house for 'InStyle.'"

"You do have a nice house."

"Yeah?" says Calvin, watching Emma approach with two pints of Harp Lager. "I don't know if I do."

Emma places the pints on the picnic table beside the gift basket. "You want to run a tab, right? So I should put these on your card?"

"Hey," says Calvin, "I see you're checking out my basket."

"Nope." Emma makes an odd smirk. "Can't say I was."

"If you want the Toblerone, you can totally have the Toblerone."

"Yeah, no. I'm good. Thanks."

Up to this point, Emma has had an aura of indifference—as if involvement with anyone requires energy she's too bored to muster—but I sense from her now a sparkle of quizzicality. Which might be why, after stepping away, she spins back to ask Calvin, "Have we met before?"

"I don't think so."

"You seem really familiar to me."

"I get that all the time. I kind of look like the guy in high school who was in the car accident that later turns out to be gay."

"No," says Emma. "We didn't go to the same high school. But I've seen you before." She frowns. "Did you go to Banff for musical theatre?"

"Nope."

"Mmm. It'll come to me. I just don't know when."

"Jesus." Calvin stares with worried eyes into his Harp Lager. "This is going to be an emotional roller coaster."

After Emma leaves, he nods at the *Toronto Star* scattered on the picnic table and asks, "Why are you looking at apartments?"

"Because I'm looking at apartments. There's a two-bedroom on Euclid for sixteen hundred. But I can't afford it. I'd need a roommate."

Reaching for his pint, Calvin says, "What about Emma?"

"Totally. We took an acting class together. But I think we're the perfect match. In fact, I've got an apartment all lined up. Here's the nightie I want you to wear—"

"It looked good on my last girlfriend—"

"It looked great on my mom—"

Calvin snorts. "Cheers, motherfucker." He clanks my pint. "Good to see you, McKee."

As his cellphone rings again, thunderclaps explode overhead, downpours resume, and the canvas tent-tops fill with rainwater.

"Sorry to be a jerk," says Calvin, reading the call display. "But I have to take this."

He moves inside, away from the storm, and it's my turn to survey the surrounding area. With the recent cloudburst, the Fringe tent has filled and the game I've been playing, in which

I'm auditioning to be the Cutest Person Present, is no longer even remotely plausible, so attractive the competition has become. I am looking at these Fringers—in their tank tops, cut-offs, and sandals—and wondering if I will ever go on a date again, when a flyer for another production is dropped on the picnic table.

It's a Pick-of-the-Fringe show called *Devil in the Dark: A Star Trek Musical*. The flyer shows a blonde woman—dressed in the gold tunic of the original series—aiming a phaser at the viewer. This woman is vaguely familiar to me.

While I am reading her name, Calvin returns from his call and sits down with a scowl. "Everything okay?" I ask.

"Yeah." He drinks from his pint. "I have an audition in LA, but the casting director's changed it three times. It was last week. It's next week. It's tomorrow. It's stupid."

"What's it for?"

He shrugs. "I might be Hoss in the new 'Bonanza' movie."

"There's a 'Bonanza' movie?"

"If it goes"—he glances at me—"I'd get four hundred grand for six weeks. Doesn't the money blow your mind?"

"Um, *yeah*. It doesn't seem real."

"I know. It's like when Farley got six million for 'Beverly Hills Ninja.' Everyone was like, 'What the fuck?'" Calvin examines what's left of his pint. "But I'll never get it. I'm up against some big-deal actors. Matt LeBlanc. Kiefer Sutherland. People actually know those guys."

"People don't know Oodles?"

"People in jail, maybe."

I pass Calvin the flyer for *Devil in the Dark*. "Remember her?" Glancing at it, Calvin carelessly shakes his head.

"That's Peyton Dean."

"Are you out of your mind?" asks Calvin. "Peyton Dean is one of the most gorgeous women we'll ever know."

"Ten years ago she was. Our friends aren't twenty-six any-more."

Calvin turns the flyer over and reads the cast list. "Jesus Christ, that's Peyton Dean," he says. "She was like Belinda Carlisle in the 'Mad About You' video! What the hell happened?"

"She was in 'Mamma Mia!' last year."

"And now she's doing a Fringe play?"

"It's all good. Everybody wins."

"Oh my God." Calvin sadly drops the flyer. "That's Peyton Dean."

EMMA FOLLOWS RETURNS to the patio. She wears a bicycle helmet and carries a copy of *NOW* magazine, the cover of which features a photograph of Calvin and the cutline "Oodles Brings It Home." Emma throws it down on the picnic table, much in the manner of a prosecuting attorney dropping Exhibit A in front of a jury, and asks, "So you're some big-shot TV star, is that it?"

"Um," says Calvin, "just trying to finish a Harp Lager, actually."

"You're in that sitcom with the alien?"

"I like to think of him as my friend."

"I haven't seen it. The bartender told me. I don't have a TV."

"Who needs a TV when you have a bicycle and a degree in musical theatre?"

"Emma," I say lightly, "this is my friend Calvin."

"Well, tell your friend Calvin his bill's been paid."

"What?" Calvin spit-takes a sip of beer. "Emma, what the heck?"

"My shift is done." She drops his Gold Visa card on the picnic table. "So there's your rainbow."

"Christ on the cross," says Calvin, disgusted. "What kind of human being *are* you?" He motions to the downpour. "And where are you going? It almost seems like you're cycling some-where. In your helmet. And defiance."

"Why?" Emma arches an eyebrow. "You have a car?"

"Well—" Calvin turns to me. "We could probably just take the limo."

Emma splutters, as if in response to a lame joke, but then, spotting the limousine on Brunswick, she asks, "You have a fucking limo?"

"Tonight I do."

"Sick," says Emma, bringing a hand to her chin to unfasten her helmet. "Give me two seconds. I'll meet you in the limo."

A frisson of intimacy has arrived in the air and, as I finish my pint, I am thinking to ask Calvin what his intentions are regarding this young woman when he becomes newly absorbed in the *Devil in the Dark* flyer. On its flip side is an image of a molten-looking space creature called the Horta. Calvin spreads his fingers above this image and, as if in the midst of a partic-ularly demanding mind-meld, pretends to be in sudden agony. "Pain!" he says, closing his eyes and jerking his head to the side. *"Pain!"*

•

THIS IS A CHRONICLE of Calvin Dover, but as you may be coming into this cold, and because my night with him sets in motion a number of adult-strength themes relating to romance, realization, and the problematics of involvement— all of which play out in upcoming instalments—it might be helpful to know a little about the chronicler, that is to say, me, thirtysomething Aubrey McKee. It's fifteen years since my last appearance, when I was a drunken man on a Halifax pier, and after fleeing that city, I became deeply entangled in Toronto with a woman from whom I have recently split. So I am, in a word, incomplete. I live in an extended remix of my own glumness and, to be honest, Calvin is one of the few people in the world I look forward to seeing.

We met in residence at the University of Toronto. I was from Nova Scotia, Calvin from Ontario. His family owned Adanac Packaging, a plastic wrapping company with offices in Calgary, Brandon, and Pickering. Calvin's visits home were mostly for holiday dinners and his little brother's hockey games. He and his brother had a private language where Calvin was Nivlac and Brian was Nairb and knits were stink. So the Dovers were rich and Calvin, presumably, could return and live in suburban comfort any day he wished. But he didn't. He stayed in town and played Tetris and read *Neuromancer*. He joined Theatresports. In certain moods he had a lunatic brightness—reminiscent of a kid I knew in childhood—and his thoughts flashed with lively invention.

Invention was often followed by Reverie, so I'm not surprised—when I join Calvin in the limousine—to find him zoned out beside his gift basket. Without altering his eyeline, he shifts the gift basket to make room for me and I recall how Calvin is always thinking of other people, whether they're sixteen streets, three time zones, or two feet away. Palpable in all directions is Calvin's respect for other spirits, and as this night goes forward, you should take for granted his interest in the common good. As Dodokin, another writer on *The Calvin Dover Show*, put it, "The fucked-up thing about Calvin is he thinks he's everyone's father." Applicable, too, is my ex-girlfriend's assessment: "Very funny, very generous, and very complicated."

"HEY, WARDELL—" CALVIN bends forward to talk to the driver. "We're going to drop off some people before the airport. You cool with that?"

"Not a problem, boss," says Wardell. "Everything criss."

"The person we're waiting for," continues Calvin, "it's a woman. I don't know if you've ever been in that situation."

A gruff chortle rises from Wardell, as if he knows only too well what such waiting implies, and for a moment we three share in an understanding of the women-dependent meanings that can seem to swirl beneath all social relations.

"So the promotion Annabel got," I say, sitting down in the back, "what's it for? Social work?"

"Art therapy." Calvin lowers an electric window. "Palliative care with the elderly. She helps them draw pictures of the pony they're going to ride to heaven on." He blows an imaginary dust speck from his hand. "What about you? Do you see Gudrun?"

"Uh—no."

"Ever talk to her?"

"No."

"Huh." Calvin slowly nods—as if I've made a surprising, but possibly very relevant, comment regarding the laws of the universe—and then pats my knee. "Probably a good thing. I mean, Gudrun? Gudrun was bright. God, she's bright. No, she's great except for the occasional lesbian affair."

There is a squeal from the patio and we turn to see Emma standing at the edge of the Fringe tent. Although the rain has subsided, the furls of the tent-top have swelled with pooling rainfall and Emma, wary of the slops of water, now makes a mad dash for the limousine. As she bounces inside, I see she has freshened her lipstick and there is a brazenness to her energy.

"I just did two bar shots," she says, pushing a hand through her damp pixie cut. She points at the mini-bar. "The bar open?"

"Drink your face off, crazy lady," says Calvin.

Emma shares with Wardell her destination—an opening night party on Dupont Street—and takes a champagne flute from a velvet glass-holder.

At the intersection with Bathurst, a squeegee kid in a soggy hoodie appears and wipes at the limousine's rain-splashed windshield.

"Ew," says Emma, opening a bottle of Prosecco. "That guy's disgusting."

"I don't know," Calvin says philosophically. "I mean, he's drunk. He pooped his pants. But at least he's in the moment, Emma. Can we say that?"

"Speak for yourself," I say. "I pooped my pants."

The light turns green, the limousine turns right, and the squeegee kid lurches backwards, his sleeve leaving a grimy smear on the windshield.

"And so," says Calvin, craning his neck to watch him, "our little homeless entrepreneur returns to the madcap world of Bloor Street West."

Emma is staring at Calvin, beginning to appreciate the workings of his mind, perhaps, or simply noting Calvin's eyes, which, in beaming summer sunlight, are Samoyed blue.

"So hey," she says, "you were nominated for an Emmy?"

"That's me. Two-time Emmy nominee."

"What's that like?"

"Pretty special," says Calvin. "You sit there for three hours to learn you lost to the guy from 'Ally McBeal.' But here's a question—" Calvin nods at a bluebird tattoo on Emma's upper arm. "Would you ever get another tat?"

"Maybe."

"What would you get?"

"I don't know." Emma pours herself a glass of Prosecco. "I don't want to get something gay. Like, I don't want to get a quotation."

"Quotations are so gay," says Calvin, nodding his head. "What about a werewolf? Like a werewolf riding a Pegasus!"

"A what?"

"Or maybe a squirrel giving the finger. Right smack in the middle of your back."

The limousine arrives at the Dupont address. It's a century-old warehouse converted into office units where some tenants, Emma's friends among them, are living illegally.

"Where have you taken us?" asks Calvin. "Whose party is this?"

"My friend Mike. From Guelph."

"Mike from Guelph—" Calvin nods as if Emma has added new and relevant information regarding the laws of the universe. "Nice."

"Why? You want to go?"

"Calvin would *love* to go," I tell Emma. "But he's on his way to the airport."

"Or he's too pussy to go."

"Let me see if I understand this," says Calvin. "You want us to crash some sleazy artistic party? Mike from Guelph may not be cool with that."

"Want me to ask?"

"I think it's the appropriate thing to do, don't you?"

"Fine," says Emma, pulling on the door handle. "And if you're not here when I get back, I'll know you pussied out."

"Don't roll your eyes at me, young lady."

Emma inserts her empty flute into the glass-holder and then, after a provocative glance at Calvin, bobs out the door.

"So, Calvin?" I say. "Stupid question—"

"There are no stupid questions. Just stupid people."

"You sure you know what you're doing?"

"That's right, Aubrey. Turn it into a problem."

"You're the guy who's flying to LA."

"You're the guy who needs a roommate. It's just an actor party." Calvin grabs the open bottle of Prosecco. "What could possibly go wrong?"

— 17 —

I'VE ALWAYS BEEN jealous of Calvin Dover because I've always wondered if I could do what he's done. Write for *Letterman*. Write for *SNL*. Star in a sitcom. So my reaction follows from this derring-do as well as his ability to walk into a hall of three hundred strangers and within twelve minutes have them all wildly laughing. I don't care who you are—circuit judge, theologian, tugboat captain—such talent is a wizardry. As indicated, Calvin's quixotics belong to the rhythms of his moods, which might be why, after Emma leads us into the party, he lingers in the outside hallway. When I check on him, he's either talking on his cellphone or picking up an empty pizza carton so he can scribble down a note or number. Finally, after twenty minutes, he joins the party—jittery, distracted—impatient for the moment to be broken by some antic turn of event.

"Yo, bro," says a heavy-set man in a Maple Leafs jersey. "You're the guy from TV? Calvin Driver? I'm Mike."

"Mike from Guelph?" Calvin fist-bumps him. "That's what I'm talking about."

"So, Calvin—" Mike watches Calvin take a Coors Light from the refrigerator. "What do you call a guy with no arms and no legs nailed to the wall?"

Calvin turns to him, delighted. "You're seriously telling me this joke right now?"

"Art," says Mike.

"Mike from Guelph *crushes* it," says Calvin, giggling. "A laser from the big man."

"Wait," says Mike. "What do you call a guy with no arms and no legs water-skiing?" Mike smirks. "Skip. What do you call—"

"No, Mike," says Calvin, "Mike from Guelph. I got one. What do you call a guy with no arms and no legs trying to answer the phone?"

Mike shrugs.

"Gerald," Calvin says simply.

"Huh? I don't get it."

"Well, that's actually his name. His name *is* Gerald. And the thing is, he can't answer the phone because he has no arms and no legs. He just knocks it over. Fucking *Gerald,* man." Calvin smiles at the room. "Anyone need a beer?"

Something in the night is appealing to Calvin. What it is, I'm not sure. It might be the result of his finishing that bottle of Prosecco, or swiftly drinking three Coors Light, or his oblique admiration for Emma's pixie cut, but, whatever it is, when I find him on the fire escape, sharing a joint with a young woman with a lip piercing, I can tell for Calvin some happy illogicality has begun.

"Anyway, this piece I'm workshopping," says the woman, "it's basically like I don't think there *is* a true personality to be expressed."

"Right," Calvin says thoughtfully. "We have no self. No one is a person. Wow."

"Because we kind of become the mask we put on."

"How true. How sad." He takes the joint from her. "And yet how human."

"I also have a movement piece I almost have a finished version of. The concept of it, it's pretty out there, and my friend's choreographing something for me for this benefit. What about you?"

"Me?"

"What is he telling you?" interrupts Emma as she steps onto the fire escape, one hand held behind her back. "Because everything he says is a lie."

"Oh, hey." Calvin moves the joint in a strange pattern in the air. "You guys know each other?"

"I actually don't know *your* name," says the other woman.

"That's Calvin Dover," Emma says.

"Calvin Dover. Why do I know that name? Do you know Tippy Friedrich?"

"No way!" Calvin drags on the joint. "You know Tippy?"

"Because I feel like I know you."

"You may have seen me," says Calvin, returning the joint. "I'm in the touring production of 'Stomp.'"

"Holy Mother of God," says Emma, half closing her eyes. "Don't listen to him."

"Okay, Emma?" Calvin pokes her shoulder. "What's up? Because it's starting to get really weird between us."

"Okay, Mr. Crazy—" Emma grabs his poking finger and from behind her back produces a tall can of Kilkenny. "Look what I found."

"Emma!" says Calvin. "You amazing space elf!"

"A what?" She swings the Kilkenny away. "Did you just call me a *space* elf? You're a freak."

"It's true," says Calvin, shrugging at the other woman. "I'm a super freak. But here's a question. Has weed changed? Because this shit's ridiculous. Like I'm flying right now. No, Emma? I'm freaking out. I'm going to have a seizure, I swear to God." Calvin lifts up his T-shirt, reaches for Emma's hand, and places it on his chest. "Feel how fast my heart's beating right now."

"Uh, *no*." Emma pulls her hand back, appalled. "Think about where you are."

"So um—" The other woman waggles her finger at Calvin and Emma. "How long have you two been going out?"

"We're not going *out*," Emma says quickly, as if the idea were repulsive. "We only met an hour ago."

"You met an *hour* ago?"

Emma turns sharply to Calvin. "Does this normally work for you?" she asks.

"If you're asking if this is normal for me, no. This is once-in-a-lifetime."

"I mean does this routine work on other women?"

"What other women?" Calvin gazes soulfully at Emma. "There are no other women. At least"—he takes her hand and holds it to the stubble of his cheek—"not to me."

"*Ew,*" says Emma, yanking her hand away and trying not to laugh. "Just—no. Stop. Gross."

Inside, a doorbell rings and Calvin, as if resigned to the day's eventualities, sighs and moves towards the door. "All right, Follows. Where'd you find the Kilkenny?"

"You're so smart, you find it."

"You think I know where everything is?" Stepping inside, Calvin spins around to face her. "Who am I—Mariah Carey? No, Emma, I'm not Mariah Carey. I can't see into the future and I don't know where everything is."

At the front door, Mike talks with a deliveryman who holds by its straps a very full pizza bag.

"What the fuck?" asks Mike. "Did someone order ten pizzas?"

"Mike," Calvin says. "Mike from Guelph, I'm on it."

"You fucking didn't," says Emma, following Calvin inside. "You bought those, didn't you?"

"Don't take it personal, Em." Calvin signs for the pizzas. "But you got beat by emcee Cee."

"This is because I paid your bill, isn't it?"

"Shit got real." Calvin carries the ten pizzas to the kitchen. "Shit just got real." He slides them onto a counter and checks the time on his cellphone. "Okay, kids. Have fun in your craptastic suck world. I'm out of here. Let me get a pizza for Wardell."

"Wait," says Emma, tugging on his T-shirt. "I'll walk you out."

At the limousine, Calvin places a pizza in the passenger seat. Then, pulling his plane ticket from his back pocket, he checks which terminal he's flying from.

"Calvin," says Emma, skipping up to him. "I want you to star in my short film."

"Uh-huh. Do I wear an eye patch?"

"You'd play my ex-boyfriend."

"So I *do* wear an eye patch."

"Can I email you the script?"

"I see where this is going. If you want my email, just have the balls to ask for my email."

"Or actually," says Emma, uncapping her lipstick, "you can just email me." She takes Calvin's plane ticket, writes her email address in red lipstick, and passes it back to him. Staring into his eyes for a flirtsome moment, she kisses his cheek, twirls around, and runs past me and back to the party.

As enchanting as this rom-com moment seems, it rather provokes in me a feeling of loss, and as the skies begin to pour again, I thank Calvin for a wonderful evening, yelling over another crack of thunder, and set off for Dupont station.

Behind me, I hear a burst of honking from the departing limousine, and when I turn around, I see Calvin on the sidewalk holding his gift basket.

"So, buddy," he says, "you up for one last drink?"

•

I WILL SEE Calvin Dover often in later life—chasing after a springer spaniel on the Venice Beach boardwalk, at his mother's memorial service at Pickering Village United Church, making his triumphant return to stand-up at Largo—but most memorable to me is this random night in July when, instead of getting myself comfortably home, I choose to walk the streets with him in drenching rain.

"Calvin," I say, "how drunk are you?"

"Drunk? I'm ripped to the tits."

"Don't you have to be in LA? What about Hoss?"

"Fuck Hoss. Let Kiefer be Hoss. He can gain fifty pounds and win the Golden Globe." He studies Emma's email address on his plane ticket. "Yeah? Like I'm going to star in your short film." He scrunches it up, pitches it into the rain, and watches an older couple scurry towards a taxi on the other side of Dupont. "Look at those weather-beaten pedestrians. Fuck them. Fuck them ragged."

Calvin is crazed, disinhibited, and without warning he sprints south, running so fast he stumbles, splashing into a deep puddle and collapsing to one knee. Jumping up, he holds his gift basket as if it were a machine gun and shoots at different spots in the street—a stop sign, a mailbox—and then he's off and running again.

I struggle to keep up, my clothes sopping, my loafers squashing, understanding that for some reason my friend *has* to do this. Do not think I am happy. For some blocks I fantasize having a firm Granny Smith apple, which—when I furiously throw it—hits Calvin smack in the temple. But in these wet minutes I only follow along, sensing my role has shifted from Drinking Buddy to Psychiatric Nurse.

Finally, on the other side of Bloor Street, Calvin slows to a walk. Although he is sodden and his T-shirt soaked to transparency, he raises the gift basket over his head as a rain cover.

"Those kids at the party," he says, "they're kind of heartbreaking. They have no clue what'll happen in the next ten years. They're still like, 'Theatre's the only thing that matters!'" He smiles. "Remember when we'd finish a taping? I loved those nights. We'd go to a bar on Queen Street, someone would be visiting from Montreal, and six hours later I'm pissing in Kensington Market."

"Sounds magical."

Calvin burps. "You ever see Jib and Dodokin?"

"Jib's in suburbia. Dodokin at Second City."

"Pete Zhu?"

"Not since they had a baby. But I don't really see those people anymore. That time you're talking about, when we were doing the show, that was a really fun time for everyone. But that doesn't exist anymore. You think it does because you left when it was still going on. But it's gone for me too."

"Everything's changed now?"

"Kind of."

"Fuck," says Calvin. "You're on and off the shelves so fast. Soon I'll be past my expiry. Like Peyton Dean. And this river of money is going to end."

"Calvin, you're on a main network sitcom."

"Yeah, I'm kind of not." He squints. "Remember first season when they sent the whole cast to the upfronts? Now it's just me. The show won't get renewed, I can feel it. And if I don't book a gig soon, I'm fucked."

"You're not fucked."

"Yeah. Something I didn't mention." He glances at me. "Annabel and I are splitting up."

"What do you mean? It's over?"

"Oh, it's over, dude. My lawyer told me not to talk to her anymore."

"You have a lawyer?"

"Her father hired this high-powered divorce firm? It's fucking hardball. I could owe her thirty grand a month for the rest of my life."

"That's not possible."

"Even if the show's cancelled, I'd still owe her half what I made when we were together." Calvin notices my look of utter bafflement. "Look, I'm contesting it. Trying to pay in a lump sum. But this legal stuff? It's not as fun as it sounds. It's actually pretty stressful."

"Calvin, I had no idea."

"No one did." Rain drips off the end of Calvin's nose. "We fought almost every day. Every day. Then I thought, 'I can't do this anymore. I can't spend the rest of my life fighting.' So two years ago, I stopped."

"So that was good?"

"No. Wasn't good. We stopped fighting, we stopped having sex. We had sex once in two years."

"I thought she wanted to have kids!"

"Before we got married she did. Changed her mind." He wipes his face. "Gets worse. When we bought the house, my folks gave me money for a down payment? Annabel paid into the mortgage, I paid into the mortgage. So it's a co-owned asset. Which means we split it in a divorce. If I want to keep it, I'd have to buy her half. That's another six hundred grand."

"So maybe you don't have a nice house?"

"Maybe I don't."

"Holy fuck. So Annabel's a millionaire now?"

"Listen, I'll give her everything. The house. The leaf blower. I just want my clothes." Calvin is abstracted for a few moments. "Annabel didn't have much of a childhood. She didn't get along with her mother. But when we got married, it was the happiest day of my life. Aubrey, you were there. You saw." Calvin is crying now, his tears mixing with the rain. "But I just couldn't do it anymore."

I watch my friend weep. I will spare the reader my rather extensive introspections—I thought if you were successfully funny then your life would be wonderful—and simply say I had much to learn.

"Calvin, I am so sorry, dude."

"So am I." He manages a smile. "It's bizarre I have to come to Toronto to talk. People in LA, they just want to hear good news. No one wants to hear about a nightmare. So you act like there isn't one. But my heart's been so twisted with this shit—" He sniffles. "I mean, it's funny? Except it's not funny."

"It's anti-humour."

"Yeah," says Calvin. "It's anti-humour."

WE'RE SOMEWHERE ON Harbord when Calvin takes a turn down Lippincott. At a certain fire hydrant, he walks between two houses and into a backyard containing a coach house, a concrete bird bath, and an upended shopping cart. He holds the gift basket under one arm and—returning to his earlier impulsiveness—bangs on the door with his fist.

"Calvin," I say, "what're you doing?"

"Waking up Nairb." Calvin opens the letter slot, bends down, and yells, "Get up, idiot!"

"He's in Toronto?"

A light flickers on and Brian Dover, no longer a hockey-playing kid but a slim hipster with an auburn goatee, comes to the door and ushers us in.

The rooms are oddly furnished—mismatched chairs, stolen garden gnomes, a mandala tapestry pinned over the front windows—but splendidly clean.

Calvin sniffs the air. "Why does it smell like Mom and Dad's house?"

"Eulene was here."

"You little fruitcake," says Calvin. "You got their house-keeper to clean your place?" He belches. "Where's the beer?"

Pleading with us to be quiet because his girlfriend is asleep, Brian directs us to the kitchen. We are given bottles of Heineken. A glass bong is produced. I sit at a slanting kitchen table as Calvin launches into a giddy description of the party and a pitch-perfect imitation of Mike from Guelph. After some minutes I am noticing that the meniscus of my beer is about seven degrees off the horizon, and realizing the entire house is on a tilt, when Brian points upward.

"Yo," he says. "Want to go to the room?"

"The room!" says Calvin, his eyes pink from a bong hit. "Let's go to the room."

Brian guides us to an attic loft, empty except for a stereo system, two giant speakers, and three La-Z-Boy recliners.

Calvin lounges in the recliner closest to the speakers, the gift basket held to his chest. I sit behind him, a Heineken in my lap.

Brian switches off the overhead light, revealing hundreds of little glow-in-the-dark stars on the ceiling. He inserts a compact disc and now begins a musical voyage, Brian playing obscure electronica, Calvin and I travelling within their floaty soundscapes.

I cannot finish my Heineken. Very soon, I doze off.

When I awake, we are still in the dark.

"Play it, Nairb," says Calvin, gazing at the stars. "You know the one."

Brian changes the music and on comes a mixtape—a recording of William Shatner performing the Beatles and Elton John in lushly orchestrated arrangements. The songs are astonishing and ridiculous, Shatner forcing emphasis into spoken lyrics like "kaleidoscope eyes" and "rocking horse people."

After some seconds of reverent silence, Calvin convulses with sudden laughter. Something about Shatner's repetition of "I'm a rocket man" sends Calvin into hysterics, his recliner tottering on the sloping floor, and as it topples sideways, he and the gift basket topple with it.

The instant it collides with the floor, the gift basket, arranged and paid for by the Disney ABC Television Group in Burbank, California, splits open and its entire contents—a Toblerone bar, six Asian pears, Carr's Table Water Crackers, Tazo Zen green tea, Napa Valley Honey Mustard Sourdough Nuggets, saltwater taffy, Ghiradelli chocolate cocoa, Wolfgang Puck European-style coffee, Baci chocolate pralines, and a truckle of pecorino cheese—spill in all directions.

Calvin is twisting and laughing on the floor, declaring Shatner a genius, when his fingers find and close around an Asian pear and as the curtain falls on this performance of *The Calvin Dover Show*, let's leave him there, this moment convincing me, more than ever, that Calvin Dover is wonderful. I love Calvin Dover.

The
Poet

1

---

poem
for dalton h

again
> i just can't
> i just can't tell you
>> you make me weak
>> you make me   want
>> you make me   kiss
>> you
>>>> over and
>>>> over and
>>>> over

again

THE POEM WAS ridiculous. I read it once and hated it. I can't explain exactly *why* it disturbed me with irritation—the lower-case letters, the cryptic initial in the dedication, the pink staples of the zine's binding—I just knew for me it wouldn't do. Female singer-songwriters were everywhere that summer, a lot of passion and glub fermenting into and out of various music festivals, and it seemed to me that young poets were collapsing into feuds or clinics on every other street corner.

I threw the zine at the kitchen window. It caromed off the windowsill and fell to the floor, pages fluttering. At the time,

I was in a shabby, cat-pee-smelling apartment in the McGill student ghetto. This was April 1986. I was with my sort-of ex-girlfriend, Gail, who turned to ask, "Why the fuck did you do that?"

"Because that's the stupidest concrete poetry crap I've ever read. How does that junk even get published?"

"*I* published it," Gail said angrily. "I'm the editor. Have you not been listening to anything I've said?"

It was true Gail had been babbling for some minutes about the politicking on the editorial board of the university literary magazine, an organization she'd recently quit, but I was only just registering that she'd created in response an upstart feminist zine called—I leaned over the table to read the cover—*Cinnamon Dip*.

"So the party tonight," I said, "it's for the launch of 'Cinnamon Dip?'"

Gail nodded.

"And over and over is going to be there?"

"Her name's Gudrun. And she's in first year. So give her a break."

"Yeah? I'm not sure it's my scene."

"Well, I know it's mine. Because I'm the editor. And just so you know, we're totally broken up."

LOOKING AT *Cinnamon Dip* now—it resides in a bookshelf of zines, chapbooks, monographs, performance programs, film festival catalogues, and other personal ephemera—I find I have new affection for its contributors. To consider gudrun peel, kat culkin, Zarqa Khan-Zwicky, Izzy Wichita, cloudpowder, Leela N'dbela, and Mary Felkin Peabody is to consider them as they were then—hurrying across the McGill campus without a coat, following an owl's progress over the McLennan Library, blackening a spiral-bound notebook with sudden inspiration. For these were their innocent, anarchic undergraduate years, a time before anyone had a car or credit card, before anyone had published a book or been married or divorced or hospitalized. In the next decades, a spate of episode would carry them into purposes mostly hidden from these, their younger selves. So reading their poems and prose pieces again, and thinking of who they were and what they dreamed on, I find I am fondly nostalgic for their frizzy hair and flannel pajama bottoms, their end-of-term cramming and independent study projects. But at the time, no. The young lunk I was resisted such a congregation of female creativity, intimacy, and identity.

Later that night, newly single and stumbling the streets of Montreal, my drunken antagonism shifted from Gail, to Gail's father, to gudrun peel, or rather the gudrun peel I imagined her to be, my profanities spilling haphazard onto Saint-Denis. Of course, everything changed the night I first saw her.

2

-----

remnants

what is this country of young men
from kingston london edmonton?
all their dreams & friends
seem like old routines
done over again

this one from montreal
so splendid & tall
an exquisite doll
decked out for a fall

another from newfoundland
singer in a noise rock band
the very model of a man
in love with his brand

there's always another
waiting to greet you
happy to meet you
all set to complete you
                      —*mile end, montreal*

OTIS JONES WAS prophetic, kinetic, eclectic—one of the more fashionable madmen of the scene—and the only person in my acquaintance who'd published a book of poetry. He was from

Bay Roberts, Newfoundland, a wake-and-bake pothead, a wavy-haired giant, a slapdash oddity, and the kind of dude who might be growing a beard or shaving his head or falling in love in a Yukon bookstore. I met him tree planting in the sundry foughten fields of British Columbia and he told me to look him up if I was ever in Toronto. So there I was on Bloor Street West, on the day I turned twenty-seven, watching Otis Jones in rubber boots approach along the sidewalk. He wore a plaid shirt, army pants, and drank from a bottle of wine in a brown paper bag.

"There he is," said Otis, waving in fellowship. "How're you getting on?"

"Pretty good. You?"

"I've been through the Boer War, my son. The Boer War."

"I wasn't aware that was still going on."

"Well, that's like everything, isn't it? You're not really up to speed. But you come out with Shannon and me. I'm sure we can squeeze you in a few places."

"Someone tried that before."

"Because"—Otis offered me the wine—"what're they going to say when they write the book about you?" He watched me swig from the bottle. "That Aubrey McKee, he'd never get up the nerve. Couldn't do it. Just sits there, the poor bugger. Never moves. Never says a word. Frightened out of his mind. That's what they're going to say."

"Where you going these days, Otis?"

"Everywhere and back."

"You want to make a night of it, do you?"

"Yes, boy. We're getting on the go tonight. You in?"

I returned the wine. "Where exactly are you going?"

WALTER WEIR WAS a hippie from Newfoundland who founded a publishing house called Wyndham and Weir in 1969. Initially situated in Rochdale College, a student-run co-op near the university, the company bounced around a few times and was saved from bankruptcy by a millionaire who, it was rumoured, slept with Walter back in the free-swinging sixties. The business was now established as a source of alternative poetry and innovative fiction and drama. But Walter Weir had Faber and Faber aspirations, wanting to move the press in a more belles-lettres direction, and towards that end he'd recently written his own autobiography—a collage of memoir, social history, essay, and correspondence—called *Beyond the Space Between*. The book launch was being held at Walter's ex-wife's house, an Edwardian mansion on Admiral Road. I say ex-wife, but it wasn't clear if she and Walter had reunited. Few relations in Walter's life, I would learn, were clear or well-defined.

The broad impressions inside were fresh-cut flowers, damask tablecloths, and crown moulding. For someone like me, who had spent the last few years tree planting and bumming around the world in a leaky tent, I felt like a muskrat in the Art Gallery of Ontario.

Otis brought me a beer and promptly walked off, a spatter of bicycle spray apparent on the back of his army pants. The crowd in the living room was segregated into middle-aged folks who knew each other and twentysomethings who did not. There were also a few solitary women sipping spritzers and looking around expectantly.

I ambled away from the living room and scaled the main stairs. I wandered into an upstairs study where, rather as if I were *in* the Art Gallery of Ontario, I leaned into the eyepiece of a telescope and pretended to be interested in a southern view of the city.

At a bookshelf behind me were two lanky young men, one sitting, one standing. The seated man had open on his lap the first volume of *The Compact Oxford English Dictionary*. He kept clearing a flop of bangs from his eyes with flicks of his head. The other man, in a camel-hair sport coat, had rusty brown hair that, probably curly and ample in youth, was now receding in early adulthood. And he seemed animated by an obscure hostility, as if something in the evening had affected him badly.

"You're from Nova Scotia, aren't you?" said the man with the dictionary. He spoke in a vague English accent. "I said to Dalty, 'That man's a McKee.' I've seen you before. Harold, isn't it? I recognize you from Race Weeks gone by. Are you a sailor? I am. Or was. I've forgotten all the odds and ends. Boring, really. Knots and such." He indicated the bookshelf. "Did you know the chap who wrote 'Don Quixote' was captured by pirates? Sold into slavery in Old Algiers. But it's because of this ordeal he was able to write a classic of world literature." He flipped his bangs. "I suppose that's my problem. Writers just aren't captured by pirates anymore."

"No," said the other man. "They're imprisoned in Beirut." He came forward to shake hands. "I'm Dalton Hickey. And this is Sebastian, my somewhat absurd brother." He turned to Sebastian. "It was tennis where we met McKee. Semifinals at the Nova Scotia Open."

Sebastian and Dalton Hickey, I remembered them now, peripheral kids from my childhood. They were townies from Chester Basin and their parents were eccentrics of some local celebrity, famous for high spirits, a trickling private income, and low-hanging begonias.

"Do you know what a freemartin is?" asked Sebastian, resuming his investigation of the dictionary. "'An imperfectly developed female calf, usually sterile, born as the twin of a male.' And do you know what a frenulum is?"

"Do shut *up*, Sebastian," Dalton said in a severe tone. "You are an embarrassing person."

"Am I?" said Sebastian. "It's all rather embarrassing, isn't it?" Just then, the dictionary slipped from Sebastian's lap and tumbled to the floor.

"And Jesus, man"—Dalton frowned at the fallen dictionary—"stop bungling."

From a nearby table, Dalton picked up a new-looking hardcover—a copy of *Beyond the Space Between*—and began leafing through it, pausing sometimes to scrutinize a sentence or photograph, and all of this done with a faint smile, as if he were someone with more pressing matters on his mind.

I asked if he planned to read the book.

"I'm reviewing it for the 'Globe,'" said Dalton. "Not sure if you've been following the reaction in the media. But what has gone under-remarked, it seems to me, is just how *awful* the book is. And I'm astounded that such a trumped-up nothing of a book can be considered significant." Scanning its table of contents, he slowly shook his head. "A memoir about nothing, from a generation no one remembers, implicating figures no longer alive. Fascinating." He shut the book. "Can you believe these people? A bunch of dropouts with mandolins and back acne? I mean, Christ, look at the title. 'Beyond the Space Between?'" He dropped the book on the table. "'Within the Trifecta of Ineptitude' was taken, presumably."

"Well," said Sebastian, "with these sort of memoirs, Dalty—"

"I've told you," said Dalton with some menace. "Don't call me that."

"Right. Dalton. Everything happens for a reason—"

"No. Rationalizations happen for a reason. And that reason is people are fuckwits who need excuses to explain away their bad decisions. We're not talking about 'People' magazine or what someone wore on a red carpet, Sebastian. We're talking about literature, a subject about which you know very little."

"Literature. Right. I'm not sure I'm interested in your game of who's smarter than who, Dalton."

"Of course not. And it's who's smarter than *whom*, by the way. But who's counting?" Dalton coolly smiled and walked past me on his way to the stairs.

I stared at the floor, oddly vexed, for in the last few moments I'd been resisting an urge to shove him into the bookshelf.

"My brother," said Sebastian, standing up, "he has this effect on people." He made a quick, lizard-like manipulation of his jaw and lips, opening and closing his mouth in an effort to clear from its edges a foaming excess of saliva. "You a writer?" Sebastian took a glass of red wine from the bookshelf. "You can't throw a fork at this party without hitting a writer." He sipped the wine. "My own novel's going rather well, actually."

I asked what it was about.

"Oh, I never talk about it. Superstitious, you know. Knock wood." He rapped his forehead. "Do you want to hear the first line? 'No one remembers when they first met Juliet Pepperhouse'." Sebastian tittered. "It's called 'The Education of Juliet Pepperhouse.'" He pursed his lips. "Or perhaps 'The Ordeal of Juliet Pepperhouse?' Not sure. But it will be my 'Zuleika Dobson.' Now, if you'll pardon me a moment"—he placed the glass on the bookshelf—"I must find the little boys' room."

SENSATIONS WERE APLENTY, meeting again two friends of my youth—two personalities, it bears mentioning, who will feature rather vividly in the next decades of my life—but my reveries were disrupted by the reappearance of Otis Jones. Following him was a young woman in a loose-knit mohair sweater.

"McKee!" said Otis, passing me a beer. "Are you meeting some Hickeys?"

"Sort of."

"That Sebastian Hickey, he's right some stunned, isn't he? I know what his mother will say." Otis cocked his head. "'He was a nice boy from Nova Scotia, but Toronto ruined him. Just *ruined* him'."

"She might say that about a lot of people."

Otis turned to his companion. "Shannon, girl," he said. "This is McKee. He was to the silver spoon born."

"Otis—" said Shannon.

"What's that, my love?"

"We should have McKee here over for supper."

"And get the Royal Newfoundland Constabulary at our door? No thank you. He may look harmless, Shannon. But what you don't know is vast."

"You're too fussy to have people over, is that it?"

"I am, girl, yes. All fuss and no bother."

Shannon airily fluttered her eyelashes. I'd noticed her earlier, when she was downstairs among the twentysomethings, and saw she was braless beneath her mohair sweater, the pink of her breasts visible from time to time as she ran her thumb beneath her necklace or traced a finger around the rim of her wineglass.

"You coming to this fundraiser?" Otis asked. He handed me a flyer for something called Cabaret Bam Bam. "We're going in a minute. I've just got to say hello to someone. But you watch yourself, McKee, or you'll be swept out to sea and no one'll know you were here."

"Someone tried that before, too."

THIRTY MINUTES LATER and Otis was nowhere to be found. For a while he'd been everywhere, delivering plates of chocolate cake, playing piano in the living room, reciting Al Purdy in the kitchen, but now that the house had filled with revellers, I was beginning to suspect I would not see him again. So I sat alone in the upstairs study reading Dalton's copy of *Beyond the Space Between*. My concentration wavered, however, and I kept reading the same paragraph over and over. I put down the book, grabbed my beer, and started down the stairs. I paused on the landing, worrying, as I sometimes do when feeling sadly isolated, if I'd made the wrong choices in my life, wondering even if I'd made the right decision to return to Toronto, when I heard two people talking on the second floor.

"But really," said a thrilling female voice, "how does it all happen?"

"Just tell me," replied an older male voice, "when's *your* book going to be finished?"

"No idea."

"But you are writing?"

"When I'm not smoking. When I'm not doing crack." The woman giggled as she clinked her glass against his. "Oop. Me spill something?"

"Not to worry. Let me get some soda."

I saw a handsome, bearded, sea-salty fellow—judging from the evening's author photo, it was Walter Weir himself—hurry to the stair-top. As he passed me on the landing, rubbing at a red stain on his linen shirt, I twisted my head to peer into the room above me.

There, framed in the doorway, was a young woman in her early twenties. Pushing a swoop of jet-black hair behind her ear, she glanced at me and smiled, as if she just happened to be smiling and I just happened to be standing there, but, as she walked out of view, I had the private sensation I alone was discovering her beauty. For there was something in her glance and aspect that made me feel her appeal had been all along unknown, maybe even to her. But in the next moment, as I came upstairs, I realized this feeling of newness and discovery must be part of her allure, and I stepped into the room.

The young woman was bending over a table of champagne glasses, her blouse taut against her shoulder blades, and trying to write on a cocktail napkin.

"I have a terrible memory," she said, not looking up. "I must scribble everything down or I'll forget. Now if I could just get this pen to work." She jiggled it. "Opa! It's working? But now I can't remember the secret note I'm supposed to remember. Oh well—" She straightened up. "That was a challenge I never overcame."

She turned her attention to a nearby dessert table, its offerings in gentle disarray. Blue plums loose in a glass bowl. Pears scattered on a marble cheese plate. A shambles of a chocolate cake. She grabbed the cake slicer and struggled to free it from a wedge of softened brie.

"Hello," she said. "I mean you, actually, not the cheese. The cheese and I aren't really connecting, I'm finding. The cheese stands alone. Are you a friend of Walter's?"

I said I knew no one and was a friend of Otis Jones.

"I see. So you're a young man from back east?"

"Yup," I said, putting on the table the flyer for Cabaret Bam Bam. "I think we're going to this thing."

"Oh?" She scanned the flyer. "So you're an eccentric scenester who goes around with Otis Jones?"

"Sure," I said, finishing my beer. "I'm like that."

Noticing my empty bottle, she said, "You know what they say about people who pull the label off their beer?"

"No, I don't."

"Neither do I. But I'm going to remember very soon." She dropped the slicer. "I had to give up on the cheese."

"No cheese?"

"No cheese. It's the cake I'm really after. As you can imagine." She wiped her fingertips on the tablecloth and held out her hand. "I don't know you yet. You're the one people are calling Harold."

"Someone *was* calling me Harold." I shook her outstretched fingers. "How did you know?"

"I had an inkling. Of that. People are calling me Gudrun."

"You're Gudrun—Gudrun *Peel*? The poet?"

"Yes. Calm down. You're going to make it." She considered the cake. Its icing, truffles, and chocolate shards were sloppily askew and it was going to be difficult to get a proper piece from its remains. "I don't suppose you'd wrap up this cake and take it home for me. I'd be forever in your debt."

"In one of the linen napkins?"

"I see what you mean," she said. "That way lies madness." Her voice rose with mock hysteria. "Madness, I tell you!"

As I followed her out of the room, she giggled at her own silliness, and I felt, with a rush of elation, that I'd never met anyone like her. In her laughter was a mix of attitudes I found beguiling, unprecedented, addictive. With every remark she seemed to say, "Why listen to me? I don't know anything and everything I say is irrelevant anyway." Yet beneath this was a consciousness of seriousness and complexity that I sensed in certain syllables, and the collective effect implied a sort of shared understanding that obviously didn't exist between us but which seemed possible, likely, even sort of inevitable.

"Have you seen the telescope?" I asked, pointing a bit wildly into the study.

"Oh?" said Gudrun. "A telescope?" She walked into the room and looked into the eyepiece. "Ah! I see someone. I'm spying on someone!" She swung the eyepiece away. "This, to me, is just not right. I suppose it's all right if you're Johannes Kepler." She stepped back. "But I am not Johannes Kepler. Nor was meant to be."

She made a melancholy sigh.

"Why sigh?"

"Because I'm doing nothing right now," said Gudrun. "The rest of my life is up for grabs, basically. It's why I have poverty mentality and want to steal cake. It's basically demolishing what's left of my self-esteem." She sighed again and retreated into private quiet—the moment curiously unguarded—then cleared her throat to say, "And I have a job interview coming up that's making me insane. It's sort of important to me, this job interview, the time of which I should just confirm with Walter, if you don't mind." She glanced into my eyes and touched my wrist. "Fare thee well, Childe Harold. God be with you. And if you change your mind about the cake, let me know."

THERE ARE TIMES when it's inevitable we see ourselves as supporting actors in someone else's story. For my part, I often skitter into circumstances and, before being consumed by drama and politicking, choose to fall away and involve myself elsewhere. This genteel book launch was such a circumstance and, while I was sort of indifferent to its many meanings, for the first time in a while I didn't want life to go on somewhere else. I wanted to be there when it happened. And it was because of Gudrun Peel. She seemed to re-create the world every few moments. Meeting her seemed one of the capital moments of my life, but, roving around the party, this rush of boldness suddenly embarrassed me and when I found her again, talking in the kitchen with Walter Weir, I felt foolish to be the stranger with a soggy piece of cake wrapped in a cocktail napkin in his jacket pocket.

She was leaning against a door frame, her head softly banging against the hinges of the open door, and gazing up into the face of Walter Weir. In the air was the residual energy of a recently told joke, and from the way Gudrun was giggling, it was as if she'd been reminded of some deeply personal embarrassment. "Oh, Walter," she said, "my virgin ears."

Walter began loudly laughing, in an affable way, in a way that made fun of his own tendency to joke around, which made me like him, but I didn't want to like him, because I was jealous of him, and when he left to get another drink, I went over to Gudrun to say goodbye.

"Harold," said Gudrun, seeing me, "you're still here?"

"I thought maybe you'd left."

"Nope," said Gudrun. "No leave. Wanted to go, but"—she flipped her hand carelessly—"people are all going to some other thing."

"So who's that guy? Is that the author?"

"Yep. That's yucky old Walter. It's his book party."

"Pretty swell party."

"I'm not sure it works, personally. But he may give me a job, so I have to pretend."

I nodded but sensed that the intimacy from before had dissipated. I thought to mention the slice of cake, to find a funny way to give it to her, but I couldn't think of anything funny, so I said, "I guess I'm going."

"I'm going too, then."

"Really?"

"Uh-oh." She covered her mouth. "That was a strange burp. Do you have any gum? I might have some, actually." She touched at a pocket. "Nope. No gum. Yeah, I think I'll go. I don't think it matters. People think I'm somewhere else anyway. It's all a scam!" She swayed into me, our shoulders bumping, and gave me a teasing look full of over-assumed familiarity, as if we'd always joked like this, and I smiled, charmed by the tipsy jostlings of Gudrun Peel.

OUTSIDE, HER FACE was flushed and warm from the party. "I'm glad we left," she said. "I was getting too drunk. I think I used the word jurisdiction in three different conversations. And vodka"—she pointed a finger skyward—"huge mistake. Vodka makes me argue. Tequila makes me insane. And red wine makes me want to make out like a bandit." She leaned into my shoulder and solemnly asked, "Did you take the cake?"

I told her it was wrapped in a cocktail napkin in my pocket.

"You take the cake!" She giggled. "You really take the cake. Thank you for absconding with it because I'm such a weirdo. I just didn't want anyone to nab me. And I'm so tired"—she made no attempt to stifle a face-distorting yawn—"I go through each day wildly exhausted."

I remarked on the party becoming fantastically crowded.

"Oh, Walter knows nine thousand people. He knows every boy, every girl, every secret thing." She looked at the sidewalk. "I hope to God he doesn't come to this cabaret."

"I'm sure he's too busy spying on people with telescopes."

"Why do the people have telescopes?" She broke into laughter. "I just cracked myself up. But, yeah, he likes to watch people. Though since I got back from Poland, I always feel like *I'm* the one being watched."

"When'd you get back from Poland?"

"Month ago. It's strange. I'm undergoing huge culture shock. I'm not used to being in a place where people understand everything I say. I feel like people know everything about me."

"Um—I don't."

"Maybe it was better in Poland, when no one knew anything. Probably I should go back."

"Good exchange. Forty zlotys to the dollar."

"Forty-two, actually." She spun the lever on a parking meter. "You're very perceptive in your way, Harold. You don't miss much, do you?"

"Some ideas I had bordered on profound."

"You're either very profound or very cagey. I should probably call and ask you what to say in my job interview."

"How can you call me? You don't know my number."

"It's an insoluble dilemma."

"So I'll never see you again?"

"Nope," she said. "That was a challenge we never overcame."

"But I *like* you, Gudrun Peel," I said, touching her hand, moving close, and lightly kissing her lips.

I'D BEEN WAITING some minutes trying to decide how to kiss her, when to kiss her. In more than a few ways, I think I'd been waiting some *years* to kiss her. After taking a step back, I expected her to say something, do something—slap me—but she only stood there, slowly blinking.

"Harold," she said, "aren't you engaged?"

"My name's Aubrey, and no, I'm not."

"That's what Otis said."

"Pretty sure I'm not engaged."

She dropped her head to one side. "God, I have to stop lying."

"Otis didn't say that?"

"No, he did. I just remembered something I said to Dalton."

"What'd you say?"

"Nothing. I was just being a weirdo. But he'll probably remember it. Whatever. Maybe I'll get a poem out of it. Who knows?" She tilted her head, as if to observe me from a new angle. "All right, Aubrey. Just so you know, I have pretty short relationships. I've got them down to one day. We decide not even to shake hands."

"That's fine, because I'm incapable of human love. But, hey, do you want to see a movie?"

"A movie? My *God,* man. It sounds so much like a date! I guess we could sit in the dark and weep."

"We could certainly try. It's only thirty dollars a movie."

"No, it went up. Thirty-two, actually."

"You have a good head for numbers, Gudrun Peel."

"It's a burden, really. A constant struggle." As we crossed Spadina, she stopped to inspect a glove flattened into the pavement. "Sure—" She scuffed it with her shoe tip. "We can go on a date. Why not? What could happen? Why do we exist?"

THE REST OF THE NIGHT I remember in flashes and fragments. Gudrun and I walking eleven blocks to Queen Street West. A Portuguese guy chasing a homeless man into an alley. People lining up to get into the Cabaret Bam Bam show. Beer was five dollars, wine was six. I bought wine for Gudrun and drank a beer. Otis appeared and bought bottles of red wine for everybody. A cute woman was staring at me from the cash-box table. I tasted Gudrun's red wine, noticing how it was staining everyone's teeth. A show began. Young men in motorcycle helmets and underwear were in a cancan line on stage. Then dancers were hanging from aerial silks. Soon it was late. People were drunk.

It was sprinkling rain when we left. Gudrun was extremely hungry, pulling a pizza slice away from her mouth, strings of cheese stretching from her lips... Then it was three in the morning and I was alone on Bathurst Street, waiting for a streetcar and reading over and over Gudrun's scrawled address and phone number on a chocolate-smudged cocktail napkin.

3

geometry

if i might subtend our love
in just a little tangent
because there was a point
at which i turned
into something new to me

i want to talk hyperbolas
and opposites adjacent
but really all i want
is a return to my amazement

our curves protracted
all proofs abstracted
circles spinning undistracted

i might talk of compasses
in the way of your dean donne
but when i'm only getting started
why end where i've begun?

—mile end, montreal

WHO *WAS* SHE? What was she like? And who were the people
in her poems? For explication, I turned to Otis Jones. "You
want to know about Gudrun Peel?" He held his gaze on me,
regarding me with suspicion. "You like a challenge, I'll say that.
She was like a lot of women at McGill. Wore her strange little

clothes in her strange little room and wrote her strange little poems. She's an interesting woman. And interesting women almost always have interesting problems. It wouldn't surprise me if she has a little pool of darkness she takes a plunge in from time to time. But I hope she keeps writing. Talented writer."

I imagined Gudrun in Montreal reading Wittgenstein, smoking cigarillos, and striding around the Plateau with an indie rock boyfriend. She seemed a strider and a striver and someone intent on forward movement. At McGill, she'd written a master's thesis on Elizabeth Bishop while working diversely as a copyeditor, exam invigilator, and music reviewer for the *Montreal Mirror*. Otis lost track of her for a while, she dropped out of view after her master's, for reasons uncertain, only to be accepted into the PhD program at the University of Toronto. Here she didn't seem to be "doing nothing," as she said, for not only had she begun a dissertation on someone named Louise Glück but she was also in the midst of a teaching assistantship and applying for a variety of other jobs. As well as working on her own poetry.

Otis had chosen one of her poems, "remnants," for *52 Girls*, an all-female chapbook he'd edited two years before, but a more recent piece I found in an anthology called *Smack: Poems from the New World Underground*. That poem, "geometry," displayed above, I read at a small press fair in the Great Hall on Queen Street. I was a graduate student in chemistry, and partial to its math-and-science motif, and the coyness of the voice and the neatness of the rhymes surprised me. They indicated a freshness of direction. Or so it seemed to me. As you can guess, I was beginning to feel drawn to this woman in ways I didn't really understand, probably because I sensed she was amazing in ways I didn't know, and, in truth, I was sort of worried, should I ever see her again, that I wouldn't fit into any category she found appealing.

After a few weeks of trying to get in touch—calling, leaving a message, sending a gift—and hearing nothing back, I realized I needn't worry. I wasn't going to see Gudrun Peel again. So I trained myself to stop thinking of her, wondering, semi-despondently, if anyone I was interested in would ever like me in return.

4

Wyndham and Weir is an award-winning independent
publishing house based in Toronto. We are seeking a
publicity and marketing associate to join our Sussex
Avenue office. This is a part-time position entailing the
promotion of titles, planning of events, and assisting staff
with sales materials and bookseller outreach. Word and
Excel knowledge required. QuarkXPress and Adobe
Photoshop an asset.

IT WAS AN October afternoon when my doorbell rang. I went
down to street level and opened the door to Gudrun Peel. She
looked prim and striking in a blue skirt suit, her black hair
side-swept and held in place by a snap-clip.

"May I come in?" she asked. "Don't worry. I'm not stalking
you or anything."

"You look very smart."

"I am very smart," she said, moving past me. "I'm also very
drunk. And now I'm going to your apartment." She jumped up
the stairs towards the second floor, a dash of colour fading into
shadow. When I walked into the front room, she was already
stretched out on the couch, her head on an armrest, her forearm covering her eyes.

"It's Gudrun, right?" I asked. "So where were you?"

"Job interview. With Walter."

"Yucky old Walter. How'd it go?"

"Great. Terrible. I don't know. Other people's lives freak me out." She sighed. "If there was a cigarette here, I'd smoke it. Do you have anything to drink?"

"I might have some beer. Or a can of soda water?"

"I'll have the soda. In the can. Please."

I returned from the kitchen and held out the soda water.

"Thank you," she said, sitting up. She took the soda water. "I'm in a weird mood. My life's not working."

"Why?"

"Because it's all about what you do. It's all about what you do. So hey—" She thumped the couch. "I lived like a nun for six months. That's okay. It was my turn to live like a nun. Now I have to live like a not-nun. God, my voice sounds squeaky. Ah, don't listen to me, I'm drunk. I've had three glasses of wine and I'm soused at two in the afternoon." She looked around the room—noticing the television, remote control, worn-out armchair, curtained window—then stared at the wall. "God, it was a really nice place."

"What was? Their office?"

Gudrun nodded. "They're grown-ups. I thought, 'Everybody else takes their life seriously and I'm an idiot.' But you know what? I don't care." She opened the soda water. "Because what a fucking weirdo."

"Who is?"

"Walter." She drank the soda water. "I had a good way to understand this a second ago. On the way over here, I had it all figured out. But maybe I'm not smart enough to know what it means. The only thing that made me not hate everything was the part about Clifford—"

"Clifford?"

"Remind me to tell you, but can we talk about why Walter would want to hire me in the first place? Because during the interview he was relating to me like I was in total control of my reality, but I don't think he *really* thought that. Either did any of them. Except maybe Duffy, the perfectly gay intern."

"Duffy—"

"Yes, Duffy, the perfectly gay intern, is a computer whiz, clever little photoshopper, and all-round office opportunist. He's an up-and-comer and adorable and I'm basically an introvert and a furtive little freaker. Everyone there was incredibly poised and smart and I just thought, why bother? Like why even bother? This is obviously what they want to do with their lives, work in literary publishing, so why would they want to hire me, neurotic, hyperconscious girl? I don't know anything about marketing. Marketing? How could I even *do* that stupid job? Sitting at a computer all day in some hermetically sealed environment. I mean, it's sort of obscene."

Gudrun sat bolt upright.

"They have these office cubicles with—you know those things—louvered doors? They've got louvered doors everywhere and bevelled glass but absolutely no windows, so I'd go nuts. I'd go out of my fucking tree." She looked at me with puzzlement. "And just why was Walter acting so sucky-uppy to me? Because that was also very intimate and entre nous like I was already employee-of-the-month. But I don't know if Walter likes me as a joke or if he wants to fuck me, because he totally grabbed my ass—" She broke off and held the can of soda water to her forehead. "God, I have to calm down. My heart's beating a million miles a minute."

"He grabbed your *ass?*"

"It wasn't totally a grab. It was more like a pat. Like a little pat-pat. I don't know. It seemed weird at the time. And then there's that awkward pause where I think seven different things but don't say anything and just try to get the hell out of there in a gracious, upbeat way which starts to feel fake but I do anyway." She sniffed. "I'm telling you, I wear a skirt and the men go crazy."

"If you wear that skirt, maybe."

She took a sip and said, "I want a trench coat."

"Excuse me?"

"I saw this woman on the subway, she was wearing the most beautiful trench coat like you wouldn't believe. Just stop-you-in-your-tracks gorgeous."

"The coat or the woman?"

"The *coat*, ding-dong. I mean, I could probably buy one in three months if I got this job."

"So you do want the job?"

She inhaled deeply through her nose, as if preparing to speak at length, then stood up and moved to the window. Standing between the curtains, she peered into the street. "I'm a-coming for you, Clifford," she said, as if it were a sort of pledge.

SHE WAS NERVOUS, upset, but it was difficult to know how upset because her exasperation was mock exasperation. In this manic state, she was many moments ahead of me and seemed to be keeping up some frantic inner discussion with herself— eyes widening in disbelief, a hand flapping in front of her face, lips briefly pouting—but her uncertainty was verging on insta-bility. The night we met, her nervousness seemed in main parts a gesture of welcome—it showed she wasn't about to dictate the moment—and it made me feel we shared certain unspoken tendencies of understanding. But such inclusiveness was nowhere now and her uncertainties seemed close to over-whelming her.

"Do you really want this job?" I asked. "A job's a job, but if you do it well, you won't be doing it forever."

"No, I know. I know all that do-the-gig-and-move-on bull-shit." She pushed open the curtains and sunlight streamed in, brightening the couch and armchair. "And I know every human action is its own thing and not something else, or whatever Spinoza said." She turned to examine the room's bookshelf. "It's just the same old story. I feel like I'm pretending to be an adult and everyone knows I'm not." Putting down the soda water, she picked out a textbook.

"'Advanced Inorganic Chemistry?'" she said, reading its title. "Why are you studying chemistry?"

"Mostly because I'm studying chemistry."

"Seriously?" Gudrun's face was full of mystification, as if my presence had become incomprehensible to her. She put back the textbook—jamming it into the bookshelf—then plopped down on the couch.

Spying the remote, Gudrun grabbed it and flicked on the television. "Oh my God, you have cable? If I had cable, I'd watch TV all the time. I wouldn't have a life. Last night, I couldn't sleep because I'm the champion worst insomniac of the world and like a zombie I watched ten hours of television. I couldn't get *off* the stuff. I watched this nature show about an impala getting eaten by hyenas and it was so horrible, I couldn't *not* watch it." She clicked through a circuit of the channels, then turned off the television as abruptly as she turned it on.

"Jesus, God, I need to change the channel on my life. Because how come when I *am* successful I feel like a bitch for not being more sympathetic to someone who's still being a loser? I mean, I always feel guilty when I accomplish something because I always imagine what someone else'll feel when they hear about it. That's why Otis is so great. He just does stuff and doesn't give a shit."

"What does Otis think about this job?"

"I don't know what he thinks." She studied a hangnail on her thumb. "But he likes you."

"He likes me? Does he like me as a joke or does he really like me?"

"Oh, he really likes you. Although he says you've got a jacked-up superego—"

"Is that good?"

"—and you try and slip the word ethereal into every conversation. But he likes you." She bit the hangnail. "But I don't want to talk about Otis at the moment. I haven't really seen him since that party. And that was a weird night for me. I was"—she frowned—"out of sorts."

"But now you're *in* sorts?"

"Not at all!" Gudrun said, dismayed. "I'm massively freaked out by this job prospect. I'm about as far out of sorts as you can get while staying in the same time zone." She snorted. "See, I like it when I make jokes like that. I would never dream of making jokes like that with them."

"Gudrun, it was a *job* interview!"

"And you have to get along with everybody, I know. Calm down. Because you have that stress of they're-not-getting-my-jokes thing. So instead you say, 'Yeah, I'm really excited about that concept.' Which I *did* say, by the way. All through the interview I was saying stuff like that and thinking, 'Why? Why am I trying to sound like Bill Gates?'" She straightened the seam of her skirt. "But maybe it's exactly the right thing to do. Work in marketing. Although I can't believe I'm actually considering working in marketing, because once you start working in marketing, then no matter what you're doing, somewhere in East Timor a child labourer is being tortured."

"Uh-huh. When do you hear back about this job?"

"Probably the epicentre of weirdness was when I had to fill out this personnel form to apply for the job and I only had that stupid friggy pen. Remember that pen? Well, it completely cacked out on me. I had to borrow one from Walter which was one of those Bic ballpoint jobs that the person chews and chews and not only does Walter slobber the end off but he peels back all the chewed-up sections like petals in a flower. It's gross and sort of masturbatory and really quite repulsive and stupidly I say, 'Oh you *would* have a pen like that.' And then he was staring at me like, 'Who the fuck are you?' Like I was challenging him on everything. Which is when I remembered Walter has a lazy eye and I don't know which eye to look at so I'm just staring at his nose and slightly panicking that he's going to bust me and I think, 'Don't betray yourself. Just keep staring like you know what you're doing'."

"It probably wasn't that bad."

"Oh, but it was. It really hit his belief structure. Because he was totally trying to zero in on who I am as a person. As opposed to who I am as an impala." Gudrun smacked her forehead. "Why didn't I get a pen before going? Fuck, if I could just *do* that, walk into a store and buy a pen without super-analyzing it a million times, then I could die happy." She took a cushion and held it to her lap. "I shouldn't have come back. This is more than just North America re-entry syndrome. This is—" She squeezed the pillow. "I think maybe I should let my hair go grey. And grow potatoes up in the rocks." She squinted. "I was trying to remember something. What was it?"

"I think it was about Clifford."

"Yes!" She smiled. "So midway through the interview, Walter gets a phone call, he has a daughter named Martha who's very smart, she's six years old, and she wants to be a boy so she's been calling herself Clifford. So Walter gets this call and it's on speakerphone and the receptionist goes, 'Can I say who's calling?' and the daughter says, 'Would you tell him it's his son Clifford calling'."

Gudrun began shaking, either with laughter or distress, I wasn't sure, but it seemed to relieve her, for soon there was quiet in her voice, as if her panic had been only a passing commotion.

"So for some reason"—she looked up—"I thought of you when I heard that story. In case you might like it or something."

"I do like it."

"Oh, *you*." She took a trembly breath. "How did you get to be this insanely patient listener? Are you like this with everyone?"

"No," I said. "I'm like this with you."

"Well, that was certainly direct. And somewhat unequivocal. But I can't have sex with you at the moment if that's where you're going. Because that wasn't part of the plan."

"There's a plan?"

"Well, there *was* a plan, but now who knows? I'm either starting a career in marketing or going back to Poland." She sniffled. "It's just—I've been thinking about you a lot so that's strange, isn't it? Don't you think?"

"It's nice to see you."

"It's nice to see you, too. And I like you and I had a good time when I met you. But you make me nervous."

"Why?"

"Because I can't quite read you. You say things like swell and ethereal but in your brain you have this parallel reality that— dum-de-dum—you live in. I mean, I know you probably come from one of those polite Waspy families that never says anything but sometimes it's hard to tell if you're being polite or just plain lying."

"What do you want to know? I mean, we tried to see a movie but it didn't happen. We broke up without even going on the date."

"I know we were supposed to see a movie, but I've had a million deadlines with school and financial stress not to mention this job interview." She pulled again at her skirt. "But I *did* want to see you and thank you for sending me the freesia and the Dentyne, it's just—"

Gudrun took her hands away from the pillow and stationed them firmly on either side of her lap. "Aubrey, look, I go off the deep end sometimes. I can get severely depressed. Really crashing depressions. It happens."

"Uh-huh?"

"I'm just saying I can be difficult and sort of fragile. And critical. Like critical critical critical. I complicate things. And you'll get sick of me."

"Don't I get to make that decision?"

"Ah—" Her shoulders slumped. "Fucknuts. I don't know how to say it or make you know it like I know it." She stood up and went to the door. "So I'm going to go. I'm just going to go. Don't follow me out." Pulling the snap-clip from her hair, she glanced at me a last time. "And don't tell anyone I was here, okay? Or maybe tell a few people—I don't know—tell Clifford." Then she was gone.

I didn't follow her out, but I listened as she hurried down the steps and bounced out the front door and I went to the window to watch her advance down the sidewalk—black hair swirling in street wind—all the while wondering, of course, if I'd met one of the world's most remarkable people.

5

ADVANCED INORGANIC CHEMISTRY
A Comprehensive Text
Cotton and Wilkinson
Fourth Edition

AND WHAT SORT of twentysomething was I? Let's just say I was a very *young* twentysomething, the sort of dolt who sings "Whip It" in a careless Asian accent while jumping up to touch an awning. I lived with two roommates at 489 Bloor Street West, above the Future Bakery, and I was playing soccer, playing rugby, and working as a banquet waiter. But mostly I was studying chemistry. Bonding Patterns in Complex Macromolecules, Valence Shell Electron Pair Repulsion Theory—those were my obsessive-compulsions, with outlying interests in astrophysics, spooky entanglements, and singularities.

I was enrolled in a master's degree at the University of Toronto, where I was under the supervision of Caesar Flame. Professor Flame's research was in superacids, he was researching proton-transfer reactions in very acidic aqueous solutions, and he strove to track reactive unstable compounds in a free radical environment. For the chemists among you, think anhydrous hydrogen fluoride, antimony pentafluoride, and the fleeting moments of cations. These are short-lived transition species that subsist for split seconds, and in my capacity as research assistant I would snatch and pattern the most momentary of their epiphenomena. How did they happen? Where did they go? What exists in evanescence?

I was grateful to have my name on a published paper—my very first byline—but the work could be onerous, I was slogging ten-hour days, and early mornings in the wide rooms of the Lash Miller laboratories, in all their acetone rinses, sample tubes, and fume hoods, became a grey monotony. Into the building by seven, lunch at my desk at noon, I was often evaluating MRI spectra late into the evening, long after the windows had darkened. But I liked it. The work gave me an identity. And the privacy and loneliness of the place reminded me of high school, those afternoons when classes have finished, when the other students have emptied into the out-of-doors, when the tiled hallways were your own private corridors.

It was a few weeks into this sameness, late October, I think, when I received the note that introduces the next section. It was written in hasty cursive on an unstamped Egon Schiele postcard and pushed through the mail slot of my door on Bloor Street West.

6

---

hey a
i just had the most delicious sleep in the whole history of
human sleeps. perhaps there are people in your laboratory
who are ready to see a movie now. call me when u get
this?
x g

"AUBREY MCKEE," SHE said, picking up the phone. "What
are you doing working till eight o'clock on a Tuesday night?"

"Just going through some anomalies in the absorption spectra of methylene. You?"

"I just opened a bottle of wine."

"I feel compelled to ask, at this juncture, is it red wine?"

"It is, yes. At this juncture. Shall I pour you a glass?"

I found her specifics—170 West Lodge Avenue, Apartment
903—and took the Queen streetcar to Lansdowne, getting off
in the softest drizzle imaginable.

Her building was a twenty-storey fortress, its directory
crowded with names like Bishundo, Thamarajah, Abukar, Ho,
Gopalakrishnan, Owusu, Chanthavong, Lu, and Kukushkin.
Beside 903 was a blank label. I pushed its button.

"Hey—" It was Gudrun's voice. "Who's there?"

"Hello," I said. "Would you tell Gudrun it's her friend Clifford
calling."

"Hello, Clifford Calling. I'll be right down. This apartment's a little hard to find with the elevators busted."

The buzzer rang to free the door, and after a few minutes Gudrun met me in the foyer, her hair in braided pigtails. She led me to a far stairwell, the building a maze of corridors and sullied carpets and defunct elevators. She was in a paint-flecked T-shirt, faded corduroys, socked feet, and going up the cement stairs she had an undeodorized smell, as if she'd spent the last four days in the same clothes. Most of the hem of one trouser cuff had come loose and a wet flap kept catching beneath her heel, leaving a smudge on every other step. I was semi-affronted, thinking she had dressed casually on purpose, choosing not to sanction the evening with dressing up. But there was a gravity and charm to her thrift store bohemia, and as she paused to see I was following her on the stairs, dipping her shoulder and smiling, I felt that beyond her odd clothes there was in Gudrun's company a tacit conferral of respect for you as an autonomous thinking person.

"Hello again," she said inside her apartment. She kissed my cheek. "Hmm. Cold nose."

"Really?"

"Little bit." One of her pigtails was beginning to unravel, and as she gazed at me, she fingered away some wisps of hair. "Hey there, Freckly Man. You look Scandinavian today."

"I'll settle for that."

"Sort of Nordic. But you must take off your shoes."

"And let my feet go bare?"

"Because they're wet. And sit down?"

I complied, sitting on a red velvet sofa, and took in my surroundings. It was reassuring to be within the intimacy of a woman's apartment, filled with so many moods and effects. The lingering smell of unknown perfume. Klimt and Chagall prints on the wall. A bouquet of upside-down roses in a window.

— 64 —

Stacks of Penguin paperbacks piled on the floor. Through passages were other rooms—a kitchen, a small serving pantry, a door that led to the bedroom. The obscure, engaging femaleness of it all quietly thrilled me.

"So what happened today?" she asked from the kitchen. "Do you want a drink? I've already polished off half a bottle of wine."

"Sure, I'd love some wine. Today?"

"Yeah. What's up with methylene?"

"Very unstable. Free radical. Crazy spectra."

"What does that mean?"

"It's the key to a lot of theories of chemical structure. But the kind of spectroscopy I'm doing, it's actually what people use to identify methylene in distant nebulae. I don't know if you know Gerhard Herzberg, but he kind of pioneered the chemical analysis of interstellar molecules—"

"Inter*stellar* molecules? Like in outer space?"

"That's the one. Now Gerhard won the Nobel for this, and if you've ever wondered how many molecules there are between Jupiter and Pluto—"

She appeared in the kitchen doorway. "There are molecules in outer space? And people *study* this? Is this real?"

"Like I'm going to lie about molecules in outer space. What kind of monster do you think I am?"

"Mmm," she said, returning to the kitchen, "I like you."

"Excuse me?"

"When you talk like this. When you talk about what you're doing. Because I'm glad you have a brain and aren't just another pretty face."

"I sure ain't that. What about you? How've you been?"

"Oh?" She came in with two glasses of wine. "The same probably." She passed me a glass. "I had to clear the decks and whatnot." She smiled, a dimple flashing in her cheek, and raised her glass. "I got that job, by the way."

"With the publishing company?" I clinked her glass. "Cheers!"

"It's Framboise."

"Sounds French. You trying to get me drunk?"

"That's my goal." She sat in an armchair. "Because you got to have goals."

I crossed my legs, my foot by chance knocking over a pile of paperbacks. I started restacking them and, after looking through the titles, asked if she'd read *Anna Karenina*.

"Well, you see—" Gudrun pulled the switch-chain on a nearby floor lamp. "It's thick and it's good. So that's a bad combination for me. I have kind of an extreme relationship to reading anyway. I read on the train, the subway, the bus going off the bridge. I think I've read 'Anna Karenina' three times? Which is weird, because I don't really like the novel. But I love Anna." She sipped her wine. "Anna Akhmatova has this theory about Tolstoy punishing Anna, actually. I don't really follow her with all the Pushkin idolatry, but the Tolstoy family gossip is wonderful."

I nodded as if I knew who Anna Akhmatova was, but really I was observing Gudrun as I could, noticing how her expressions revealed her to be beautiful.

"I was thinking this week," she went on, "that I should be one of those people who doesn't have books. Because you sort of have to take care of them. And I hate the idea they're just sitting around unread. I feel like I should give them away."

I said I'd read whatever she had.

Gudrun touched away another wisp of hair. "McKee," she said, "thank you for being so nice to me when I arrived like a madwoman at your place."

"Gudrun," I said, "why else am I alive?"

She tilted her head to one side, considering my comment, the smoothness of her throat displayed in lamplight, and I was aware of the possibility of kissing her, that of course the whole evening was a prelude to kissing her, when she put her wine-glass on the floor and stood up.

"That's romantic," she whispered, kissing me, her lips soft on my own.

RAIN WAS BATTERING the windows, it was three in the morning, an ambulance siren wailed somewhere in the streets below, and I was in Gudrun's bathroom in a tizzy of half thoughts. After we had sex, I was not able to sleep and worried I would snore. As I lay on my back, Gudrun's sleeping head on my shoulder, I kept my mouth closed because I had an idea I wouldn't snore this way. I began to fall asleep, starting to dream—bizarre dreams of searching the telephone book for Gudrun's name in lower-case letters and encountering my own name five times—and I remember touching my tongue to the parched roof of my mouth, a connection that twitched me out of sleep. I eased myself out of bed and went to the bathroom, where I was now staring at everything—a red Altoids tin on a shelf, a smeared Q-tip in the sink, control top pantyhose on the showerhead, and, in the wicker wastebasket, our used condom, speckled with rust-coloured blood. I was full of neurotic ideas—if I was going to mess up this relationship by being too available, if Gudrun wanted to put her finger in my ass—just quirky, ridiculous ideas mostly inappropriate to everything, but they occupied me nonetheless, along with some unstable queasiness that ebbed and swelled so unstably I was convinced I was having some sort of nervous breakdown—

IN THE LIVING ROOM, Gudrun was lazing on the red velvet sofa under a child's blanket, watching television and softly humming to herself. Beside her on the floor was a bottle of Orangina.

"Hey naked man," she said.

"Hey yourself."

"You all right?" She studied me. "Did we fuck until you puked?"

"Not yet."

"But did you sleep?"

"No, I did not."

"Why not?"

"I felt weird," I said. "I was worried about my pelvic floor."

"Hmm-mmm." She changed the channel. "You're having a panic attack, I can tell. That's all right. I had mine this morning. Now I'm just having separation anxiety."

"But I don't have panic attacks."

"Of course you don't." She flicked to another channel. "Ooh. 'Law and Order.' I like the stuff with Ben Stone. I think that's Michael Moriarty. And I *love* Steven Hill." There was a burst of rain outside and Gudrun drew the blanket around her bare shoulders. She squinted at me and smiled, as if happily disoriented.

"I can't really describe you," she said. "You're sort of charming. You're one of the few people I know who could be described as charming."

"I'm actually flattered when someone likes me."

"I do like you. As soon as I heard your voice on my answering machine, I knew I was going to like you. But I don't know. I must seek you guys out. British guys with brown hair parted on the side. You guys have been haunting me since junior high. But why were you in the bathroom for so long, may I ask? Was it my period underwear soaking in the tub?"

"I had a weird dream and couldn't sleep."

"So did I!" Gudrun reached for the Orangina. "I had two dreams, actually. The first was the normal stuff where I'm driving a car from the back seat and my head falls off and you kick it out the window. That old chestnut. But the second one! I dreamt I had a second bathroom somewhere in this apartment. I was so happy to find it. There was like a secret passageway to another bathroom."

"Sort of like Narnia. Except to a bathroom."

"Yeah," she said. "Sort of like Narnia." Gudrun examined the Orangina label. "I was trying to finish a sentence again. Which one was it?"

"Having two dreams?"

"No, I think it was about why aren't you kissing me anymore is what I want to know."

I leaned over and softly kissed her.

"Oh—" she said. "I hope you always kiss me like that." She made room for me on the sofa. "It's hard to sleep on the first night. But I don't think we should worry. We don't have to figure it all out tonight." She offered me the Orangina.

I drank from the bottle. It tasted wonderful. I would forever associate its sparkling taste with this night, this apartment, the rain outside.

"So you're okay?" asked Gudrun. "You sure it wasn't the period underwear?"

"No, I was just having a premonition we'd fall in love and our lives would turn upside down."

"We won't fall in love. My socks are too stinky for that." She gazed at me. "Uh-oh. I'm having it again."

"What?"

"Separation anxiety."

"But I'm sitting right beside you."

"I know—" She gently kicked my foot. "I'm just making sure you're here."

As I set the Orangina on the floor, I was sort of amazed by the random turn of circumstance, as if it wasn't extraordinary to start the day in my own apartment and quite unexpectedly end up in someone else's life.

"Mmm," said Gudrun, rising. "I might keep you, naked man. Even with your clicky jaw." Taking my hand, she placed it over her stomach and led me to the bedroom. "God," she said, "it's so nice just to be touched."

IN THE BEDROOM, she wanted me to hold her down and bite her, not softly, but so my teeth caught and pressed on her skin. As I moved to kiss the tender inward of her thigh, she pushed her head back into the futon...the smell of her unperfumed body in the bed, her fingers grabbing at my hair...then she wanted me behind her and that stunning moment when she reached between her legs to hold and guide my cock within her and I wondered is there a verb for this? Then how foolish to think in words at all and the gorgeous bewilderment of being inside her overwhelming me and what I recollect best were her moans when, flipping on her back, she moved to touch herself, her head in profile on the bedsheet, her words dissolving into nonsense swearing, the quick movements of her fingers below and how wet she was, drawing me towards her as she came, her face warm with blushing, and then, the murmurs of our bodies subsiding, I collapsed on top of her, a trace of semen, like a melted pearl, gathered in her belly button.

7

Let him kiss me with the kisses of his mouth:
For thy love is better than wine.
— *highlighted in Gudrun's copy of the Song of Songs*

SHE WAS SNOW WHITE with tangly hair. Snow White in falling-apart corduroys. Snow White confronting the unknown. To see the colour rise in the cheek of Gudrun Peel was like the completion of a prophecy. I wanted to be the first she saw when she cleared her hair from her eyes, the first she thought to tell a funny story, the first to hear her views on everything.

I dreamt often of her face and waist, wondered why her fingers smelled faintly of peppermint, my awareness of her addictive, increasing, circumambient. I loved how smartly she thought about the world. She had an elliptical intelligence and her intuitions for the movement of beauty—behind the curtain, around the bend—quirked often into a sort of genius.

Sometimes, fearing things were moving too fast, she'd kick me out and midnights would find me walking home dazed and disoriented. But soon we seemed to spend every night together, my clothes at her place, hers at mine, every evening a fascination. We saw movies the world remembers—*Goodfellas, Miller's Crossing, The Grifters*—and movies the world does not—*The Russia House, Henry & June, The Nasty Girl*.

On weekends, we'd wake near noon, go for newspapers, and walk with croissants and coffee. We'd wander Queen Street or simply return to bed. "I think I'm actually *sore*," she said happily. It was intoxicating to have someone kiss you, miss you, wish to be with you. I think we were daring to be in love and beginning to prepare, in some not-too-distant future, a place for ourselves together.

"I DON'T KNOW," Gudrun said one night when we were both in her bathtub. "Maybe this year's gone all wrong."

"How's that?"

"Because I was sort of planning to have three lovers. Two men and one woman. That's what I was planning in my head. When I got back from Poland. And I was going to arrange it so they had different nights and never meet. It was going to be very sophisticated and discreet and very—something." She passed me a face cloth. "Ah, if I had to do it all over, I'd be a dyke. Wash my back?"

"You would?"

"I don't know if I really would. But I'd be more adventurous. I tried to pick up a woman once."

"I've tried that. What'd you do?"

"And wash up there? Oh, I sprawled on her bed and tried to look sexy."

"How'd it go?"

She shrugged. "Didn't happen. I mean, I've thought about being with a woman, but it'd probably get too confusing."

"I'm washing here too. I just think I should've slept with more people in college."

"I wouldn't worry about it. You've got a cute butt."

"Yeah? I'm so grateful when my butt works for someone. Though then I always feel sorry for them."

"Oh God," said Gudrun. "I've played that game. The what's-wrong-with-them game. I used to think every person attracted to me was sort of defective."

"Wait—I'm defective?"

"You know you've thought that too. I mean"—she laughed at the ambiguity—"that people attracted to you were." She stood up. "Listen to us. We're doomed. Only a couple of goombas would talk like this."

"So—" I watched the water stream from her shoulders. "When do I get to read what you're writing? I thought you said I could read a poem."

"I don't remember that. Must've been one of your other girlfriends. Must've been your fiancée." She stepped to the bath mat and reached for a towel. "No, I don't think I want you to read anything, Clifford. Not now." She wrapped the towel around her waist. "I know I'm being weird, but I had this vision of you talking to people about it and it freaked me out. And Dalton, when he read my stuff, well, I was absolutely sort of destroyed by his reaction to my work. Probably because he was right."

I watched her wrap a second towel around her head. "I have to tell you something," I said. "When I first read a poem by you, I threw the zine at the window. I didn't like it."

"It was probably something I wrote when I was eighteen. I was kind of a jerk back then. I mean, most of my poems are flops in one way or another." She picked up a toothbrush. "There's this long poem I've wanted to do for years, but it's just not working. I mean, all my poems are barely one page."

"You're probably not a real poet until you write a six-pager."

"It's sort of gross doing work you're not proud of. I'm always thinking, 'Am I writing something sucky?' And most of the time, yeah, I am. And stuff recently? Terrible. Like worse than undergrad." She blew out a sigh. "Being a poet is one of the stupidest things ever. No one cares if there's another book of poetry in the world. And how do I even *talk* to people about what I do? It's like an AA meeting. 'Hi, my name is Gudrun and I'm a poet'." She grimaced, conscious of difficulties past and present, and rinsed the toothbrush under the tap. "I just want to do something real. Not a stapled-together zine. Or a poem in a journal nobody reads." She squirted Colgate onto the bristles of the toothbrush. "I do all this shit. I do a bunch of random jobs. All I want is one 'Gretel in Darkness' and my own book. Is that so much to ask?"

She gazed at me in the mirror. "Because without a book, Clifford, I'm sort of fucked. I won't get a proper job. I won't get a placement. I don't want to be thirty years old without a book. No one will take me seriously."

"I will."

"You're sweet, Aubrey. But you're not the world." When she was finished brushing her teeth, she glanced at me. "I'll write you a poem if you want."

"Yeah, right."

"No, I promise."

"Will you put rain in it?"

"As you wish."

"Will it rhyme?"

"Well," she said, "a poet never knows. It's only in the writing that you find out."

"Sounds complicated."

"About as complicated as your butt."

"Let me see *your* butt. Lift up that towel?"

"Oh, I see what you're thinking"—she glanced into the tub—"you little floater."

"Maybe I am. I don't know."

Gudrun suddenly shut her eyes, as if in sharp pain.

"Clifford," I said, "are you all right?"

"Oh my *God*, you make me want things."

"What things?"

"All of it. I don't know. Weddings. Babies. Houses. Stuff I never really considered before." She pouted. "Maybe we should've met after a couple more relationships."

"Well, we've known each other almost two months now. I think we should worry about our relationship *way* more. Like, put aside time each day to be horrified."

Gudrun jiggled her head, as if to concede her histrionics, and asked, "You coming to bed?"

"Give me a kiss?"

She bent down and gave me a toothpastey kiss. "I might have to just fall asleep tonight."

"Cool. I'll lie in bed and stare at your ass."

"Ha!" said Gudrun. "That's the real McKee. You should do that more."

LYING IN BED, as she slept beside me, I kissed her shoulder, her ear, the nape of her neck, and stared at the line of her profile. She seemed perfection itself—her hair so black, her complexion so fresh—her beauty as stark as a comma typeset on Japanese paper. I don't think I'd ever felt closer to anyone in my life.

"Gudrun," I whispered, for my movements had wakened her, "I love being with you."

"Mmm-hmm," she murmured before falling back asleep. "Me too."

8

now I lay me down to sleep
with fuzzy socks upon my feet
if it rains please let me know
eenie meenie miney mo
yours truly,
dostoevsky's vulva
p.s. want to do something later?
—*a Post-it Note left on my bathroom mirror*

SEBASTIAN HICKEY WAS a strange and handsome young man. He looked seventeen. He was twenty-six. He was a writer, a painter, a playwright. He knew a thousand fopperies and could talk for hours about Saxo the Grammarian, Edmund Blunden's marriages, or the proper placement of an antimacassar. He seemed to belong to an era of crumpets and bugles and champagne. I liked that about him. It was reassuring somehow. He looked a bit like the young Michael Palin. You'd see him strolling around town with an expression of genial confusion, as if he'd taken a wrong turn at the East Putney Tube station and was only now beginning to grasp he was somewhere in North America. Just where he acquired his English accent—his four years at Royal Holloway College, family holidays in Pucklechurch—was anybody's guess. He certainly spoke like no one I knew from Chester Basin. His general tone was ingenious. It allowed him to sound both exquisitely sincere and preposterously affected. Everyone sensed his tricksy humour, his vulnerability, his shyness, but Sebastian Hickey hadn't quite managed to develop an adult personality and, when nervous, withdrew into deferential politeness. This made him seem nerdy and inconsequential— qualities he deplored—and in such situations he might turn snobby and cruel. And then he really would seem like a snoot and I'd be embarrassed for him and keen to adjust the moment so he'd feel at home and secure and happy. Which was why, when I saw him one day on College Street, I greeted him warmly, waving my arm and calling hello.

He wore this day a purple bow tie, scarlet blazer, and lengthy silk scarf of the sort you'd see on a pilot boarding a Sopwith Camel. It was an ensemble I rather admired.

"Sebastian Hickey!" I said. "How goes it?"

"Oh," said Sebastian, bleary-eyed, "I've been immersing myself in a bath of Oliphant Smeaton."

"Is that safe? Is it even legal?"

"It's for 'Othello.' I'm the dramaturge for Cabaret Bam Bam."

"Right. The theatre company. And what's Dalton up to?"

"Something fiendish and malevolent, I'm sure." Sebastian wiped his mouth. "Do you know Dalton has a journal filled with the people he hates? Really absolutely loathes. I tried it for a while, but it's exhausting keeping up." He yawned. "Now McKee, you have this reputation for being an interesting chap, what do you think of the Canadian Securities Course? Do you think I should take it? I'm a bit of a financial illiterate, but you have to know a lot of maths and I'm good at maths."

"What about your novel? What's happening with Juliet Pepperhouse?"

"Oh, that. I've done some writing, but I keep waiting for the characters to *do* something, you know. I stare at the pages, daring someone to charge off somewhere. Even tried telling them to go fuck themselves. Still nothing. Strangest thing."

"Sounds like you've made a start."

"I fear the geist has gone out of my zeit. Not sure what's next."

Rather immediately, as the day would have it, Gudrun Peel sprang out of a taxi. She was returning from the university after delivering the first three chapters of her dissertation and looked quite glorious in a navy blue peacoat. I was happy to see her smiling because for some reason I'd been worrying all day she was going to dump me.

"Did you *smell* what came out of that taxi driver?" she said.

"Should we?" asked Sebastian.

"I just thought," said Gudrun, "something was in his bum and now it's in my nose."

"It's not all blossoms on College Street," said Sebastian.

"Between the falafel in the front and what he was farting into the back, it was just too much."

"Sort of a concerto grosso, was it?" Sebastian swung his scarf around his neck. "You don't have to tell me. I went to this Mexican establishment and came out absolutely reeking. Damn near ruined my best dirndl."

After a moment of hesitation, Gudrun began giggling, charmed by the possibilities of this new life form. "Aubrey," she said, "who's your marvellous friend?"

"You haven't met? Really?" I wagged a hand in introduction. "This is Sebastian. Sebastian, this is Gudrun."

"Gudrun?" Sebastian repeated, rather sharply, as if the name for him signified real and present danger. "Gudrun *Peel?*" He stepped back to inspect her. "You mean *you're* the gorgon? Well, yes, I've heard all about you. You're positively gorgonian. You devour men. But I bet they never leave you alone, do they? With those eyelashes. And that porcelain skin." Sebastian bent down, took her hand, and kissed it. "Where does one sign up?"

THE MANNER IN which Gudrun organized her friends and affiliates often baffled me. She seemed to have a network of connections whom I heard about but never saw. There was Pascal in Berlin and Cruikshank in Brooklyn and Kat in Montreal. "I miss all my friends," she'd say. "But I miss Kat the most. I mean, you're lucky, dude. You have friends here. People you can talk to. I'm not sure I do."

But Sebastian Hickey would become someone Gudrun could talk to, and he grew to be special among her Toronto confidants. That first afternoon on College Street we stayed in Bar Italia—drinking espresso, beer, spirits—as Sebastian re-enacted conversations he'd had with his college tutor, his mother, his mother's friends. He'd called one of his mother's Vassar classmates to say he was travelling to Manhattan and would she like to meet?

"'Whose son are you?'" said Sebastian in a quavering mid-Atlantic accent. "'Lolly Smith? Oh, *Smitty!* Well, of course I can see you in the city, but you must come visit us in Montauk'."

It was stratagems such as these that intrigued Gudrun Peel.

"What kind of man," she asked later, "takes the bus to New York City, stays at the YMCA, buys six pairs of boxer shorts at Brooks Brothers, and takes his mother's childhood friends to lunch? He's absurd. The man's absurd. And bow ties? Like, is he gay or what?"

I said I thought he might be beyond all that.

"Aubrey, he drinks *sherry*." Gudrun spoke as if this alone were worthy of strict attention. "And what does he do again?"

"I think he works in an antique store."

"He *is* an antique store. He's living in his own private Bloomsbury. And he's trying to write something?"

"Apparently."

"But does he write, though? God, he's a funny creature. He's such a snob. I don't think I've ever met such a snob. But I kind of love him. The repressed smart boy who nurtures quirky comic genius. He's sort of like me."

"I don't know if I've ever met someone so affected."

"Well," said Gudrun, "his affectations might be the only thing keeping him together. He's certainly not like anyone else I know, and I have no idea what's going to happen to him, but—Clifford?" She reached for my hand. "I think we just made our first friend together."

9

Othello by William Shakespeare directed by Istvan Boda.
The Bard's timeless tragedy gets an experimental revamp.
Presented by Cabaret Bam Bam outdoors under the Strachan
Avenue overpass. Opens November 5 and runs to
November 21. Pwyc.

CABARET BAM BAM was dedicated to work that explored difficult topics by radical, provocative, and visceral means.
"Purveyors of Cultural Disruption since 1988" was the slogan
on their posters, and the enterprise was under the supervision
of émigré artistic director Istvan Boda.

Now, Istvan Boda was a complicated guy. He and his wife
arrived from Serbia in 1984 and formed Dufferin Theatre Projects. Music was central to their vision—wailing sopranos and
pounding tom-toms—and the people onstage were always sort
of flying or falling or committing suicide while Istvan himself,
naked in a white shroud and lying flat on his back, screamed
the Book of Revelation backwards. That was the sort of show
they did. But Istvan grew impatient with the compromises
forced on him by that theatre company, as well as that marriage, and broke free of both to create Cabaret Bam Bam.

Soon thereafter, he was staging experimental dramas in
starkly non-traditional settings. Recent work included *No Exit*

in a freight elevator, *The Ghost Sonata* in an abandoned dry cleaner's, and *Maimed,* an original play, presented in Istvan's own kitchen, where two street kids pretended to be Bob and Billy Barton, two real-life brothers who'd been convicted of a series of murders in a Parkdale housing project.

Shrewd, passionate, alcoholic, perpetually searching romantically but currently living with a woman with muscular dystrophy, Istvan Boda was a *very* complicated guy. He was strongly built and Slavically handsome, in a look-into-my-eyes-and-understand-the-universe sort of way, and when strutting into the opening of a gallery exhibition or the launch of a designer's fall collection, he often put womenfolk in a fluster. His production of *Othello*—which Otis Jones was stage managing and for which Sebastian Hickey was dramaturge—was to be performed outdoors under the Gardiner Expressway. Whether Cabaret Bam Bam had permission from the city for such a site-specific production, I didn't know. I suppose if the authorities tried to shut it down, so much the better, for that would be political theatre of another kind. But was the show any good?

"It's sort of nightmarishly perfect," Sebastian told me. "But of course I *am* biased."

The show itself, an amalgam of dance, opera, and prison riot, was forgettable. What was not forgettable was Istvan Boda, who, after the performance, stood in his sweat-soaked Iago jockstrap in the exit area, wanting not only to shake hands with each and every audience member but to hug them all good night.

I was, by this time, used to other men checking out Gudrun— gawking, ogling—but nothing prepared me for Istvan Boda's unremitting hawk stare.

Afterwards, making our way up Strachan, Gudrun walked in sullen silence. I wasn't sure if Istvan had done something objectionable or if she was simply cold from sitting outside for two hours, but I sensed it was better to say nothing and, while walking beside her, positioned myself so I was the one closer to the curb.

"Why'd you do that?" Gudrun demanded. "Why are you walking over there now?"

I explained I was taught to walk between the street and my female companion.

"Yeah? Maybe it starts with walking next to the street and ends with roofies and date rape."

"Roofies and date rape? How'd you get that?"

"Figure it out." Gudrun resumed walking up the sidewalk.

I stared after her. "You want to tell me why you're mad?"

She stopped at Queen Street, marshalled her thoughts, and turned to me. "Okay," she said, "I know what it is now. It's that play."

"It's the *play?*"

"That's the first time I've seen 'Othello.' I know it's famous, but that play doesn't work for me. Because let me see if I understand the story. It's all right to murder your wife if she commits adultery, is that it? Oh, but it's a tragedy she *didn't* commit adultery and he kills her anyway? So we should feel sorry for him? Why? Because he's Black? So it's *his* tragedy? Even though she gets murdered?" Gudrun spat at the street. "That logic is just so hideous and sick-making, I can't tell you. I can't tell you how much I despise it." Her voice grew shrill. "It's like 'Betty Blue.' Please don't say you like that movie. In fact, if you say you like that movie, we have to break up—"

"I haven't seen it."

"Good. Don't. I'll tell you what happens. It's about a French chick who goes crazy and dies but she looks great doing it. It's sort of the key to French cinema."

"Why does she die?"

"Because she has a lot of sex. And because she has a lot of sex, she *has* to be crazy and die. So her boyfriend can feel poignant

— 83 —

about what happened." Gudrun scoffed. "I came out of that movie wanting to punch the filmmaker in the face. It's as ridiculous as—" She glared at me. "Have you seen 'Zorba the Greek?'"

"No."

"It's this movie where—" She sputtered. "It's so fucked! Why is the most beautiful woman on the island killed by the men? Because she has sex with someone the men don't want her to have sex with? And widows aren't really supposed to *have* sex. Not unless they're raped. Oh, well. Let's just end the movie with two men dancing on the beach. Because ultimately it's a celebration of the circle of life. And the murder of a woman." Her face twisted with revulsion. "*Think* what that does to a young girl growing up. What kind of message that sends her."

"How old is that movie, though?"

"It's a very fucked-up message is what it is. Women in this culture, they're not supposed to have an original thought. They're not supposed to say uncomfortable things. They're supposed to act polite and smell nice and dress as sexy cats on Halloween. You know this, right? I mean, it's not like I'm addicted to witnessing all the sick punk rock shit that goes down, but if I pretend this *isn't* real, in fact if I don't incorporate an understanding of this shit into my vocabulary, sooner or later it will be used against me. Like, what am I supposed to do? Pretend it's not there?" She jerked her head. "Christ, Aubrey, it's just the culture's so endemic with this stuff—and I know I'm getting all militant right now, but fuck it—because sometimes I'm reminded how deeply the masculine epistemology is embedded in our society and it makes me fucking crazy."

"And all of this is applicable to me walking on a sidewalk?"

"It's not *in*applicable! Because, yes, it's actually fucking relevant." Gudrun went quiet. "Uh-oh. I'm having that feeling."

"What feeling?"

"The feeling I'm going out with someone who doesn't get it."

— 84 —

"Get what?"

"The world. What's going on. What needs to be done." She covered one of her eyes. "Fuck, I don't know now."

"Know what?"

"Because—" She scowled. "What am I to you? Just some fun fuck. But in five years you'll want another life. Nice house. Nice things. Nice wife."

"Why're you *saying* this?"

"Because it's true! I know what happens. Jesus Christ, you rich kid fuckers—"

"I'm what?"

"Nope," said Gudrun. "Not doing it." With those words, she spun away and strode down Queen Street.

EPISTEMOLOGY—IT'S ONE OF those words like eschatology or teleology that I'm murky about and have to look up. Which I just did. Epistemology is the study of knowledge and the structures of knowledge. It's about what we believe in and why we believe it. And what distinguished Gudrun was her instinct to question our structures of knowledge especially if they seemed to her unfair or unjust. That she was so engaged with her own point of view fascinated me. She questioned everything and made *me* question everything. I've not been able to see *Othello* again without thinking of Gudrun. I still haven't seen *Betty Blue* or *Zorba the Greek*. But Gudrun's later criticism of *American Beauty*—"Oh, so if Mena Suvari's character *wasn't* a virgin, it'd be okay for Kevin Spacey to fuck her?"—still resounds years later. These jolts of judgment astonished me with their electricity. Gudrun was exploring an alternate epistemology—hers was a universe still actively developing—and even if she had not fully worked out her opinion, her surges of intolerance were a means to understanding. I was much more conventional in my views. "I feel like I'm dating someone from the Eisenhower administration," she told me once. With Gudrun I was self-conscious of the conservative and conventional life I'd led. I think, back at this time, I often behaved as if I didn't really have feelings. Certainly not to speak of. My own chemistries, for a variety of reasons—familial, social, tragical—skewed mostly inorganic.

WHETHER THAT PRODUCTION of *Othello* was our first fight, I don't remember. I think it was. Gudrun came to my apartment the next afternoon. She wore her navy blue peacoat with the collar up and sat rigidly on the couch. "Going out with someone—" she said. "Being with someone is complicated." She ruminated for a moment. "And sometimes I get mad because a relationship reminds me of the person I'm *not* going to become. But maybe that wouldn't happen with a normal person. Maybe that's just my feelings of weirdness."

"Unless," I said, "going out with someone actually shows you the person you *can* become. Don't you think there are relationships fluid enough that they allow people to develop into whoever they want to be? Isn't that what a good relationship is supposed to do? Gudrun?"

10

Sebastian Hickey's Lemon Cake

6 tablespoons shortening
1 cup white sugar
2 eggs
½ cup milk
1½ cup flour
1½ teaspoon baking powder
½ teaspoon salt
Grated lemon rind
Lemon juice

Cream shortening and sugar. Combine eggs and milk in a
separate bowl. Combine dry ingredients in third bowl. Add
alternately to shortening and sugar mixture. Always start
and finish with flour. Add grated lemon zest from one
lemon. Put in bread pan and bake at 350 for 45 min. While
warm, glaze with ⅓ cup sugar and juice from one lemon.

THAT WINTER WE WERE POOR. Gudrun made eleven hundred dollars a month, but rent and groceries and student loan
payments took away a thousand. My own funds were dwin-
dling. At the beginning of December, I borrowed sixty dollars
from eleven different people to cover my rent. Broccoli-and-
instant-noodles was a standby meal. Christmas travel wasn't
possible. We planned to spend the holiday at my place—my
roommates were elsewhere for ten days—and we decorated a

little spruce tree in a terracotta pot with paper snowflakes. A snowstorm filled the city on the solstice and I remember Gudrun asking if Sebastian was in town.

I said I hadn't seen him in a while.

"Call him right now."

I dialed his number and he promptly picked up.

"Sebastian," I said, "what news?"

"Oh," said Sebastian, "just leafing through 'The Sylvia Plath Cook Book.' Almost finished. I've got the oven at three-fifty."

Gudrun picked up the other extension. "Hickey? Get over here. You're coming for dinner."

"Look here," said Sebastian, "I've wanted to have *you* chaps for dinner. I mean, I'd invite you to my hovel, but it's such a disaster I can't prepare a meal for myself without vomiting."

"Invite us another time," I said. "Tonight, come here."

"Well, I do have some peach schnapps I'd like to get rid of—"

"We don't care what you have," said Gudrun. "Just come."

"May I bring my new companion?"

"Your new companion?" Gudrun said excitedly. "Of course. Let us know if there's any dietary thingamajigs."

"Will do. Cheerio."

Gudrun hung up the phone and looked at me in wonder. "A new companion? Who do you think it is? Is Sebastian *seeing* someone?"

FLURRIES WERE SPINNING WILDLY when Sebastian arrived at the front door, making him appear like a figure in a toy snow globe. He wore a peaked hat with lowered earflaps, a burgundy overcoat with matching half cape, and a leather satchel on his back. "I know, I know," he said with weary finality. "I look like Mycroft Holmes." His new companion, wrapped in an angora blanket in his arms, was a fluffy creature, a male puppy, and I asked his name.

"Whipple," said Sebastian as he trudged up the stairs. "A schnauzer-poodle cross. And he's a perfectly horrid little beast, aren't you, Whipple?" At these mentions of his name, Whipple poked his nose out of the blanket and sniffed at Sebastian's coat.

"Oh, he's weak," said Sebastian. "He's always been weak."

"Hello, Lovey," said Gudrun from the open doorway. "Can I get you a drink?"

"Thought you'd never ask. I did bring that bottle of schnapps, but I'll have whatever's going round."

Inside, I hung up Sebastian's snowy coat in the bathroom. When I came into the living room, he was sitting in an armchair and talking about Christmas shoppers.

"These ladies from Yorkville, they stumble into the shop, full of martinis and vitriol, no *idea* what they're buying. Put it all on hubby's Visa." After placing his satchel on the floor, Sebastian flicked a Christmas ribbon in Whipple's direction. "We're having a special this week on knick-knacks, incidentally, if you're interested in purchasing a trinket." The puppy, ignoring the ribbon, shyly advanced towards Sebastian's socked feet. "Oh, Whipple, you're hopeless. Hopeless." He lifted his empty wineglass. "This was rather good. May I?"

"I'll get it," said Gudrun, grabbing the wineglass and twirling to the kitchen.

I asked Sebastian what he was immersed in these days.

"I've been reading this new biography of Jackson Pollock. Not sure where I found it, but I can't put it down. These two homosexuals wrote it and they love to psychoanalyze everything. I think Pollock *was* a pretty mixed-up sort, but for these two everyone's completely bent."

"But Hickey," said Gudrun from the kitchen, "what about you? Are you painting? Are you writing? Because I'd love to see whatever you're working on."

"Ah, my book," Sebastian said ruefully. "My one-volume novel. I've applied for a grant, but they seem to be giving them out to other chaps at the moment. No, I think I have to chuck it. Rather hard to write a book. We can try, I suppose. For us there is only the trying. Is that the phrase? 'Four Quartets,' I think. Poor Tom. Poor Tom's God's vicar."

Returning with glasses of wine, Gudrun almost lost her balance with bursting laughter. "Did you make that up?" she asked. "Poor Tom's God's vicar?"

"That is one of mine. Made it up as a schoolboy. Poor Tom's God's vicar. Who hasn't seen the moment of his greatness flicker?"

"I *love* that," said Gudrun. "That's kind of genius." Passing him a glass of wine, she asked, "What kind of schoolboy were you, Sebastian?"

"Oh? A quiet, bookish sort. Often on my own. Rivendell. Oz. Lilliput. I've been to all of them." He looked to Gudrun with an air of interest. "And Miss Peel, what kind of child were you?"

"Me? Sheesh. I was a weird little kid. I didn't have a lot of party dresses, let's put it that way. Hey—" She waved her hand. "I have an idea." She pulled a red Altoids tin from her back pocket. "You guys want to do something bad?"

"Do you mean to tell me," said Sebastian, standing up, "you have curiously strong mints in there?"

Gudrun pried open the tin to reveal six joints.

"Oh my," said Sebastian. "Are those marijuana cigarettes?"

THE EVENING BECAME somewhat non-linear at that point, a hazy, dazey sort of evening where the soft focus of a scene might abruptly sharpen with the green lip of a wine bottle, a flick of bangs, a squirming puppy. We smoked three joints from Gudrun's stash, dined on takeout barbecue chicken and roast potatoes, and had for dessert Sebastian's lemon cake.

There was something loose and warm in the apartment, something besides Whipple, though perhaps something inspired by Whipple, because what we felt for each other was affection. We giggled. We gossiped. We drank. And I realized we were most rich being poor. Most of the time I didn't think to marvel at the good fortune of our lives—to have dinner with friends, to go to movies, to listen to music—and as the scented candles burned lower, and as we finished even the peach schnapps, we seemed a spontaneous family of four.

Somewhere near midnight, I was feeding Whipple a last crumble of lemon cake when, confused by my fingertips, the puppy jumped sideways, as if being attacked.

"He's a fickle little fiend, isn't he?" Sebastian said. "Yes, Whipple, I'm talking about you. J'accuse! You berserk little creature. You don't get any more because you're a naughty little baggage. But Whipple, my sweet, we should go. But before we do—" Taking hold of his satchel, Sebastian approached Gudrun, who was on the couch dreamily listening to Erik Satie. "I have a small gift for you, Gudrun Peel. Plucked from the liver of Prometheus, brought to earth in the beak of a griffin, and presented here tonight like the fabled apple of the apocalypse. Voila."

He fetched out a small oil painting. It was a framed seascape with splatters of yellow and scarlet, a sky of Moroccan blue.

"Who's the artist?" I asked. "Is it from the antique store?"

"Perhaps I *should* sell these at the shop," said Sebastian. "They'd never know the difference. I'll tell them Marsden Hartley did it."

"No, Clifford," said Gudrun, taking the painting. "Sebastian painted it." Gudrun gazed at the seascape with steady admiration. "Oh, it's beautiful. I love it."

"Well," said Sebastian, "I should return to my burrow. Come along, Whipple. We'll tootle off before we're snowbound." He pointed at the red Altoids tin. "I mostly stick to wine. But those are rather good. Do you mind if I take one with me?"

OUTSIDE, FLURRIES BLEW in bursting squalls, newly fallen snow sparkled under lamplight, and sloping drifts hushed the empty streets.

I wished Sebastian happy holidays and a safe journey home. "Dalton's well?"

"Dalton?" said Sebastian, buttoning up his burgundy over-coat. "I think"—he leaned forward to whisper—"he has a lover in Ottawa."

"A lover in Ottawa?" I smiled. "Good heavens, no."

"What about you?" asked Gudrun, appearing beside me. "Do you believe in love?"

"Of course," said Sebastian, attaching a leash to Whipple's collar. "Love's always there. Lurking around the corner for the next chap."

"I mean you."

"Oh, yes. I'm here too."

"Because," said Gudrun, "I think you're lovely and wonderful."

"And you're ravishing, Lady Peel. Everyone falls in love with you at some point." Taking a deep breath, Sebastian spoke to the sky: "Oh for a muse of Gudrun Peel that would ascend the brightest heaven of the holiday! A city for a stage, writers to act, and the world to view our common scene. Then should this starlit essence assume the part of Venus and, at her heels, leashed in like schnoodles, should half the world chase after."

"Hickey-Wickey," said Gudrun, her eyes moist with sudden feeling, "that's about the nicest poem anyone ever wrote me." She ran in socked feet in the snow and took Sebastian's face in her hands. "Thank you for coming." She kissed both his cheeks. "And Merry Christmas."

Sebastian made a waving salute and spun away, raising his hand in the air with a flourish.

We watched as he and Whipple walked in tumbling snow towards the Spadina subway station. After a moment of reflection, Gudrun turned to me and kissed me on the mouth. "Aubrey," she said. "Do you want to move in together?"

11

---

morning

stretch out
and i will sing our days
in wistful madrigals
with each breath of air
you rise

MOVING DAY WAS Good Friday and the afternoon of an Easter procession in Little Italy. There were six thousand participants and road closures till six o'clock. Because we were moving into a second-floor flat on Grace Street, not far from St. Francis of Assisi Church, we were forced to watch the floats, altar boys, torchbearers, penitents, choirs, Roman centurions, and three Jesus Christs parade for hours past our new address. The first Jesus wore a hemp robe and New Balance sneakers. The second, middle-aged and paunchy, sauntered by eating a panzerotto. And the last, in a crown of thorns and heaving a full-size cross, collapsed in front of our very house.

"Clifford," Gudrun said, "we're either close to April Fool's or the neighbours are going a little heavy on the symbolism."

What was that first weekend like? SAMPLE CONVERSATION: "Um—Aubrey? I know you survived in the outback eating squirrels, but you're in civilization now. You don't have to cook hot dogs in a kettle." "Hey, I did that two times. Three, tops." "And pillowcases and matching towels are our friends. They're not the enemy." "Matching towels. Fucking pink-and-teal matching towels." "Why don't you eat this apple? You should always have one for your blood sugar issues." "Maybe *you* have issues." "Okay, Clifford, come here and let me give you a kiss."

I tended to wish *all* conversations finished with kisses. I was new to the whirlings of a live-together relationship and my emotions were sometimes disordered. And now that my emotions are on the page, maybe it's appropriate to offer some commentary on this version of Aubrey McKee.

I WAS WAYWARD, clever, obstinate, and as I watch myself in memory carry moving-boxes up the stairs and stack them in the rooms of the Grace Street flat, I will explain now what I didn't think to think of then. Living with a girlfriend was new to me and the situation prompted new feelings.

I was not a very sexually experienced sort—Gudrun had had many more partners—so I was insecure about that.

Likewise, Gudrun had a drove of admirers—her high school English teacher still sent her birthday cards—and she was often invited out in the city and I was not. So I was jealous of that.

Plus, there had begun to be, on the last Sunday of every month, pot luck dinners at Walter Weir's new apartment. These were for employees only, and because I felt this was bullshitty and didn't like to be separated from Gudrun in this way, I could be made anxious about that.

And even though I was given to insecurity, jealousy, and anxiety—as well as the vexation that issued from my inability to express such feelings—I wanted to be understood as emotionally intact and I think I imagined, if someone *were* to write a book about me, that I'd be described as "heroic and stoic and mature beyond his years." But, you should know, I wasn't.

So the weekend of our move I was in an odd mood. On Easter Sunday, when Gudrun was getting ready for yet another pot luck at Walter Weir's, I was on the sidewalk waiting for Otis Jones and his El Camino. He'd agreed to help me transport my filing cabinet and bookshelf and Gudrun's red velvet sofa.

Now, Otis Jones had marvellous availability and to be in his presence was to be reminded of daring idiosyncrasy—you might see him with *The Dharma Bums* jammed into his pants, you might notice lavender nail polish on the fingernails of his left hand—but the guy was flaky. He smoked a lot of dope. He returned one phone call for every three received and often double-booked outings with friends. Did it matter? Otis Jones was Otis Jones, and in the latitudes below Bloor Street, he was trending up. His new book of poetry was about to be published by Wyndham and Weir, and Gudrun, not one to subscribe to classic models of masculinity, decided she *adored* the book.

She especially liked a poem called "Cupids," an ode to the town of that name in Newfoundland, and she found so much to like in the poem, and rereading it made her so happy, that she often recited its opening line, "I am the morning in Conception Bay!" when making a first pot of coffee, say, or running from a Canada goose in Trinity Bellwoods Park, or protecting herself from the frustration of being unable to find her other winter boot. And when she passed me carrying tea biscuits on her way to the pot luck, she sang it in my ear and made me promise to tell Otis how much she loved the line. But I didn't. He was late. Otis Jones was often late. And I became grumpy as I worried about completing the move before a storm broke later that day.

MOVING THE BOOKSHELF and filing cabinet went well, but at the end of the afternoon, nine storeys up on West Lodge

Avenue, when we considered the unwieldiness of Gudrun's red velvet sofa, my mood worsened. As quaintly Victorian as it once appeared, this dilapidated three-cushion sofa, with its sagging back, exposed down stuffing, and walnut carving, seemed to me ridiculously cumbersome. And the elevators were *still* broken, so we half carried, half slid the contraption down all those flights of stairs.

I came away from West Lodge Avenue grimly silent and it was while we were driving up Lansdowne, on our way back to Grace Street, that Otis made a prefatory sort of wheeze.

"So, uh..." He cocked his head, as if having trouble remembering something. "How's it going with you-know-who? What's-her-name. Dark hair."

"Gudrun?"

"That's the one." Otis nodded. "How's it going with Gudrun? Where's she tonight?"

"At a work thing."

"Go on," said Otis. "Walter's got her there on a Sunday?"

With this reference to Walter, thoughts of his beard and pot lucks—as well as his rather entitled chortle—began uneasily in my mind. I had presentiments of steep complication and abruptly asked, "So what's the story with that guy? He's from Newfoundland, right? Is he a friend of yours?"

"Not exactly. Walter's from town. From St. John's. I'm more a bayman."

"What's a bayman do?"

"Ties knots and fixes things. The town folk, they wouldn't know how. Too lazy."

"You think he's lazy?"

"Would it surprise you?" Otis smiled. "But you take a fellow like Walter and plunk him down in Toronto and what do you think's going to happen?"

"He starts a publishing company?"

"Well, yes. Technically, he did do that."

"Are you going for the big fish from the small pond thing?"

"More like a little fish in the Big Smoke."

"So you don't trust him?"

"Well, McKee," said Otis, guiding the El Camino towards a last parking spot on Grace Street, "there's different types of bullshit."

"Because I don't trust the guy at all."

"There you go." Otis switched off the engine. "A fish called Walter."

AT THE NEW place, with the red velvet sofa teetering off the back of the El Camino, Otis and I were confronted by the twin challenges of the front door and the narrow stairwell. We hoisted, we tipped, we toppled and turned, and finally, after unhinging the front door and unscrewing the sofa's wooden feet, we managed to press it through the entranceway and hump it upstairs. There we set it down amid the moving-boxes, random furniture, and unfilled bookshelves.

I stood there a moment, my shirt damp with sweat, and offered to take Otis for pizza and beer on College Street.

"On a Sunday night?" said Otis. "Maybe another time. You come to the Ship one day and we'll make a night of it."

"Well, then." I found and passed to him a quart bottle of rum. "Thanks for helping."

"You got it, boy." Otis felt the weight of the bottle. "You may want to talk to Gudrun Peel about all this. You know"—he tapped my chest—"let her know what's going on with you."

LATER, FOLLOWING A shower on this first evening alone, I walked naked to the bedroom, where I was surprised to see, on our newly made bed, a red Cortland apple on the midmost pillow. And this moment, as tiny as it was, as irrelevant to everyone else in the world as it might be, this moment meant so much to me because it showed Gudrun had been thinking of me and had in her heart a sweetness and light and I got into bed a-daze with thoughts unpredicted and new-starting...

WHEN GUDRUN ARRIVED home near midnight, she touched me awake and thanked me for moving the sofa when she'd been so—she found the word—*delinquent* and outside a distant thunderstorm broke and Gudrun, shedding her clothes, slid lissome into the clean sheets, smelling of boozy coolness and perfect girlhood. She climbed on top of me, straddled my thighs, and began French-kissing me, bringing my fingers between her legs to feel how smooth she was, how *wet* she was, and, after some moments, she fell beside me on the bed, reaching for my cock and wanting me on top of her. As I moved within her, she touched herself, her fingers nimble against my tautened stomach, her upper lip in sneer-spasm, for she was trembling, shivering, and as she came, her beauty transfigured by a sort of torment, all my worries vanished, all my feelings made gorgeously irrelevant, for this was, I thought, what a relationship *should* be, what I wanted it to be, and I write these lines not for anyone else's prurient benefit but to fasten with details into remembrance one rainy Sunday night making love with Gudrun.

12

———

Tonight on CBC **Radio One** Author and poet Otis Jones
discusses his writing process, the passions that shape his
new poetry collection, and all things meteorological as we
join him and his father hunting for moose in
Newfoundland and Labrador.

DALTON HICKEY COLONIZED all materials. There was no
one he hadn't read, nothing he didn't know, nowhere he hadn't
travelled. His intelligence disturbed me. He used words you
didn't recognize, like pelf and flyte and heuristic, and seemed to
take everything from you, make it his own, and, far from your
fumbling attempts to articulate a response or a differing view,
vault it away in the safe of his opinions. In my company, he was
never warm or generous or encouraging. He was always vaguely
adversarial. Rather than assuming you would become what you
wanted to become, there was much in his behaviour—his doubt-
ful gaze, his telling silence—which more than suggested you
would *never* become what you wanted to become and, further,
that you were probably failing at whatever it was you were trying to do now.

"Dalton Hickey?" Otis Jones said. "Yeah. He can be what the
Germans call a real fucking douche."

So I was disturbed by Dalton Hickey, intimidated by his achievement, and to Gudrun I seldom mentioned his name. That the two had gone in and out of some long-form relationship at McGill, a relationship that may have involved codependency and manipulation and who-knows-what-else, confused me. Their present friendship—which combined rivalry, fear, affinity, admiration, exasperation, mockery, and even outright revulsion—might attenuate from time to time, but the two never seemed to completely separate from each other.

She thought of him often. She was worried, for example, what he'd think if she flunked out of her PhD. "Wouldn't that be perfect?" she asked. "So then everything Dalton's said about me can become true and I can slit my throat." But I wondered if in some way Dalton's imagination actually *helped* Gudrun, if his conception of her work, and his sense of difficulty and complexity, created some space within which she might develop. Who knew how they affected each other? It often felt as if there was something sick and compromising and corrupt about their relations. It was beyond simple formulation, whatever it was, even if it had dissipated, and because I didn't understand to what extent they were fond of each other, or obsessed with each other, or cruel to each other—or any of the interior finagling that led to and from those dynamics—my reactions to Dalton Hickey were ambivalent and complicated.

In those first few years of our life on Grace Street, I mostly, and mostly successfully, avoided him. So to learn we'd been invited to dinner by Dalton Hickey and his new girlfriend did not, to borrow a phrase from a famous comedy of manners, exactly inspire me with feelings of unmixed delight. In the days beforehand, I was fretful and jumpy and finally asked Gudrun why she and Dalton Hickey broke up.

"Oh," she said, "it was fucked-up in twenty-two different ways. I don't know what they were, exactly, but I didn't need to figure them out. I just knew it was time to go. Before it got really juvenile and terrible. So, yeah, I'm glad you kind of swooped me away. I didn't want to be messed up my whole life."

"What do you mean, messed up?"

"With Dalton, I think it was masochistic what I was doing. Plus some other stuff happened and, well, I don't know if I ever got my power back." She sniffed. "I'm probably going to have a cigarette tonight, just so you know."

DALTON'S DINNER WAS a housewarming as well as a celebration of American Thanksgiving, his new girlfriend being from Connecticut. The couple had purchased a small carriage house near the university, on tree-lined Borden Street, and one icy Saturday in November, Gudrun and I walked from Grace to Borden, arriving with numb noses, freezing fingers, and cold trapped inside our overcoats.

Dalton greeted us at the door. Gone were the thinning curls and camel-hair jacket. His hair was shorn to a bristle and he wore a blue blazer, white shirt, grey flannels, and polished black oxfords.

"Hello, Gudrun Peel," said Dalton with a smile. "Don't you look delicious? And this is your beau? We've met before, haven't we?"

I said we'd met at Walter Weir's book launch.

"Oh?" said Dalton, frowning, as if forced to recall something disagreeable. "Did you like that party? A lot of expensive art on the walls, as I remember. None of which I particularly liked. This rage for Lawren Harris I find tediously suburban. Then again, that's Walter for you. Shackled to the boomer past. But it's Gudrun who has to work with him. Not me. Gudrun, darling, may I take your coat?"

Jennifer Hunniwell, Dalton's new girlfriend, was a gangly woman in diamond earrings, cashmere turtleneck, and slacks. Her braided blonde ponytail looked like something you'd see in a hayloft. Although she gaily waved to us from the kitchen, she was very busy with trays of filo pastry, bottles of red wine, and a baking dish for Arctic char. She and Dalton had dated sporadically, the Hunniwells owning a cottage near the Chester Yacht Club, and the year before, after a failed engagement to a Yale classmate, she'd spent the summer in Nova Scotia, where romance with Dalton had unexpectedly reawakened. Deciding to move with him to Toronto, she'd taken a job with a television production company.

There was among the women quite a discrepancy in personal presentation. Jennifer wore pastel eyeshadow, blush, and pink lip gloss. A thirtysomething woman with a slight French-Canadian accent, who had been in a serious-sounding telephone conversation since we arrived, had on winged eyeliner and red lipstick. Then there was Gudrun, with no makeup at all. She was, however, someone whom other women could not stop assessing, which was probably why, mindful of being the centre of attention, she flapped a hand melodramatically over her head and asked, "This is your *house?* You guys own it?" She considered the exposed brick, perfectly set dining room table, and shelves filled with books and compact discs. "Jeez, Dalton. It's stunning."

"Is it?" Dalton puckered his lips, as if, for better or worse, he was stuck with the place. "Bought it for seven-fifty. Probably paid a hundred thousand too much, but that's Toronto real estate for you."

"He's such a prince," said Jennifer. "He sold his dream car to help with the down payment."

"You sold your Spider?" Gudrun asked. "Really?"

"He was so *fond* of that car," said Jennifer.

"Fiat Spider," said Dalton, adjusting his collar. "Sold to a Portuguese chap. Wait till he sees how much oil it burns."

"He really loved that car," said Jennifer. "He *talked* to it."

"That's commitment," Gudrun said cheerfully, glancing at me.

"Better to move on," said Dalton, taking Jennifer's hand. "Anyone for a beverage?"

SOON TO JOIN US were the poet Charlotte Lister and her lawyer husband Peter. Though they drank like sailors, it was pretty obvious Charlotte and Peter Lister came from a world of Hermès scarves, *Town & Country* magazines, and Spanish holidays. They too had met in childhood, their family cottages side by side on Lake Rosseau, and they'd both attended Queen's University. Peter, a partner at a Bay Street firm, was grey and stooped at twenty-nine, and, despite slamming back an espresso, drowsy at seven o'clock. The last two arrivals were a husky fellow named Gogarty, Dalton's editor at *Saturday Night* magazine, and Freda Gubbins, a sprightly young intern at same, who left after two appletinis to see a show at Lee's Palace.

The remaining guest, the French-Canadian woman who'd been on the phone, was introduced as Marie-Josette and it took me a moment to realize this was Marie-Josette *Beaulieu*, the host and executive producer of *Beaulieu on the Arts*, a television program that aired every Sunday night from the nation's capital. There was something deftly attractive about her presence. In every motion and glance, she expressed sanity, elegance, and self-possession. I had a sense everyone was trying to impress her, so I treated her very casually, as if she were one of my sisters, one of whom she vividly resembled, and after a run of rather strained small talk, I chose to ask Dalton about Sebastian.

"My brother," said Dalton, "is in Nova Scotia as far as I know."

"Gudrun and I saw that production of 'Othello' he worked on."

"Did you?" Dalton turned to Marie-Josette. "My brother volunteers for this ragtag theatrical company. Cabaret Bam Bam, I believe it's called. For my birthday, he gave us a subscription to their season. I think we saw four plays?" Dalton smiled brightly at Gogarty. "Just the worst sort of hipster drivel. Pulverizingly inept. I mean, the last productions were so abysmal we almost forgot how horrible the first ones were."

"Gudrun," I said, noting her empty glass, "you're drinking white wine? Chardonnay work for you?"

"Sure."

"Peter?" Charlotte Lister elbowed her husband. "Why can't you be more like him?"

"Which one you mean, Shmoop?"

"This one." Charlotte Lister pointed at me. "I have never seen a more thoughtful boyfriend."

"Well-trained, is he? I'm sure he'll make a fine wife someday."

Charlotte Lister looked at Gudrun. "What makes you so lucky?"

"True," said Gudrun. "If I hadn't met Aubrey, I'd probably be dead in a ditch somewhere."

"What a charming thought," said Dalton. "Shall we move to the table?"

AND IT WENT on like that. The meal, I will say, was magnificent—red pepper and cucumber salad with sesame seed dressing, Arctic char, risotto, fresh squash. But the energy and dialogue seemed performed. We were mostly new to each other, behaving as if we weren't, and playing the parts of Entertaining Dinner Guests, rather as if we were auditioning to be panellists on Marie-Josette's television show.

Gudrun's thoughts were elsewhere—I was worried she was not enjoying herself—and when she excused herself from the table and didn't return, I thought to check on her. I went upstairs—only to be startled by Charlotte Lister, who came bumping out of the bathroom's pocket door.

"Whoopsie!" She undid a blouse button and smiled at me. "Did you want to use this?"

"Just looking for my date."

"Who isn't?" She smiled again, as if we might be fated for more intimate encounters later, then squeezed past me. "Try Dalton?"

Dalton in the kitchen was looking for something on the marble countertops, the kitchen island, and within the glass cupboards.

"Hey," I said. "Seen Gudrun?"

Dalton—continuing to search—didn't appear to hear me.

"Is there something I can help with?" I asked.

"Hmm?" Dalton said vaguely.

"Never mind. Do you know where Gudrun is?"

"She borrowed my lighter to set fire to something. I believe she's outside." He opened the dishwasher and looked through it. "But where is my salver?"

As I moved to the back door, I tried a last time to make conversation. "So Sebastian's in Nova Scotia? Are you there much?"

"Oh, I like Nova Scotia." From a high cabinet, he took down a silver tray and arranged six crystal champagne flutes on it. "Very pretty."

I asked if he'd ever go back.

"You're asking do I want to *live* there?" Dalton grabbed a bottle of Veuve Clicquot from the refrigerator. "Do I wish to return to polyester hoodies and camouflage utility shorts? To the permed and sunburned and continuously pregnant? Do I wish to spend my days reminiscing with the indigent and morbidly obese and those collecting pogey? While the alcoholic on the hill argues with the radio?" He popped the cork. "No, Aubrey McKee, I do not. I like a room where you can mention Proust and not be jeered for being a homo. I like a boulevard where a woman can walk in high heels and not be labelled a slut. And I do like, as despicable as he seems, the scruffy, goateed scenester in the corner Starbucks doodling sonnets in his pocket notebook. However horrible the sonnets. And, believe me, they will be." He filled each champagne flute. "I am interested in ideas and works of art and how these things affect the hemlines of political and cultural thought. And scallop fishermen and fork-lift operators on workmen's comp are not. At least not in my experience. And my experience"—Dalton picked up the tray and returned to the living room—"is what I'm interested in."

GUDRUN I FOUND at the far end of the backyard. She was coatless, shivering, an unlit cigarette in her lips, and feeling in her front pockets for the lighter. She was preoccupied, eyes half-closed, as if registering multiple narratives.

"Hey." I clomped through the snow. "This is like dinner with the grown-ups."

"Yup." Gudrun lit the cigarette. "I don't think we'll be playing beer pong."

"It's very coupley. Like a dinner party full of couples."

"It's like a reception for a Top Ten Under Thirty article. It's a media power list."

"So what are *we* doing here?"

She took the cigarette from her lips. "Exactly."

"I miss Sebastian and Whipple."

"Clifford misses puppies." Gudrun flicked her ash over the backyard fence. "I just can't believe Dalton has a fucking house. I'm so jealous it's making me insane."

"Not really getting a warm feeling from the guy. He's smart, though. Everyone's smart."

"Everyone's so one-uppy." Gudrun dragged on the cigarette. "I don't know. I'm not from here. Where I'm from is not perfect.

It's not powerful. It's not sophisticated. But it's honest. And you know who your friends are. In Toronto, the idea of a friend is sort of tactical. It's about how you can use someone to advance your career. But I'm not sure it's healthy. And I'm not sure I know how to do it."

"Marie-Josette's pretty great."

"Isn't she? She's one of those perfect French-Canadian women who speaks flawless English, graduated from the London School of Economics, and has a walk-in closet with sixty-three pairs of shoes." She exhaled. "I have a huge crush on her. She's so intact."

"What's she doing here?"

"She's here because Dalton's probably fucking her."

"Is that a joke?"

"My guess is she's the lover in Ottawa."

"Really? He'd invite his mistress to dinner?"

"Why not?" Gudrun coughed. "He invited Jennifer for dinner when I was with him."

"He did? Fuck this guy. Why'd you go out with him?"

"If you want me to apologize for being cheated on, I'm not sure I should do that."

"Oh," I said, "I didn't mean it like that. Gudrun—"

"Whatever." She dropped the cigarette in the snow and stamped on it. "I'm sorry I'm not a virgin, Aubrey. But I did date other men." She blew a plume of smoke and looked at the lighted windows of the kitchen. "I just can't believe he has a fucking house."

THE BACK ENTRY—a sliding glass door—was locked and I had to pound on its glass to get someone to notice. After some minutes, Dalton spied us, slid open the door, but did not immediately speak. His head was held to one side for he was listening to a radio program emanating from the living room stereo.

"I believe it's Mr. Jones," he said, finally letting us in. "On location somewhere."

Since leaving Toronto, Otis Jones had been on the go. We'd received postcards from Lowell, Massachusetts, and Bangor, Maine. This week he was moose hunting with his father in Buchans Junction, Newfoundland, and the escapade was being broadcast on CBC Radio.

"Otis Jones," said Charlotte Lister, reaching for her wine. "The man, the myth, the legend. He's a man for all seasons."

"Is he?" Dalton moved to the stereo to adjust the volume. "Not sure I'd take that bet."

"Which one is he?" asked Peter Lister. "The poet? He's a disaster. He's the sort of guy you see living in his car."

"You're just jealous," said Charlotte, "because he's tall and dreamy."

"Ah, yes," said Gogarty. "The sly wit and offbeat charm of the Newfoundlander. Whether it's genius or codswallop is up to each of us, of course, but it's a bit much, this preoccupation with the folk art of Newfoundland."

Marie-Josette looked to Dalton for a more balanced inter-pretation.

"Well," said Dalton, "I can admire Otis, but I rather take Gogarty's point. And I'm not sure the idea of Otis Jones as Holy Fool, sprinkling his Newfie fairy dust over the country-side, is one I care to endorse over the long term."

"Turn it up," said Charlotte Lister, listening. "They see some-thing."

Dalton spun the volume and into the living room came the sounds of Otis Jones and his father tramping through a woodsy marsh a thousand miles away.

"Quiet now, Pop," said Otis. "You'll spook him."

"Aw, look," said the father. "Ain't he something? Oh, I loves being in the woods, boy. Aim for the neck—"

"*Shh*, Dad. And stay in sight, would you? Don't wander off."

"Jesus," Peter Lister said. "Can we turn this off before someone gets shot?"

At that moment, there was the crack of a rifle shot, but Dalton perversely switched to piano music—Glenn Gould's *Goldberg Variations*—and returned to the table.

"Now we don't know who's been hit!" said Charlotte Lister.

"Isn't it better that way?" asked Dalton. "Anyone for a refill?" He picked up the Veuve Clicquot and raised it over Marie-Josette's glass. "Un petit peu?"

"Ça suffit." Marie-Josette covered her glass with two fingers. "I'm fine."

Jennifer was announcing dessert and taking requests for coffee and tea when Marie-Josette, who had been quietly attentive to Gudrun all evening, turned to address her for a first time.

"What about you, Gudrun?" Marie-Josette asked, her fingers shifting to play with her earring. "What did you think of the radio piece?"

"Well—" Gudrun was staring at the curved tines of her dessert fork. She put it down and quickly fingered some hair behind her ear. "I've never been to Newfoundland or anything, but it seems sort of easy to me. Otis is doing the life-lessons-in-hardscrabble-poverty thing, but he sort of wants to make a groovy aesthetic out of it by essentializing moose hunting as an authentic scenester-related activity. Which I find seriously upsetting in about four different ways, but mostly because I think what the fuck? I haven't met Otis's father or anything, but there's something—I don't know—beautiful about a moose. I mean, it's kind of fucking majestic. And the idea that they want to go into the woods with a gun and blow it away kind of disturbs me. I mean, just because they have a house in Newfoundland doesn't mean they should be allowed to watch child pornography, does it? Hunting's *fucked*. To take an animal's life? It just feels like some big-ass circle jerk."

The silence at the table was salient. For Gudrun had gone where no one else had ventured—she'd risked being emotional—and her voice in her last words had shaken with feeling. No one said anything until Marie-Josette, who had not taken her eyes from Gudrun, raised her chin to ask, "Would you like to come on television to talk about that?"

13

Selkirk is a town in the western province of Manitoba twelve miles north of Winnipeg on the west bank of the Red River. It has a population of 9,701. Mainstays of the local economy include tourism, a steel mill, and a major psychiatric hospital.

"I CAN'T GO ON television and slag Otis Jones. He's one of Wyndham and Weir's authors. I'm supposed to be publicizing him, not dissing him in the national media. I love Marie-Josette, she's totally fabulous, but I'd lose my fucking job. I mean, do you think I'm being crazy? Holy shit, that dinner made me feel weird."

Dalton's dinner wedged inside Gudrun for several reasons. Not only because, shortly after, she fell sick with a persistent cough, but because she was convinced that hers had been conduct unbecoming to a literary professional.

"I get so snippy and acerbic at those things," she said.

"You were hardly snippy and acerbic."

"And I don't want to drink anymore. I don't like myself when I drink."

"You weren't that drunk."

"Yeah, no, I kind of turn into this bitchy opinionator. And I don't want to be one of those people who has to drink to get through things."

But what really obsessed her, for she mentioned it more than a few times, was how Dalton and Charlotte Lister had met their respective spouses. "Meeting your partner because your cottages were next door to each other, that's not really my heritage, Clifford. I'm not a rich kid. Like you and Dalton are Halifax rich kids—"

"He's not from Halifax. He's from Chester Basin."

"Well—" She briefly tipped her head. "I can't always keep track of the Nova Scotian diaspora. I'm just saying I'm the only one with a poverty-class background." She sent a stern look my way. "I didn't grow up in a perfect family, dude."

"Not sure I did either."

"We grew up in different houses, Aubrey. I didn't go to private schools and tennis camps. And when my dad was alive, I didn't have a lot of friends over, because my parents were drunk most of the time. I mean, I imagine you with my uncle Dwight and it just doesn't work. Waspy middle-class people make my family look like a bunch of twitching loogans."

AS I WAS getting involved with Gudrun Peel, I was also getting involved with the dramas of her childhood, which might be best summarized by the tabloid headlines DEAD DRUNK DAD and BORN-AGAIN MOM. Gudrun was twelve when her father died, hit and killed by a drunk driver when he himself was drunk on a crosswalk. She'd loved her father and often wore his wristwatch as her own—a wide-strapped curio so loose on her wrist it slid up and down her forearm— but his drinking she despised. He had been the lead singer in a Winnipeg bar band—think the Guess Who that didn't make it—but fell into drunken purposelessness. First beers were at eleven in the morning and thereafter he'd drink till drunk. There was something tragic and sinister and horrible about it.

"Everybody in Selkirk knew what was going on," she said. "Someone should've called Children's Aid. But no one did anything. I remember I was at this birthday party, my father was supposed to pick me up, but he never came." Embarrassed to be seen waiting, ten-year-old Gudrun walked the six miles home. "When I got back, my dad was passed out in his truck." She shuddered. "Alcoholized diarrhea is not really a smell you forget. You know the smell of liquid pig manure? That's pretty much it. And that wasn't even the worst day. My parents—" She wiped at her eye. "My whole life's been sort of determined by my parents, and my parents weren't sophisticated people. They were very young when they got married. Teenagers. And I came along and, well, just think of any sort of comfortable middle-class life, like Anne Murray and wagon wheel tables and cherry Pop-Tarts, and think of those things as a completely impossible dream. My family's from the sticks, Clifford. I grew up poor. Like food banks and welfare cheques. I don't know if you can understand that if you didn't live it. You and your sisters had advantages I didn't have. And sometimes it makes me resent you."

"Resent me?"

"I'm not saying it's logical. It's just that feelings are powerful." She sighed. "When I think of my father? I really did love him. I don't know why he drank. His brother died when he was young and I don't think he ever got over it. But I don't know. Things usually happen for more than one reason. And alcoholism becomes its own pathology."

Gudrun's mother in widowhood became sober, born-again, Pentecostal. This was thought to be a temporary development, following from Alcoholics Anonymous meetings in church basements, but she continued fiercely pious and Gudrun's memories at this time, as a country girl tween, were of church meetings in prairie towns—oatmeal cookies, Styrofoam coffees, stilted conversations with the elderly devout.

"I'm not sure you understand, Aubrey. My mother's a Bible-thumper. An evangelical. She thinks she's going to meet Jesus on the mountaintop."

The few times I was uncomfortable in Gudrun's presence were when she spoke on the phone with her mother. In these conversations, Gudrun's voice had a forced cheerfulness that she used to misdirect her queasy feelings of anger and pity and sadness and exasperation.

"I'd prefer it if my mother just came out and said she disapproves of me," she said. "Just anything besides this gratuitous Christian distortionism."

"Gudrun," I said, reaching for her hand, "I wish you had a sister."

"Why?"

"So you had someone to go through that with."

"Yeah? But maybe being an only child made me resilient. Because I knew I had to get good grades. If I didn't, I'd still be there." Her eyes welled up. "So now I'm in Toronto with crippling student debt, but at least I'm here."

"I'm *glad* you're here—"

"No, I know."

"And I don't mind if you talk about this stuff."

"I know." She pushed away a tear. "I don't talk about it too much because it makes me feel too shitty."

"Gudrun, you are an amazing person who has come very far—"

"Some of that stuff is hard to even think about. I know everyone has to create their own life, but some shit just devastates me. And I don't really want to fall into another depression. And I don't want to drink. So it's kind of like, what else is there?"

14

Zoloft®
TAKE 2 TABLETS BY MOUTH EVERY DAY
Sertraline Hydrochloride equivalent to 50 MG Sertraline
MAY CAUSE DROWSINESS

TO COUNTERACT FEELINGS of devastation and depression, that winter Gudrun stopped drinking, stopped eating junk food, and went on an antidepressant called Zoloft. The pills flattened the extremes of her moods, but there were side effects—emotional numbness, reduced libido, weight gain. "None of my jeans fit me anymore," she said forlornly, looking at herself in the bedroom mirror. But Gudrun had resolved to move forward responsibly, properly, professionally. While she waited to hear back about the first draft of her dissertation, she began a crusade of increased expedition.

In her capacity as marketing associate at Wyndham and Weir, she was obliged to attend all of their functions, but she opted now to check out every literary happening—every book launch, poetry slam, fundraiser, and open mic. Socializing in such circles was one of the skills she sought to acquire, she applied herself with the keener fanaticism of an A-student, and in three months I think Gudrun met every unshackled poet within a hundred miles of the CN Tower.

POETRY—I'D NEVER REALLY set my thoughts to the writing of poetry. Gudrun and Otis Jones and Charlotte Lister were committing themselves to an institution of words, seeking to transform Days Lived into Poems Written, and for no foreseeable return except a nervous nod of appreciation from a stranger in a moth-eaten cardigan at a poetry reading.

Now I tended to throw all poets in a drawer labelled *Crazy Fucking Poets,* but I was learning there were divisions among them. The conceptual poets chased their own ideas, the speculative poets their own realities, and the confessional poets their own feelings. And the mere mention of John Ashbery could provoke a fist fight.

Gudrun had little patience for such divisions. Or divisiveness.

"People dismiss each other in these knee-jerk distinctionalist ways which don't really work for me. I mean, Jesus, God, we're here for such a short time. Can't we just get along?" She duly supported *all* members of her poetical family, congratulating them on their grants, attending their events, buying their books.

But what was she trying to prove? And for whom? She was in the midst of her job, her thesis, still hacking with coughs from that November dinner—and traipsing everywhere in damp winter boots—and I worried she was depleting herself. So when Charlotte Lister asked her to participate in Stop the Silence, a poetry reading and benefit for the Toronto Rape Crisis Centre, I suggested she skip it.

"I have to go, Clifford," said Gudrun, brushing her hair. "I don't feel much like a poet anymore, I haven't written a fricking poem in a year, and this would be my first reading in Toronto. Don't worry"—she sneezed—"you don't have to go. If I bomb, it's better no one's there."

"But how're you feeling?"

Gudrun sneezed again, a spasm so violent she was unable to speak. When it was over, she leaned over the toilet bowl and spit out a gloop of sputum. This sputum, dissolving in the toilet water, was murky with psychedelic colours.

"Peel," I said, "that infection's gone to your chest." I touched her forehead. "How long have you been running a fever? You sure you want to do this?"

"I promised. I want to support Charlotte. It could be really good. It could be amazing. I mean, if life is essentially meaningless, you might as well try to be amazing. Or—I don't know—get a job in marketing."

WHEN YOU SUPPORT your friends by going to their shows, you are in some sense participating in their efforts, sharing your hopes with their own, and contributing to their careers. Gudrun had high hopes for Charlotte Lister's evening, but when she returned, I saw she was saddened by the formlessness of it all.

"It was just so almost." She sat on the bed and pulled off her snow-wet jeans. "Charlotte's almost political. She's almost radicalized. She's almost brilliant. But I'm not sure she's enough of any of those things to make it. And because she's so pretty, I don't think people will take her seriously until she actually has something to say." A convulsion of sneezes passed through Gudrun, and as she got under the covers I passed her a clean cotton T-shirt to sleep in. "I'm interested in magic, you know? And when something doesn't come up to expectations, I feel like I've wasted my night. Because a lot of poetry readings are death. They're just nothing. And I'm bored of all this nothing. I'm bored of non-events. I'm bored of nights when someone says their friend is great and they turn out to suck so bad it's embarrassing." Lying in bed, she twirled a hand in front of her face, as if summoning spirits out of the air. "I want amazement. I want enchantment. I want something so stellar I will always remember it. And I want to feel something is happening." She sniffled. "I just wish for something to happen. Is that too much to ask?"

15

CULKIN W LUV 2 PEEL SONY METAL SR-60

Tom's Diner	SUZANNE VEGA
If She Knew What She Wants	THE BANGLES
You Don't Need	JANE SIBERRY
I Only Want To Be With You	THE TOURISTS
Retard Girl	HOLE
Bodies in Trouble	MARY MARGARET O'HARA
Here's Where the Story Ends	THE SUNDAYS
Jolene	DOLLY PARTON
Easy	TIMBUK 3
Lorelei	COCTEAU TWINS
Johnny Are You Queer?	JOSIE COTTON
Walkin' After Midnight	PATSY KLINE
Hope Road	ANNE CLARK
2000 Miles	THE PRETENDERS
Hate My Way	THE THROWING MUSES

AND THEN IT GOT COLDER. Two months of winter storms left the city craggy with cold. The skies were grey, streets salt-stained, sidewalks crusty with frozen snowfall. One night in February, in the waning hours of an all-day blizzard, with streetcars disabled, I plodded home in blowing flurries from the Lash Miller building. Toronto this night was a city made alien by temperature, it was really too cold to be outdoors, and I saw no one, not a single person, on any sidewalk. I felt lost in mid-winter. So did Gudrun.

The week before Valentine's Day, there had been bad news from professors Folliot, Block, and Bugbee, her thesis advisory committee. Because I once remarked the names sounded like a Calgary law firm, Gudrun now referred to them only as "that fucking Calgary law firm." To wit: "Can you believe that fucking Calgary law firm rejected my dissertation?" The rejection was damaging and her feelings of defeat and failure, coincident with her desire for excellence, began to disable her. She took a leave of absence from the publishing company. Some days she did not get out of bed. And she had continued sickly. Her moods were not good. I'd return home to find her sobbing, coughing, unable to calm down, obsessed with some new slight or setback. She spun through a spectroscopy of sadness—blue sorrows, red meanies, dead greens—and melancholy blackened many days.

"I don't know if I can see anyone," she'd say, "when I'm going through all this."

So I did not know what to expect as I climbed the stairs to the Grace Street flat. Wiggling off my winter boots, I was encouraged to hear music in the front room. It was a favourite mixtape of Gudrun's, sent by a friend in Montreal, and the cassette's cardboard insert, which had been reversed—and which I'd read many times—showed the track listings on the front flap and a note, *Culkin w Luv 2 Peel*, written in mauve eyeshadow pencil, on the spine.

Because Gudrun's tape player had a function for continuous play and because she often fell asleep without attending to it, a cassette might play for six hours or more, and this tape had been played so regularly it was full of whistles and pops and high-frequency fall-off. It made me sad, somehow, to understand it was disintegrating, when the songs had been sent with love, and as I walked to the bedroom, softly calling Gudrun's name, I resolved to respond to her darkened moods in the same spirit of love.

She was sleeping in a jumble of blankets and pillows and papers. On the floor around her were containers of Zoloft, Extra Strength Tylenol, Robaxacet, and Gaviscon, as well as bottles of NyQuil and Benylin, teacups of NeoCitran, crumples of Kleenex, and, somewhat randomly, a pint of Jack Daniel's.

Gudrun seemed a different version of herself. Her skin showed signs of eczema, her waist was pudgy, and her black hair stringy and damp. But gazing at her hair, as it stuck in wet wisps to her temple, brought on for me a sentimentalizing awareness of all the people she'd met. A kid on a playground who saw her once and remembered her forever. A guidance counsellor in high school recognizing her talent. A McGill undergraduate astonished by his TA's beauty. And here she was now, in the bed I shared with her, sleeping, dreaming, just now stirring.

SHE AWAKENED WITH a lurch, coughing as if something had gone down the wrong way. She looked around the room, bewildered, and rubbed her eyes. She wore a purple hoodie, frayed black leggings, and heavy grey work socks. Rising up from these bedclothes was a smell of sweat—a tang of wetness on top of older perspiration.

"Is it still snowing?" she asked.

I said it was.

She dislodged herself from the blankets. "My neck's sore." She massaged under her ear. "My neck's always sore."

Striving for a cheerful tone, I asked how she was feeling.

"The same. Horrible. I'm so bloaty and gross." She sat up and, slouching slightly, rested her back against the wall. "I'm sorry you have such a lame and horrid girlfriend."

"I don't have a lame and horrid girlfriend. I have a very sick girlfriend."

"Yeah, no, with me it's all misery, all the time." She sniffed. "Clifford, sometimes I think you should go out with a normal person—"

"What's that?"

"—because you're too nice to be with a sick, hysterical freak."

"Hey—" From my shirt pocket I brought out a pack of Wint-O-Green Life Savers. "I got you a treat. It's methyl salicylate. It sparks in the dark."

"Christ O'Malley," said Gudrun. "You've given me so many treats. You don't have to give me any more." She spied the container of Zoloft beside the bed. To reach it without moving, she had to slump somewhat lower on the wall, but this new position proved unstable because—when she groped for the Zoloft—she tumbled sideways, her elbow cracking on the floor and her wrist knocking over a teacup of NeoCitran.

"Why is everything such a *trial* right now?" Gudrun asked, staring at this spill.

Using some Kleenex, I wiped up the NeoCitran.

"And why," said Gudrun, "have I been sick for three months? It's not fair. It isn't. I don't always want to vent to you, but nothing's really gone right. I hate my job. I hate grad school. I hate my thesis—" She shoved a heap of papers off the bed. "Why can't they just take it as is?" She sucked her lower lip. "There really is only success and failure."

I said there were other ways to think of it.

"No, there isn't. This dissertation is like a referendum on my talent." She snuffled. "I just wish I was smarter. If I was smarter, I wouldn't have to work so hard."

"Gudrun, you're one of the smartest people in the city—"

"Then why do I feel like I'm going to fuck this up? Because I *am* going to fuck this up. I couldn't finish my poetry manuscript. I can't finish this dissertation. I was scared when I was little I was going to be a fucked-up person. And now I finally

— 122 —

am." She sighed. "Aubrey, I can honestly say I have never been happier in my life. I didn't even know someone could *be* this happy. And it's because of you."

"Or it's because of us together—"

"But—I don't know—I feel like I'm starting not to have a personality anymore. Or I'm losing it. Or I don't know where it is. I can't explain it. I feel so weird. It's those *pills*—" She glared at the Zoloft. "Those pills are fucking with my brain chemistry. I don't feel sexy on those fucking pills. And I've gained so much weight—" She made a frowny smile. "I'm fat. I've never been fat. And I'm a fucking whale."

"Gudrun, it's the middle of winter. Everybody gains weight."

"Hey—" She rolled on her side, shook some hair from her eyes, and glanced over her shoulder. "You still want to do me?" She saw me looking at a rupture in her leggings. "You want to slam this new fat booty, is that it?" Gudrun wiped her runny nose. "We can do the side-by-side thing if you want. But I'm warning you, I'm not moving. I'll just face the wall."

"Sweetie—"

"Because I know we haven't had sex in months."

"We don't have to think about sex right now." I picked up the container of Extra Strength Tylenol and shook it. "We out of Tylenols? I can do a drugstore run." I tucked her in, smelling again the sourness of the bedsheets. "And maybe I should change the bed."

Gudrun dabbed her nose with Kleenex. "And maybe I should have a baby."

"Excuse me?"

"Would you like that? I'll just give up and have a baby."

"Because that's the way a child should enter the world."

"Well," she said, "I know I'm sort of joking, but sometimes I think we should've had a baby when we moved into this place." She folded the Kleenex. "Listen, bud, you should knock me up when you have the chance. You want a cute little baby? It'd give me a chance to try out these new honking boobs."

"Not sure that's the reason to have a child either."

"If we had sex now, you probably *would* knock me up, I'm so out of it. I feel like I haven't got my period in months."

"Okay, Peel." I grabbed one of the papers from the floor and pulled out a pen. "Tell me what you want at the drugstore. Tylenol, Benylin—"

"And Robaxacet." She flicked her hair behind her ears—middle fingers moving in tandem—and added, "And Fisherman's Friend."

"Anything else?"

"Kleenex and Popsicles. Actually?" She got up. "Fuck it. I'm going out." Gudrun slid to the window and peeked at the blizzard. "I'll have a shower and go with you. Because this is ridiculous."

"In a snowstorm?"

"Fucking A. Let's hit up some titty bars."

"Sure. I'll get my snow pants. Gudrun, you can barely see straight."

"I can't stay inside anymore!" She stamped her socked feet. "It's been three weeks! Where's a towel?" Gudrun was sliding towards the bedroom door and reaching for the bath towel draped over it when she slipped on a piece of paper. She tumbled sideways, her face striking the cut-glass doorknob, and promptly fell to the floor.

I knelt beside her. She was barely conscious, she looked as weak as a child, and for the first time I realized she might be, as she once described herself, fragile.

"Gudrun?" I carried her to the bed. "Can you hear me?"

"Stupid," she said. "So stupid."

"You rest a minute."

"No," she whimpered. "Titty bar."

"Please rest, Clifford."

"Clifford dead. New name Smudge. Smudge stain everything."

"Sweetie," I said, examining the welt on her cheek. "Do you want to go to Emergency? What do you think?"

Seized by a violent and protracted coughing spell, Gudrun rolled on her side. Bringing her knees to her chest, she hacked up something from inside her lungs. When the coughing subsided, she spit into a fold of Kleenex.

"I know I'm disgusting," she said, "and I know what you think of me." She cleared her throat. "You don't have to sleep here if you don't want."

Needing a moment to myself, I stood up and went to the closet. There, in the dust of the floor, was a black ballet flat, the sheen of its inside edge worn away, and I remembered that for some weeks we'd been unable to locate its pair. I was wondering how we could possibly lose a shoe in this tiny apartment when Gudrun groaned on the bed.

"Oh, Aubrey," she said, staring at the wall, "have you ever not wanted anything?"

"Not wanted anything?" I looked at her. "But then it's like you're dead."

"That's right." She gazed at a crack in the wall. "All I have to do is die." She tried to touch the crack, the moment seemed very important to her, and murmured, "The only thing I have to do is die." Her fingertip fell just short of the wall, and in order to make contact she was forced to stretch over a pillow. This pillow bunched beneath her hips and the blankets fell away, exposing the partial nakedness of her ass-cheek.

My girlfriend had just talked about her own death, but the smell of her rank sweat, the plumpness of her ass, and the aura of feminine defencelessness aroused in me a reaction rather inappropriate to the circumstance, so when the doorbell rang, I was both grateful for, and frustrated by, the interruption.

"It's eleven o'clock!" I said loudly. "Who's ringing doorbells at this hour?"

As I trooped down the hall, a swell of sexual confidence rose in me and I imagined a time when I would be on top of Gudrun, controlling her upraised ass with my thrusting hips, and moving towards the front door I felt an erection buckle in the fabric of my underwear. While I was sticking my hand down my pants to unkink myself, I heard Gudrun call out, "I don't want to see anyone!" Nodding in response to Gudrun's plea, and to any number of other exigencies, I pulled open the door.

THERE ON THE LANDING was a snow-speckled scarecrow. She wore a pink acrylic ski mask, a scarlet overcoat with a mink collar, and carried a canvas zipper bag. The ski mask was dappled all over with snow, in fact her entire person was dappled all over with snow, and as I noticed further details—an infected eye, the drooping tassels of a scarf beneath the coat hem—I was deciding to make clear she was at the wrong address when there was a squitter of movement behind me.

"Kat?" Gudrun whispered, limping down the hall. "Is that you?"

From the visitor came a barely perceptible nod of the head and Gudrun squeaked with joy.

"Oh, Culkin," she said, "I am *so* happy to see you, I can't tell you."

Gudrun shuffled up and flung her arms around the visitor's snowy shoulders, embracing her as if she were the one creature in all the world who had any real claim to understanding her.

16

---

night zoo

a frog in my throat
it's all in my head
a flea in my ear
it's all in my head
here's mud in your eye
now get up off the bed
like a crow freed at last
rising up from the dead

KATHRYN CULKIN HAD been a contributor to *Cinnamon Dip,*
Gudrun's roommate at McGill, and a kindred spirit. Five foot
three, willow-thin, with slanted blue eyes, Kat Culkin was a
girlish grown-up who reminded me variously of Little Red Riding Hood, Lizzie Borden, and someone with a personality
disorder. She exhibited that first night an epilepsy of expressions—glares and starts and involuntary smirks—all of them
sourced in suffering. She had not slept in two days, she'd
thrown up on the train from Montreal, and she was shell-
shocked, short of breath, and shivering. She did not make eye
contact—she seemed afraid to look at anything directly, lest
she interact with malignancy—and indeed, in the front room,
where Gudrun sat her down on the red velvet sofa, Kat peered

into the corner as if she fully expected a spiny lizard to pull itself out of a crack.

To have Kat's behaviour in our apartment unnerved me. She seemed like a rescue animal that, abused in youth, never quite recuperates no matter where it's re-homed. And even though she was petite, there was something awkward about her, something disjointed in her anatomy, as if one of her shoulder blades didn't fit correctly. There was just something gorky about everything she did, and as I stood in the hallway, watching her, I took an instinctive step back, repulsed by her haplessness. I returned to the bedroom, closing the door behind me, and began tidying up the Zoloft, Robaxacet, Gaviscon, NyQuil, Benylin, teacups of NeoCitran, dissertation papers, and crumpled folds of dried snot.

FOLLOWING SEVERAL MINUTES of subdued conversation, I heard Gudrun leading Kat on a tour of our apartment. I couldn't make out the words, but Gudrun's tone I understood—soothing, practical—her inflections implying she was not showing the place to a close personal friend so much as guiding a disabled person through a possibly hazardous new environment.

When they entered the kitchen, because of the acoustics of the flat, their soft-spoken exchange sounded with exacting clarity in the bedroom.

"So Kat? Look at me?"

"Mmf?"

"There's always food in the fridge. Here's cheese and prosciutto—"

"I'm vegan."

"There's carrots and beets in the salad drawer—"

"I only eat white foods. Rice. Parsnips."

"Okay."

"But I'm on a cleanse, so I'm not really eating."

"Sure."

"Do you have hazel water?"

"Just tap."

"For my colitis, I need hazel water."

"Right."

"And does this kitchen have pots that haven't been used to cook meat?"

WHAT WAS MY response to this absurdist dialogue? Picture this in split-screen, on one side Gudrun is taking Kat on a guided tour, on the other I am pacing here and there, stunned at the words I am hearing, repeating in shocked whispers the words I am hearing, and generally waving my hands and muttering, "What the fuck?"

When Gudrun returns to our bedroom, I say, "She only eats white food? So she's a food racist?"

"Shh," Gudrun says, closing the door.

"And hazel water?" I whisper. "What the fuck is hazel water?"

"Dude—" Gudrun steers me away from the door. "Kat has maybe a screwed-up relationship to food, but gaunt and pathetic isn't a bad look for her."

"Gudrun, she looks like Crackhead Number Two."

"Yeah?" Pulling off the dirty bedsheets, Gudrun balls them up and tosses them in the corner. "She sort of needs to get her power back."

"Get her power back? I'd be surprised if she could eat cereal."

From a closet shelf, Gudrun takes down some clean linen and, after a moment of pensiveness, starts changing the pillowcases. "Kat's been through a lot and I don't think she has anywhere else to go. Her parents sort of disowned her when they found out she worked as a stripper."

"Oh, God."

"I mean, Kat's not like you. She doesn't really have a family. So maybe go easy on her troubled mind. You're not exactly seeing her at her best."

"I don't mean to be an asshole—"

"You're not being an asshole. You're being a guy. And guys don't have to go through what she's going through." Gudrun stares at the uncovered futon. "Oh, Culkin. Something's going on. She wasn't like this at McGill. Kat was the star—scholarship, prizes, publication—but I don't know." Gudrun flings the fitted sheet over the futon. "She started doubting herself at a certain point."

I move to the other side of the bed, stretch the fitted sheet over the futon corner, and ask, "Has she ever seen a therapist?"

"Is there a therapist she *hasn't* seen?"

"Or did something horrible happen when she was young? Because she reminds me of somebody who wants people to be as messed up as she is so she can hate them instead of herself."

"Oh, I don't think it's that." Gudrun shakes out the flat sheet. "Kat maybe has some low-grade emotional issue, but I don't think it's about hating people. It's more like she's so afraid of rejection she rejects everybody else first. But Aubrey—" The sheets now changed, Gudrun returns the blankets to the bed. "I'm sorry if you have to suffer through all this dysfunctional girly-bop. Kat's just in a very specific situation in her brain right now. I think she's stuck. And I kind of need you to not freak out over her issues."

"Um—okay."

"I think"—Gudrun slips out of her clothes and gets into bed—"Kat just needs to be a little crazy right now."

"Uh-huh? So how long do we have to live with a crazy person?"

17

if anything happens with kat, call me at work. i'll be home late. xo

I REMEMBER THOSE first days with Kat as a series of linked dramatic scenes, call them *The Kathryn Culkin Dialogues,* with our house guest sitting catatonic in the front room and Gudrun, when she was home, trying to tenderly connect with her. I don't think anyone was really counting on these scenes transferring to Broadway. My own hope, after Gudrun alerted me to Kat's history of self-harm, was simply to keep adding to our apartment's tally of Days Without Accident or Injury. Learning that Kat had been anorexic, that she'd cut and burned herself, and that she'd been hospitalized after a suicide attempt worried me that more drama was in the offing. Kat was full of problems—insomnia, migraines, nausea—as well as some spastic bowel issue, and the flush and bubble of her sickness became another in the litany of weirdness you couldn't really mention. For good or ill, I began avoiding her altogether, choosing, when I came home, to sneak past the front room, where she was camped out, and get to the bedroom as quickly as possible.

But one day, when I tripped over a winter boot and sent it tumbling down the stairs, Kat gasped at the noise and I realized I couldn't pretend I wasn't there.

"Hey," I said cheerfully. "Just a boot. I think it's going to be okay."

"Sorry," said Kat, "I'm in your apartment all the time. It's probably weird to have a stranger on your sofa weeping like an idiot. But I don't have to be here. I can go to a Starbucks."

"Why? You want tea?"

"Do you have camomile? Or—um—what's the tea for self-mutilators?"

"All out of Cutter's Rapture, I'm afraid. We do have Lemon Zinger."

"I guess I could get zinged." She smiled feebly. "Thank you."

I plugged in the kettle and returned to the front room. "You're not really cutting yourself, are you?" I asked. "Because we just had the floors done."

Kat swiftly shook her head. "Been there. Done that. Third year McGill, I used to walk around with a nail file in my vagina—"

"Who didn't?"

"But it gets kind of old."

"It certainly can. How are things today?"

"I'm trying to figure out if I should call someone back."

"Is that why you're crying?"

Kat nodded. "I know he wants me to. I'm the only person he talks to. I mean, he and his wife haven't kissed in twelve years. And he got some bad news this week. A blood test."

"But how're *you* feeling?"

Kat snivelled. "Not so amazing."

"Maybe don't call if you're feeling not so amazing."

"I guess. I don't know. I feel—I think—I worry I may not be doing the right thing." Kat brought her shirt sleeve to her mouth and began sucking on it. "But he needs me. I can feel it. The day I left, he called me three times." She glanced at me—looking me in the eye for a first time—and asked, "Should I call him back, though?"

"It's probably okay to take some time for yourself." Hearing the kettle whistling in the kitchen, I stood up. "I don't know if you have to make all the decisions in the world right now."

"Maybe I'll sit here." Kat chewed her shirt sleeve. "Under the ceiling. Reeling. Dealing. Silently squealing." She opened her mouth very wide, her mandible reconfiguring with a sudden crack. "I can't feel my face. My face is so numb—" She flicked her cheek. "It feels like my face is falling off my jawbone."

AND WHAT OF Gudrun Peel? She was still sniffly, she still coughed, but within a few days demonstrated an almost supernatural recovery from months of illness. Her colour came back. Her spirits returned. She bought a new skirt suit, went to work early, stayed late.

Returning that day at midnight, she placed her new suit jacket on the bedroom doorknob and tugged at the skirt's zipper. "How was Kat today? You talk to her?"

"She was crying all day because of some guy."

Gudrun paused mid-zip. "What guy?"

"Some guy whose wife hasn't kissed him in twelve years."

"I knew it." Gudrun sucked in a breath. "I fucking knew it."

"What do you know?"

"Fuck fuck fuck." Gudrun tightly shut her eyes. "She's seeing him again."

"Seeing who?"

Gudrun dragged a hand down her face and pinched her lower lip. "When Kat was in undergrad—don't fucking tell anybody this—she had an affair with her art history professor. Romulus Hogg."

"Romulus *Hogg*?"

"And when she was with him, her life was a mess. No one saw her. You only see Kat when she's between boyfriends anyway,

but when she's with Hogg she's totally isolated in Hogg World."
Gudrun stepped out of her skirt. "It all feels counterphobic."

"What does counterphobic mean?"

"That she's so afraid someone like him *wouldn't* like her, she's trying really hard to make the relationship work to prove that that's wrong."

"Oh."

"When this happened last time, I told her it's a pattern of masochism with Hogg. She's not in love with him. She's in love with being treated badly. She's never as unhappy as she is when she's with him and I bet she fucked up her life again by seeing him. And she won't face it." Gudrun sat on the bed and pulled off her pantyhose. "It's why she dropped her last therapist. She said she couldn't talk to him about sex, because he was asking about her sex life, but I think it's because he was getting too close to the truth and she couldn't handle it."

"She's having an affair with her professor? I have to say, I do *not* see the attraction. I mean, Kat looks like an abused street kid."

"Oh," said Gudrun, "you'd be surprised. Kat's a little shape-shifter. She gets into things. She'll meet a guy and crawl around his head, believe me."

"But if she's being treated badly, why crawl around?"

"Well, Kat has this anthology—it's with this Montreal publisher that Hogg sits on the board of—and I think she thinks if she waits around long enough, it'll happen. But Jesus Christ, Clifford, that anthology should've been done two years ago."

"What's the anthology?"

"It's this anthology— Wait." In bra and underwear, Gudrun left the bedroom.

"Kat?" she said, walking down the hall. "You awake? I have an idea for you. What if—What're you doing?"

Following Gudrun into the front room, I saw Kat sitting at Gudrun's desktop computer, her eyes glowing with the light of its screen.

"Sweetie?" said Gudrun. "What are you doing on my computer?"

"Checking email." Kat bit her thumb. "He keeps emailing."

"Who does?" Gudrun looked at the screen. "Romey?"

Kat nodded. "Just to see his name in my inbox was like trauma."

"Uh-huh?"

"I don't know if I can deal with the input." Kat was about to double-click on the dial-up icon when she suddenly switched off the computer. "Like this morning? I had so many panic attacks I had to do five sun salutations in a row." She shuddered. "But do you think I should email back? Or maybe just call him."

"Oh," said Gudrun, "I don't think you should call him."

"I should email?"

"Why?"

"I could email to say, 'Stop emailing me'."

"No, I wouldn't. I mean, Kat?" Gudrun led her away from the computer and sat her down on the sofa. "You should do what's right for you, but you need calm. You need to feel safe."

"I *do*. Because do you know what it's like to feel worthless? Like a piece of toilet paper blowing down the sidewalk? That's what I feel like. A ripped-up toilet paper stuck to someone's shoe." Kat scratched herself. "And I feel so fucked-up I let this happen to me."

"Kat," Gudrun said firmly, "you didn't *let* this happen to you. That's victim thinking. It wasn't you who did it."

"No, I was weak. I shouldn't've gone back to him."

"Girl, it's not your fault."

"I just feel so sucky—"

"Look," said Gudrun, "you're allowed to have emotions and it's okay to have low self-esteem right now. But you're also allowed to remember how you valued yourself before you met him. Who got the scholarship to McGill? Who won the poetry award?"

"Gudrun," Kat pleaded, "he's published fourteen books. I mean, there are conferences about his work, about his thought and theories, and he listens to me."

"I don't care if— Wait. No, I *do* care if people are listening to you, Culkin. But I don't care if there are academic conferences and learned societies supporting the bullshit and teachings of Romulus Hogg. I really don't. I care about you. I mean, Kat? Straight up?"

Gudrun waited for Kat to nod before she continued.

"I don't want to be a cunt, and you can tell me to fuck off if you want, but I have seen you go in and out of this relationship for six years. And before?" Gudrun smiled. "You used to laugh a lot. You used to joke a lot. The funniest nights of my *life* were with you—" She regarded Kat. "But I haven't seen that side of you for a while."

"I've been sad?"

"What do you think?"

"Yeah." Kat blinked away a tear. "I've been sad."

"And Boss Hogg, I'm just going to say it, I kind of feel like he's a motherfucker."

"Gudrun, he just emailed to say he *loved* me—"

"And how'd that make you feel?"

"Um," said Kat. "Confused?"

"If he was a good person, I don't think you'd feel confused. I think you'd feel happy."

"I want to feel happy—"

"You deserve to *be* happy. Look, Kat, I can't tell you what to feel, but he's fifty-six years old. You're twenty-seven. How's that going to work big picture? Seriously."

Kat scrunched her nose. "I should maybe go for someone younger?"

"Maybe."

"Oh, Gudrun—" Kat made an odd smile, a smile both helpless and incomplete, and twisted her face to one side. "My judgment's bad. It really is. Two weeks ago, he got me so drunk I gave him a blow job in the taxi before we even *got* to his house. Like, is that love or what?"

Gudrun tilted her head, noncommittal.

"And being away from him now?" said Kat. "I just feel so hollow and fucked-up and meaningless. Like oblivion. Like the worst ever."

"Well, Kat," Gudrun said, "do you die?"

"No—" Kat wiped her nose. "I do not die."

"What do you do?"

"I see." Kat sat up straight. "I scream. I fight."

"If you want to, you do."

"We all scream," said Kat, staring at the floor and beginning to sob uncontrollably.

18

Zuppa del Peel

> 2 onions, finely chopped
> 3 celery stalks, diced
> 2 carrots, diced
> 1 cup green beans, washed and sliced
> 2 zucchini, washed and cut up
> 28 oz can of kidney beans
> 28 oz can of whole tomatoes
> 3 potatoes chopped
> 3 shallot cloves minced
> ½ cup fresh Italian parsley
> 1 quart chicken broth
> 2 cups penne pasta
> 1 tablespoon butter

Melt butter with vegetable oil in pot on lowest heat. Add onion, shallots, celery, carrots and sauté 5 minutes. Add beans, tomatoes, zucchini, potatoes, broth. Turn up heat and bring to boil, partially cover, and reduce heat. Simmer 45 minutes till vegetables are tender. Add pasta and fresh parsley and simmer 20 minutes. Salt and pepper to taste and serve hot with grated cheese.

AFTER THAT IMPROMPTU intervention, therapy appointment, and deprogramming session, Kat started to improve. And, as the winter lifted, so did her depression. Various ailments pursued her, there were good and bad days, but the general trend was positive.

She went to yoga. She went for walks. She drank tea. She had two bowls of Gudrun's homemade—and very colourful—minestrone soup, Zuppa del Peel as she called it, and I remember a Sunday morning, probably Week Four of *The Kathryn Culkin Dialogues*, when she came into our bedroom as we were waking.

"Gudrun?" She sat on the bed. "I did it. I deleted all his emails. No more Hogg."

"How's it feel?"

"Good. No throwing up. No bladder infection. No can't-breathe feeling. And healthy poops."

"So you're coming out of it?"

"I don't know if I'm a fully functioning human, but I'm not a suicidal piece of toilet paper anymore. I was just so j'en ai marre, you know? It was just so fucking dingue. C'était complètement dingue. C'était dégueulasse. It really was."

"You had me worried, girl."

"Hey," said Kat, wiggling Gudrun's toe through the blankets. "You said you had an idea for me. What was it?"

Gudrun *did* have an idea for Kat. Since publishing a book of poetry, Kat had been working on an anthology of feminist theory, polemic, poetry, fiction, interviews, and art. Two years earlier, she'd submitted the manuscript to Poèticule—this was the Montreal publishing house Romulus Hogg was associated with   and was still waiting for a response from the senior editor.

"I don't know if they'll take it," she said. "They keep wavering. So I'm in a limbo of a hundred winter popcorns. But this anthology is huge for me. It's all I have. Take that away and I'm fucked."

"Well," said Gudrun, "what if you did it here?"

"Edit here?"

"Publish here. With Wyndham and Weir."

"Hold up. You can *do* that?"

"I can certainly try. What do you think? Want me to ask?"

SCENE: THE GRACE STREET APARTMENT. *TIME:* A SUNDAY
IN MARCH. In the bathroom, Gudrun is just stepping out of
the shower. I am doing dishes in the kitchen. In the sunlit front
room, Kat looks through a draft copy of the new Wyndham and
Weir publishing catalogue. The proofreading of this industry-only
booklet is just one of many items on Gudrun's to-do list. Other
tasks include copyediting a soon-to-be-released Wyndham and
Weir poetry sampler, approving the artwork for an advertisement
intended for the *Globe and Mail* book section, and, for Otis Jones,
the stuffing of twenty manila envelopes with press kit materials.
The press kit comprises an information one-sheet, an author
photograph, and a copy of the issue of *Canadian Vacations* that
features a topless Otis Jones zip-lining in Glacier Mountain Park.

Leafing through the publishing catalogue, Kat calls out, "Can
you believe Charlotte Lister calling her book 'The Burgeoning?'"

"I don't mind Charlotte," says Gudrun from the bathroom,
"but I'm not crazy about that title."

"The burgeoning of what, exactly?"

"Oh, it's fine," says Gudrun. "Charlotte's about the sister-
hood. She's doing the feminism thing."

"What kind of feminism, though?" Kat picks up the poetry
sampler. "All-intercourse-is-rape feminism or she-really-knows-
how-to-stretch-a-pot-roast feminism? Because the more you
meet these Rosedale ladies, the more you think, 'What the fuck?'
I mean, Charlotte Lister's kind of bougie and consumerist,
isn't she?"

"Well—"

"Like, she's all about the resistance, but really it's more
like, 'Thank you, Charlotte, for your tax bracket and artistical
preferences'."

As Kat reads "Esker," a poem by Charlotte Lister in the
poetry sampler, Gudrun walks into the front room wrapped in
a bath towel.

"That's like half a poem," Kat says when she's finished. "Or half a poem from three different poems."

"That's my total nightmare and fear," says Gudrun, re-draping herself. "That if I ever publish a book, I'll be Little Judy Midlist who publishes boring Canadian nowhere poetry."

"Fuck that shit," says Kat. "I don't care about divulging the fractals of the Ontario woods. I mean, I *get* it."

"It's an inexpressible geography—"

"Now fuck off." Kat picks up a copy of *Canadian Vacations*. "Good God, it's Otis Jones. What's he doing now? Is he in Toronto?"

"He was. He's got another book at the press."

"He was so ridiculous at McGill. He was like this bardic Heffalump. He wanted everyone to read Baudelaire."

"Like that'll solve everything."

"Be drunken."

"Exactly. Be drunken. Smoke dope."

"Snort coke—"

"That's all there is to it."

"Ask what time it is?"

"Drunk o'clock." Gudrun shrugs. "I'm a little over Otis Jones."

"It's all so boner-centric," says Kat. "I mean, Otis acts like he's got some big Volker Schlöndorff in his underpants, but has anyone seen it? Because Gudrun—" She brandishes the copy of *Canadian Vacations*. "This is all sort of man-porn, you know?"

Gudrun makes another shrug, sits down on the sofa, and inspects the polish on her toenails.

"Otis Jones, Otis Jones," Kat says. "Oh for God's sake, Otis Jones. Otis Jones and Buffalo Lukashevsky and all those other Man Poets of Nature. Jason Teezergang. Bryden Tovey. Give me a fucking break, Otis Jones. Stab me in the fucking head, Otis Jones. He's out there, exploring the furze and sphagnum, teaching us important philosophical knowledge with his heart and words and majestic testicles."

"Majestic testicles?" Gudrun hoots. "I *love* that."

"Please. I'll never be one of these Man Poets of Nature. I'll never be Spoken Word Joe."

"Spoken Word Kat!"

"I can't even. What has it decided? Or provided? What findings and rhymings shining in hiding from the soul of the blah-de-bloo-de-blah?"

"Kat," says Gudrun, "you had me at shining."

"Done." Kat turns to look again at the Wyndham and Weir catalogue. "Gudrun," she says finally, "no offence. But this is dorky. This catalogue. It looks like a Bank of Montreal annual report."

"I know, I know."

"It isn't you. It isn't anywhere *near* you."

"I'm not on the editorial board, dude. I'm just a part-time marketing peon."

"It's kind of fucking cringe, you know? And you want me to bring out a book with these people?" Kat sneers. "They won't get it. We'd have to show them the vibe of it. Because we can't blame everybody else for what's happening. Then we're just whiners." She sniffs. "We need a new hermeneutics."

"I'm listening, Susan Sontag."

"Because if I'm going to do an anthology with these fuckers, it better be great, right? Or why do it? Because if their brand is Otis Jones howling into a microphone?" Kat hotly shakes her head. "Fuck that shit. Let's do our own thing."

"Are you serious?"

"Why not? Let's do a show that's the vibe of the anthology."

"Culkin—" Gudrun stands up. "You're brilliant. You're totally right." Gudrun stares at Kat as a current of ideas passes between them. "There should be music and performance—"

"And babes in bustiers—"

"An official photographer—"

"Fuck, I'll produce it."

"Or Kat? We'll both produce it. We'll make it the night *we* want. We'll make it the most fabulous—"

"First annual whatever the fuck it is."

"I want it to be really—"

"Gashy and spectacular."

"And if Walter Weir doesn't get it?"

"He can eat a big dick."

"I'm quitting."

"Done."

19

The Rivoli presents "Spring Bust Up," an all-girl celebration of voice, writing, sex, and song. Hosted by poet Kathryn Culkin and featuring Tao Jones, Deandra Johnson, Lucy Lucy Lucy, Kiki Noir, Horgasm, and many more. Tuesday May 9 at 8pm. $10.

FABULOUS IS THE word I associate with these next weeks. Fabulous wasn't just a word. It was a cause, a commotion, a call to action. Kat made an out-and-out performance of the sound, lingering on the fricative first letter, vocalizing the vowel with a playful squeal, and finishing the syllables with a lingering sibilance. Fabulous was beauty and confidence and excitement. For Gudrun and Kat, there was no discrepancy between high and low culture. Everything belonged to a continuum of achievement. Grace Jones and Joan Didion were genius. David Bowie and Heather Locklear were amazing. The false ending of "Cannonball" was brilliant. *Exile in Guyville* was a masterpiece. Christopher Marlowe was dope as fuck.

The two women seemed excited in ways and styles I didn't know and perhaps might never approach. It felt as if their favourites were imbued with some quintessence that, if you didn't immediately "get it," you would never properly understand. But the two friends were in perfect covenant. They were their own glimmer twins. There weren't a lot of boundaries between Gudrun and Kat. Not back then. And Spring Bust Up, the show intended to create interest for Kat's anthology, became for them a convergence of fabulousness, zeal, and rebellion.

WE START THAT day in the Grace Street flat some hours into the getting-ready timeline. Kat has found employment at Stilife, a nightclub on Richmond Street, a place she calls "primo douche central," and with her bartending earnings she has begun contributing rent as well as bringing into our lives a proliferation of cosmetics. I'd grown up in a House of Many Sisters, so this new clutter—Finesse texture-enhancing shampoo, Pantene Pro-V conditioner, MAC Volcanic Ash exfoliator, L'Oréal Mega Volume mascara, and Revlon metallic lip liner, as well as various emery boards, eyelash curlers, bobby pins, scrunchies, and hair elastics—I find strangely reassuring. Inevitabilities, romantic and professional, will soon send Kat into new worlds and so the following represents one of the final fragments of *The Kathryn Culkin Dialogues*. We join our cast in the midst of final touches on Gudrun's hair, makeup, and wardrobe.

"What do you think?" asks Kat, looking at Gudrun in the bathroom mirror.

"Holy Mother." Gudrun studies her reflection. "Putting eyeliner between the lashes is such a good idea."

"Isn't it?"

"I would've never thought of that."

"Let's see the dress. Where's the safety pin? Don't move—"

"Careful, Kat. I'm not wearing underwear."

"Stay still, freak."

"Ouchies."

"Don't jump around."

"But do you think I should wear the stripey dress?"

"No, I don't like you in stripes. I like you in solids."

"Do you think it's too skanky?"

"Pah!" Kat fires up a hair dryer. "A little late for that, Peel. Let's see how the hair's holding."

After some moments of shaping, Kat clacks off the hair dryer. "You are fucking hot, girl."

"It's not too slutty?"

"No, you look bitching."

"Dress is a little tight."

"It'll stretch over the evening. Don't eat anything. I like it. Do you like it?"

"If I got it, flaunt it, right? Before I become Miss Booby Bumdrop. 'There goes Booby Bumdrop,' they'll say. 'I knew her when her ass was high'."

"Close your eyes," says Kat. "I'm perfuming!"

I HAD SEEN Gudrun once before in lipstick. And a few times I'd seen her wearing eyeliner. But I'd never seen her go maximum glam. That is to say, in four years I'd never seen my partner fully made up. The specifics were twisted updo, cat-eye makeup, red lipstick, and a low-cut dress made of crushed black velvet, but the gestalt effect was overwhelming. It was like being face to face with a movie star.

"Holy smokes," I say, "I have a gorgeous new girlfriend."

"*Who?*" asks Gudrun, alarmed.

"I mean *you*, lady. You're all dolled up."

"Oh," says Gudrun, pushing her eyebrow back and brushing a clump of mascara from her eyelashes, "I have no doubt you'll leave me for some bimbo."

"What if you're my bimbo? Let me give you a kiss—"

"No!" Kat pushes us apart. "Don't muss my creation, freak."

I gaze at Gudrun in the mirror. "You look absolutely fabulous, Gudrun Peel."

"I'm having premonitions of weirdness but whatever."

"Weirdness? Why?"

"Well—" Gudrun views her reflection and, as she shivers, I feel for a moment what she wants for herself, as well as the deep contradictions that both fuel and frustrate her. "What if no one shows?"

"Oh, they'll show," I say. "People have been talking about it for weeks."

"Something's going to happen," Kat says, squeezing our hands. "I can feel it."

LIKE MOST STRAIGHT men, I have in my head a ready-reference Map of Extraordinary Women, that is to say, I remember where in the city I have seen someone whom, should the occasion arise, I would like to see again. So you may assume in these years that I carried with me, in some dreamy part of my imagination, ideas about the Pre-Raphaelite amazon who worked at West Camera, or the Jamaican dreamboat who ran the Nightwood Theatre reading series, or any of the servers at Terroni. I suppose these ideas belonged to an interior fantasy world, "Aubrey's Spank Bank of Hoes," as someone would later describe it, but to walk into the Rivoli that night was to see all my ideas collected, that is to say, *in the same room.*

When we arrived at six o'clock, I was the only man in a room of thirty-one women. Guests were gorgeous severally. There were a lot of spiky dreads and Chuck Taylors but just as many corset tops and peep-toe boots and everywhere perfume, musk, fragrance. These elements—together with candles and roses and a diversity of highly expectant women—put a tremor of sexual energy into the air for which I was wholly unprepared.

I remember a Rivoli staffer coming in to prep the back bar—this was David the Undead, so named because he worked nights and slept days—and, while slicing his lemons and limes, he'd glance up from time to time to see yet another exceptional-looking woman prance into the room and he'd shake his head in astonishment, as if to say, "Holy *fuck* am I glad I took this shift." The woman he was presently considering wore a faux fur cowboy hat, platinum pigtails, a Farrah Fawcett T-shirt ripped open to display the word *Kinderwhore* on her breasts in black Magic Marker, pink bikini bottoms, and knee-high black boots. This was the Montreal pop star Kiki Noir. She'd been marching here and there, looking for Gudrun, and she was now, after a less than perfect sound check, finally speaking to Gudrun, but speaking in rapid French. Gudrun had put me at the merch table—I was to sell the zines, compact discs, graphic novels, artwork, and buttons from the contributors—but, from the way she was staring at me over Kiki's shoulder, I knew she wanted me to rescue her.

Just as I approached, Kiki stomped off to the green room.

"Nightmare," said Gudrun, closing her eyes in annoyance. "Soon as Walter gets here"—she spoke with a raspy throat—"I'll give you guys the float and you can get started. But after that, your new girlfriend's going to be crazy and she won't be able to pay attention to you."

"Got it. Who am I working with?"

"And"— she spun her finger to indicate the room—"stay out of trouble, okay?"

Sitting down at the merch table, I was clearing my head of earlier daydreams when a young man with green hair, no older than twenty, slung himself beside me on the banquette. He had a camera around his neck and wore a mesh tank top and jeans that drooped beneath the waistband of his plaid boxers. In one hand he held a martini and with the other he made a shooing motion.

"Scooch over, would you?" he said. "I'm literally falling off the edge here."

As I slid closer to the wall, I examined the camera. It was a Nikon single-lens reflex with a stuck-on flashbulb unit. It seemed a gadget more appropriate to a squinty-eyed veteran of ACME Newspictures than a young man with green hair and a martini.

"So we'll be working together?" he said, his voice lazy and flippant. "You snap the names, I snap the photos?" He surveyed the room. "Isn't this place out of this world? Sort of backroom of the recording studio. Like black box theatre in a community college. But so dour, you can't believe it. It's so dour and transgressive. It's all so transgressive." He swirled his martini then lightly extended his hand. "I'm Duffy the Boy Friday at the publishing house. I do a little of everyone."

"Duffy?" I shook his hand. "Yes, I've heard of you."

He wiped something off his lip and lifted his martini. "So how do you know Gudrun? Don't tell me you're obsessed with her like everyone else."

"We live together."

Duffy choked. "You're the famous Aubrey?" He nudged my shoulder. "Oh, Aubrey. You're so mysterious. You're just like me." He sipped his martini. "Well, I love all my co-workers equally, but really I'm Team Gudrun. It's done. It's decided. She is so good at everything in all of recorded history. What can I say? She's the real deal. She's an artist. She's a writer. I mean, she could be a model and she chooses to be a poet? That's commitment. Truly, she is one of the greatest things on planet earth. For sure. So Aubrey, tell me—" Duffy leaned into my ear. "Where are you going with all this?"

Before I could reply, spinning out of a cluster of people, as if expelled from an unbalanced revolving door, came Sebastian Hickey. He wore a lavender twill shirt and seemed charmed if befuddled, but he soon adjusted, seeing me, and walked over with a fond smile. Now Sebastian had always looked slimly boyish, like an undergrad on his way to audition for the *Cambridge Footlights Revue*, but tonight he was changed. He was still as Arthurian as ever, but he looked pasty and stout, as if on antidepressants. And he may have been. For he wasn't drinking.

"I haven't had a drink in a twelvemonth," he told me.

"You want to break the seal?" I said. "I'll buy you a beer."

"Maybe just one. Where's Lady Peel?"

"Backstage mobilizing."

"Hello," Sebastian said, bending down to Duffy. "We haven't met. I'm Sebastian Hickey."

As Duffy took his fingers from his martini to properly shake hands, the merch table was bumped sideways by a charging Istvan Boda. Oblivious to his clumsiness, Istvan strode to the centre of the room, rather as if it was *his* night, then beckoned to his followers and selected a table close to the stage, a table where, two minutes earlier, Sebastian had left his burgundy overcoat.

"Hmm," said Sebastian, attentive to these troop movements. "Would you chaps mind terribly if I sat with you?"

"Um—" Duffy said uncertainly. "This is the merch table?"

"It's just that I'm not speaking to Istvan at the moment. Bit of a falling-out. I don't mean to cause a fuss, but I'd rather not get hacked to death by some deranged Serbian alcoholic."

Sebastian slunk towards the front of the room, trying, as inconspicuously as possible, to retrieve his burgundy overcoat.

"What is this guy's issue?" Duffy asked, watching Sebastian. He leaned back and grimaced, as if concerned about impending conspiracy. "And is he wearing guyliner?" Duffy stood up to stare at Sebastian. "He *is*. He is fucking wearing guyliner." Duffy glanced at me. "I have no idea what trajectory is being explored here. You tell me. Is this man transitioning or what?"

"Who—Sebastian?"

"You and I both know what's going on here, Aubrey."

"We do?"

"Because this is a *serious* obfuscation." Duffy grabbed his martini and promptly downed it. "Who is this man, really? And what am I supposed to be feeling right now?"

THE ROOM WAS filling up. Latecomers were seeking out empty chairs at *any* table, stragglers were huddled in a Standing Room Only area beside the bar, and servers were hustling last-minute pre-show drinks. For a moment, Gudrun had been in hushed consultation with the soundboard technician, then she was poking around the stage, searching for something. Gone from her face was any consciousness of how magnificent she looked. She stopped by the merch table to say, "Can anything *else* go wrong?" before rushing past Istvan Boda, completely unaware of his presence.

But Istvan Boda *was* present, with open arms, ready to embrace Gudrun in greeting, but, the moment done, he returned to his table and kicked at his chair.

"Istvan," said Duffy, taking out a tube of lip balm. "I mean, I like him? He's obviously very talented, but it bugs me he's such a whatever he is. Wizard. Hobgoblin. Super-fiend."

Duffy quickly applied the lip balm.

"I don't know what his trip is," he went on. "And that style, theatre artist gone bad, gone bohemian druggy bad boy, that style's less and less appealing the older you get. He can be a disgusting little humanoid, that's for sure. He's just so heinous and demented. And hostile? Wow."

Duffy smacked his lips together.

"But who am I to say? If that's his prerogative, so be it. I mean, I don't really need bad karma with his people, you know?"

Duffy looked around the room as if to see who might be listening, then leaned in to whisper: "Apparently he just gets crushes on psychopaths. That's what I've heard. Istvan just gets crushes on psychos. What can you even *say* about that?" Duffy was sitting back, his eyes wide with revelation, when a shriek from Gudrun sounded at the back of the building.

I found her in the green room trying to bash open a one-litre bottle of Evian.

"Hey," I said, "I think I saw Marie-Josette."

"Great. That's all I need. The person I admire most watching me horribly fail." Abandoning the Evian, Gudrun turned to me. "Walter's not here, so I don't have a merch float. Kat's delayed, so I don't have an emcee. Three of the performers called to say they're late, the closing band's drummer broke her wrist, and there's no sound system because we dropped a Sennheiser." She scowled. "I have to abort this mess."

"Okay," I said. "It's your call, but there's two hundred people back there. They've all paid ten bucks. They're kind of expecting a show."

"Well, I don't *have* a show, do I?"

"The performers will get here. If they called, they'll get here."

"Fucking God," said Gudrun. "Marie-Josette. Dalton. Everybody. I'm fucking done in this town."

"Why isn't Walter here?"

"Some emergency at the press. But I can't sell the contributors' stuff without a float."

"How much do you need? I can get cash from a bank machine. That's one down. You can probably borrow a microphone from the Horseshoe. That's two. What performers *are* here?"

"The other musical acts."

"Put on whoever you have."

"I want to *close* with the musical acts. One of the writers should go first. We need to introduce the idea of the anthology."

"So you go on."

"I'm not a performer!"

"Tonight you might have to be."

"With this sore throat?" Gudrun made a pained face. "I can't emcee. I can hardly talk. It's not going to work."

I grabbed the Evian, twisted off the cap, and passed it to her. "Who's going to announce the show's cancelled?"

"Well, doof," she said, taking a drink, "*I* am."

"If you're going to talk to the audience, why don't you just announce a first act?"

"If this doesn't work"—Gudrun cleared a tangle of hair from her eyes—"I'm probably going to have to kill you."

WHAT DO I REMEMBER of the show's first half? Holly Yuen saving it. She was the violinist in Horgasm, the all-girl metal band slotted to close, but she went on twice in the first half, once with the dancer Suzi Chukwu, who improvised a solo to Holly's cadenzas, and again on her own, entrancing the crowd with what was for most of us a first exposure to live looping.

Deandra Johnson, one of the anthology's poets, recited a poem called "Granny Bailey," about the woman in Regent Park who raised her after Deandra's mother killed herself, and she silenced the room in the last line when she revealed Granny Bailey had died the night before at Toronto General.

"Goosebumps," Duffy said to me, moving forward to photograph Deandra. "Everywhere. Seriously."

No easy task for a comedy act to follow such a panegyric, but when Lucy Lucy Lucy came on as a trio of nuns presenting scenes from a new musical, *Reservoir Gods,* and closed the first half with blood packs bursting through their starched white tunics, the buzz in the room was palpable.

At intermission, something came free in Gudrun's mood. David the Undead brought her a complimentary vodka shot, sent from someone in the audience, and she tossed it back like a veteran. The show went on. Highlights continued.

Tao Jones performed a monologue from the point of view of a kid trapped in a basement.

Fucknuts von Trapp read from her teenage diaries about loving her boyfriend, hating her boyfriend, and dumping her boyfriend—material so charming and disarming and hysterically relatable it made us feel we'd all graduated from the same high school.

In a room already humid with body heat, Kiki Noir et Les Queues de Castors, a neo-burlesque act, bedazzled the room to sweltering extremes.

With Horgasm and Kat only moments away, Gudrun returned to the stage and walked into the spotlight. Her cat-eye makeup had become blue bruises, her lipstick a slash of red, but she didn't care. She was happy. She thanked the performers, the Rivoli staff, and all of us for coming. If she might ask for a few more minutes of our time, she'd like to read a poem by Kathryn Culkin, the editor and guiding light of the proposed anthology, and then the night would be ours for music and dancing.

Gudrun cleared her throat. She drank from the bottle of Evian. Then, stepping up to the microphone, she opened her copy of Kat's book and started reading the first poem. I knew she loved the poem and wished to convey that love in her reading—and whether it was stage fright, some errant consciousness of persons, or something else undefined, I don't know—but she wavered in the second line and lost her breath in the middle of the third. She was quick to make such faltering into a form of entertainment, curtsying to concede her mistakes, and then, smiling to show she was equal to the situation, she resumed reading.

But when she botched a next line, mispronounced two words, and lost her place on the page, a blush appeared in her cheek. She stuttered. She squinted. She pushed some hair behind her ear. And then, as she struggled and failed to find her place in the poem, she began to hyperventilate.

Stepping away from the microphone, she picked up and swigged from the Evian.

"I wasn't really prepared for this," she said.

"Prepared for what?"

The voice from the crowd, bold with booze, was Istvan Boda's. He sat at a front table, presiding over a graveyard of empty beer bottles, and glared at Gudrun as if wanting to wipe the lipstick off her face. Like many men in the city, Istvan was both interested in Gudrun and resentful of the possibility his interest would be rejected. It was Istvan who had sent her the vodka shot, possibilities of interaction very much in his mind, but when once he'd hugged and chatted with Gudrun—at the Cabaret Bam Bam fundraiser, after *Othello*—tonight he'd been unacknowledged. And unnoticed. And he was fixing to change that.

"Prepared for all this," Gudrun said from the stage. "I hope that's all right."

Istvan grunted. "We'll tell you after the reading."

Gudrun peered into the audience. "Fuck you, Jack," she said.

Which is when a beer bottle smashed on the wall behind her.

I wondered for an instant if this was part of the show, but from Gudrun's look of fright I understood it was not.

Still holding the Evian, Gudrun walked offstage and, correctly identifying Istvan as the culprit, began emptying the Evian over his head. Istvan, for his part, bore his punishment stoically. He was secretly pleased, I think, to be at the centre of what was not only a very spontaneous bit of street theatre but a moment charged with his own brand of uncertainty, subversion, and confrontation. When Gudrun shook out the last dribbles of Evian, Istvan crossed his arms and spun away in his chair, like a king spurning an incompetent emissary. But the applause that began was for Gudrun, not Istvan, just as Duffy's photograph was to be of Gudrun, not Istvan, and as Istvan grabbed a beer bottle and flung it carelessly above his head, shattering it on the ceiling and propelling a hunk of glass into Gudrun's face, the flash on Duffy's camera went off, capturing Gudrun as she fell to the floor, her fingers touching at the spot where blood was already seeping from her gashed-in temple.

20

***

Forthcoming from Wyndham and Weir: *Keening* is
an anthology featuring writings by and interviews with
sixteen feminists and lesbian activists on subjects
sacred and profane. About the editors: Kathryn Culkin's
first collection of poetry, *Tatterdemalion*, won the
Tilson-Burkett Poetry Prize. Gudrun Peel is a PhD
candidate in the English Department at the University
of Toronto. Her poems have appeared in *52 Girls, Smack:
Poems from the New World Underground*, and *Nancy
Sinatra Is Not Dead*.

BLOODSHED AT POETRY READING was the headline in the
Toronto Star. The article was picked up by a national wire service and appeared as a kind of curiosity piece in a variety of
newspapers across the country. Accompanying the text was
Duffy's photograph—starkly dramatic, instantly memorable—
a high-contrast image of an elegantly dressed woman with a
bleeding head wound. It would become the first mass market
photograph of Gudrun Peel, one of the more distinctly iconic
images of Queen Street West, and go on to a lingering afterlife
as poster art for a death metal band called Dream Baby Suicide.
For many years following, I would see Gudrun's face flapping
in the wind on an infinitely extending sequence of Parkdale
telephone poles.

That Rivoli show made Gudrun famous in the city. She was talked about by people she hadn't met. She became someone whom people *wanted* to meet. Invitations began. Would Gudrun like to take part in "Women and Song" at the Halton Hills Literary Festival? How did she feel about moderating a session on feminist poetics for Word On The Street? What about appearing in a pink lamé miniskirt in Fingerbird's new music video? Gudrun was bemused by these distractions. "Everyone wants to know me now. It's sort of annoying. Where were these people before?" To all proposals, Gudrun said no. The only gig she really considered was a research position for a documentary Marie-Josette was producing. But the money was less than she earned at the publishing house, she'd have to start right away, and Gudrun respectfully declined. What became her focus, now that Kat had made her co-editor, was the anthology. The editorial board acquired the title and planned to bring it out in Spring 1995. The idea was to pursue foreign sales at the Frankfurt Book Fair in October. Which meant the book's images and text had to be finalized by the end of August. "Walter wants to expunge all the shit-and-piss poems," she told me. "But I'm fighting for every last one." She was going to see *Keening* to market. She wanted to stay the course at Wyndham and Weir.

•

AND WHITHER AUBREY MCKEE? I have not itemized my professionalizing in a while—there may be space to do so later on—but essentially, after starting and then dropping out of a doctorate in chemistry, I'd been diverting myself with reading and writing. A few years earlier, on the back of a spectroscopy printout, I'd written a skit about "The Testing of Abraham" as told from the point of view of an eavesdropping Isaac, if anyone remembers him, and on a whim I'd sent it to my college friend Calvin Dover. Flash-forward some months and Calvin is putting together a one-person show for the Edmonton Fringe Festival and calls to ask if I have anything else. I duly write more stuff. He takes six of my scribbles, two he likes enough to include in all his sets, and when he calls to say he's performing in Toronto, I ask Gudrun if she'd like to go.

"A play? I don't really want to see a play. And I have a conference call."

"It's not really a play."

"Are people on stage?" asks Gudrun. "Talking in front of an audience? Then, yeah, it's a play. Same cringe. Clifford, I think you're a genius, but what even *are* these plays where Pocahontas meets Robert Oppenheimer in a Bulgarian restaurant? Just— no." She flips her hand. "Why don't you take Kat?"

"Seriously?"

"Sure. Have a playdate with Kat."

"I'm down," says Kat. "Which theatre is it? Show me the experts of German theatre."

"Yo, ladies," I say. "It's not theatre. It's not a play. It's a showcase."

IT *IS* A SHOWCASE. Execs from the Aspen Comedy Festival are in town scouting talent and the evening is an invite-only gathering of the city's alternative comedy community. Lucy Lucy Lucy, Butt Jump United, Apocalyptic Monkey Chatter, Frumkin and Frumkin, and Calvin Dover are among those set to perform. For reasons best known to her, Kat puts a turquoise streak in her hair, marks her eyes with heavy eyeliner, and dresses entirely in black. She looks like a psychedelic raccoon. I am embarrassed by her. Downtown comedy types are not the most fashion-forward of citizens. Most look as if they've pulled their wardrobe from a Salvation Army donation box. So when we arrive at Clinton's Tavern and are informed the place is at capacity, I'm relieved to abandon the outing.

"Well, that straight up sucks," says Kat. "The experts of German theatre can suck my balls." She takes my arm. "What do you want to do instead?"

SETTINGS: DOONEY'S, THE VICTORY CAFÉ, AND LEE'S PALACE. TIME: SUMMER 1994. There is on this night simultaneous action in multiple venues and spectators should feel free to follow the participants from location to location. For those of you now arriving at Dooney's, that's me in the front window ordering lemon tea and there's Kat coming up from the bathroom, holding in her hands a copy of NOW magazine. She is turning to its middle pages, scanning the club and concert listings, and pausing at a two-page spread of live music advertisements, when who should walk in but Coyote Head, the band headlining that night at Lee's Palace. For me, all indie rock guys tend to distort into a fuzz of E minor chords, wispy goatees, and ripped-up jeans, but Kat, I can tell from her discerning gaze, is alert to their every nuance. While she investigates this foursome, my tea is delivered in a glass hottle and, using rock glasses taken from the bar, I divide it into two portions.

"Oh, the joy of the indie rock boy," Kat says, walking over, "when they've recorded their first album, when they're still sleeping on someone's couch, just before their first real tour. That's the best time in a band's life."

"I'll take your word for it. You want this tea?"

Kat looks perplexed. "Me no understand." She sits down with the NOW magazine. "Where'd this other tea come from?"

"I poured it from mine. It steeped enough."

"It steeped? Huh. Aren't you the sweetest thing? Yeah, I worked the coat check at this place in Montreal, so I saw a lot of fucking bands."

"What place?"

"Club Soda." Kat sips her tea. "It was like the epicentre of a lot of people's lives. But it was just so hardcore, the tribal polities of Montreal, I couldn't handle it anymore. Mainstream anything to them was just ground zero repulsive. And each new band had to be sort of Mile End approved, you know? If you had a different attitude, you were sort of excommunicated from the cult. And I didn't really need to be in a turf war with the Montreal punk scene. Godspeed whatever and fuck off. It was exhausting."

I ask if she would ever go back.

"To Montreal? I don't know. It's weird. You're tired all day and then it's dark. But everyone's like we're at Biftek or Bar des Pins or some other old-man dive bar." Kat shifts in her seat. "Thing is, I like old-man dive bars. And I like old men. Why, universe? Why?"

Kat impresses me, the way she's speaking now, revealing further discernment without needing to prove herself, and I sense a candidness I have not understood before. Which makes me wonder if her work contains similar candour.

"Hey Kat," I say, "I'm sorry I haven't read your book yet."

"You don't have to read my book. You gave me tea. You zinged me. I mean, my book?" Kat glances at the members of Coyote Head, who, after reading the menu, seem to be reconsidering their choice of restaurant. "It's weird only having one thing in the world that's supposed to represent you. That's why I'm doing this anthology. It's other voices, other vibes. But I think—and this is my one true thing of the last year—inside every problem there's a poem. And you can decide if the world's a problem or a poem. It's up to you."

"I like the title. Was it always called 'Keening?'"

"It used to be called 'Servant Monster.'"

"Is that from 'The Tempest?'"

Kat watches the band file out the door then sends me a puzzled smirk. "How could you possibly know that?"

"I did it in school. 'Servant monster, drink to me'."

"You're a fucking weird person." Kat sips her tea and then immediately puts it down. "You're different than how I thought you'd be."

"You thought I'd be a lean, mean fighting machine?"

"No, I thought you'd be this chemistry guy who studies elementary particles. But really you're a comedy dude who reads 'The Tempest?' That's weird." Kat sternly shakes her head. "And your last name's McKee? So are you a Scot?"

"Well, I'm Scot-*ish*. I'm from Nova Scotia."

"Mmm, yeah. You're sort of funny. You're not like Wocka Wocka funny. You're more—"

"Hunka Hunka funny?"

"No," says Kat, wincing.

"Walla Walla funny?"

"Fuck, no. Please stop."

"*So* close! I was so close!"

"No," says Kat, trying to stay stern but beginning to smile, "you're sort of—I don't know—gaytarded funny. You're like this gaytarded version of your other Scottish self. You're in love with Batman and Baby Shamu and your own private unicorn. Little tip? That's kind of gay."

"Being in love with your own private unicorn isn't gay. How is that gay? That's not even the first thing of gay."

"You know what?" Kat pushes away the tea. "I want a fucking beer."

ACTION MOVES TO the Victory Café, a corner bar with a leafy courtyard, patio umbrellas, and picnic tables. Kat seems to me now a slinky invention. In her turquoise streak, darkened eyes, and black outfit, she radiates self-confidence. There may be moments when she's gorky, but there are many more when she's keen and real and fluidly present.

"What should I get?" asks Kat, dropping her NOW magazine on the picnic table.

I suggest a Hoegaarden.

"Me not know Hoegaarden. What is Hoegaarden?"

"See that guy? He's drinking one."

"Done. Two Hoegaarden."

When two half litres of Hoegaarden arrive in very wide glasses, Kat cups her glass and sniffs it.

"Scheiße!" she says. "That's a fucking sweet-ass beer. And this glass is *huge*. I feel like a woodland creature who has just found a giant flagon of mead." She lowers her mouth and sips the froth. "This is *so* good. I am literally jacking off to it right now."

"Um—Kat? I don't think you're 'literally' doing that. Because I can see both your hands and you happen to be holding the beer."

"Okay, just—" She grabs my elbow and starts shaking it. "Do you always drive people this crazy? Hey—" Kat stares intently at me. "Are you a Virgo?"

"How could you possibly know that?"

"I *knew* it!"

"Just a second. How did you guess that?"

"Because you're so *detaily*. And you have a good memory and you like to help people but you're such a freak it's ridiculous. You're the most ridiculous person anyone's ever met." Kat drinks half her Hoegaarden. "Me want more. Me have to pee first. You order?" Kat leaves the table, yelping as she slips on a maple blossom. Recovering her balance, she bobbles her head, as if to indicate the many mysteries of life, and moves to the stairs.

As she climbs the steps, I notice how her low-rise jeans sag to reveal pink thong underwear. I am still thinking about this pink thong underwear, and how a dart of its fabric rises within the cheeks of Kat's ass, when a hand closes around the back of my neck.

"HEY YOU," says Charlotte Lister. She releases my neck and gestures to Sebastian Hickey. "We were just talking about you. Mind if we join you?"

"Ooh," says Sebastian, noticing the second Hoegaarden. "Not sure about that."

"Sebastian, darling," says Charlotte, "are you having qualms again?"

"I had a qualm once." Sebastian brushes at his lapel. "European, I think. Kept soiling the carpet. Had to be put down. Not the nicest story. Sorry, chaps. Don't have any qualms. Moral there. No, no, sweet Charlotte. It's just—" He points to the other side of the picnic table. "Aubrey may be on a date of some sort."

"A date?"

Just then, Kat trundles down the steps and shouts, "That's my Hoegaarden, yo."

"Oh?" says Charlotte, observing her. That Kat has turquoise hair, wears a tight Lycra top, and is probably a size zero are features not lost on Charlotte Lister. "You're sitting here?"

Kat sits down and slurps her Hoegaarden. "That really *is* a sweet-ass beer." She gazes up at Charlotte. "Yep. This is my spot."

"So," Charlotte says, intrigued, "how do you know Aubrey?"

"Oh, you know—" Kat bobs her head enigmatically. "When I was destitute, he and Gudrun took me into their Home for Wayward Girls."

"Uh-huh?" says Charlotte. "How wayward?"

"Kat's being modest," I say. "She's a writer and editor. The Rivoli show was her idea."

"Really?" Charlotte stares at Kat. "How do I not know you?"

"Crazy, isn't it?" Kat shrugs. "Je est un autre."

"Well," says Charlotte, "that night was amazing. Wasn't Gudrun ruthless?" She glances at Sebastian. "She was absolutely ruthless, wasn't she, Sebastian?"

"She was certainly qualmless," says Sebastian. "Not a qualm in sight."

Kat points at the diamond ring sparkling on Charlotte's left hand. "That's quite the rock," she says. "Somebody must really love you."

"I certainly hope so," Charlotte says brightly.

Kat cocks her head, as if to imply another of life's mysteries, and drinks from her Hoegaarden.

"So," Charlotte says to me, "come have a drink if you want. We'll be inside with our wine."

"Don't have wine, bitch," says Kat. "Hit up some Hoegaarden."

"Hoegaarden," Charlotte says, moving with Sebastian towards the stairs. "We'll keep that in mind."

When Charlotte and Sebastian have gone inside, Kat slowly nods her head. "So that's what Charlotte Lister looks like," she says. "Nice rack."

Kat turns to the personals in the back pages of *NOW* magazine. These are crammed with advertisements for full-body massage, phone sex, and upscale companions. Pink and magenta seem to be preferred colours.

"Okay, then, Scotty," Kat says. "What do you look for in a lady, anyway? Obviously you're with the most happening babe in the city, but what about someone from Belarus? Or how do you feel about—" She bends down to read the fine print. "She-male Tulip?"

"You want to know what I like?"

"Not really." Kat closes the *NOW* magazine. "I know what guys want. At first they want some hot tushy, then later they want the love of a good woman." She drops her head sadly. "Not some random goony sketch-bag."

"Whoa, Kat. You're not *that* random."

"You think?" She slaps me. "I'm just fucking with you. You're an idiot anyway. Hey—" She plucks at her top. "You want to do some shots?"

PROPS AND SETTINGS change a few times—Jamesons in the Green Room, Jim Beams at the James Joyce—and then Kat and I are walking on Bloor. She struts beside me, eyes glittering, voice buoyant, these details, together with a dozen others, becoming for me a blur of sexy indiscernibles.

"Hey," says Kat, pulling a zip-around wallet from her jeans, "do you want to smoke a joint? I think I have a joint from New Year's." Rummaging through her wallet, she removes a business card. "What the fuck?" She flicks it at the sidewalk.

I pick it up and see it belongs to someone named Brian Bristol at BMO Capital Markets. "You know this guy?"

"Oh, you know." Kat shrugs. "Bay Street guys come to the club where I bartend and give me their card because maybe they want to go for drinks."

"Right."

She glances at me. "Or maybe just splooge on my face."

"Bay Street splooge? I'm all *about* that."

Kat giggles. "You know when you're talking to a guy and he's listening but really the whole time he's thinking about splooging on your face?"

"Totally."

"So it's like blah-blah-blah, splooge-on-your-face. Blah-blah-blah, splooge-on-your-face?"

"This is eerie we're so alike. 'Splooge on My Face'? That's like the theme song of me."

"Who *are* you, Aubrey McKee?"

"Me? I'm—"

"Titty-smack!" Kat slaps my nipple and races across the street, laughing chaotically.

WHAT AM I thinking? My mind is awhirl with the sting of her slap and the back-and-forth jiggling of her dashing ass. When I catch up to her at Lee's Palace, she's reading through the concert schedule posted in the window box, but the deliberateness of her gaze implies an awareness of me, and my coming near, and everything that has passed between us. The next moments feel like a dare. But whether I'm being dared to do the right thing or the wrong thing, I can't tell.

"So Culkin," I say, "you're going to some rock show?"

"Maybe." Still gazing at the schedule, she hooks a finger in a belt loop of my jeans. "What're you doing?"

"What works for you?"

"That's a big question."

"Is it?"

"Could be," says Kat, tugging on the belt loop.

I put my hands on her hips and I'm moving my mouth to hers when she twists away, my lips sliding weakly along her cheek.

"Kat," I say nervously, "I wasn't going to really kiss you. You know that, right?"

"Of course not. Because I wouldn't've let you." She moves towards the doors and then—yanking on my beltloop and whirling back to me—she bites my throat before fading into the darkness of Lee's Palace.

My girlfriend is asleep when I get in bed drunk, my thoughts travelling in seventeen different directions. I'm proud I've behaved appropriately—or *mostly* appropriately—but I'm fairly confused and four hours later I awaken from a sex dream with the most obstinate pee-boner of my life. Sitting on the toilet seat, I direct my erection into the toilet bowl only to have my cock, in a spasm of jumpiness, squirt urine through the gap between seat and basin. When I'm on my hands and knees, mopping up this spill with toilet paper, I hear the front door open. Knowing I am drunk, wearing only a tiny Sleater-Kinney T-shirt, and embarrassed I've pissed all over the bathroom floor, I return to the bedroom, get into bed, and fall asleep, my dreams alive with all manner of fever, thong, and woodland creature.

•

GUDRUN AWOKE EARLY, wanting to read over the notes from her conference call, and I remember her look of consternation as she heard, through our apartment's curious acoustics, a man in the kitchen gargling over the sink. Grabbing a bathrobe, she advanced to the hallway, where she was disturbed to see on the hardwood floor several empty beer bottles and a single Blundstone boot. It was at that moment when a tousled young man, one of those at Dooney's the night before, sauntered down the hall to retrieve the Blundstone. This was the drummer in a band called Finbarr Pinto. That was actually the drummer's name, not the band, the band was Coyote Head, but the rather preposterously named Finbarr Pinto was also rather preposterously cute, in a Black Irish way, and to see him in person was to understand the half-million circulation numbers of *Tiger Beat* magazine.

After Finbarr Pinto departed, Kat sat on the red velvet sofa, wrapped in a bedsheet, and explained the two had met at Lee's Palace the night before. Following the gig, she and Finbarr closed Sneaky Dee's and spent the night in our front room.

"We didn't have sex or anything," she said, pulling the bedsheet tight. "We just made out. With extras. And I'm trying to be a proper grown-up, but I'm so going out of my mind right now. Like, how can he *be* that cute and not give a shit?" She blinked at Gudrun. "Why am I obsessed with him? Please help me."

"Well—"

"He is literally my favourite thing ever. He reminds me of myself from—I don't know—a thousand doors ago. Did you see him? Isn't he stunning?"

"He's gorgeous. But Kat—"

"Mmm?"

"He's *nine*teen."

"But did you see how beautiful he is? He is possibly the cutest human." Kat bit her thumb. "I like him so much. I like him *so* much." She looked to Gudrun. "Should I catch his bone, though?"

"Do whatever you want, woman. Just—you know—if you want to be this complicated in your personal life, then be it, but I care about you, girl."

"Thanks, sweetie." Kat pouted. "I care about you, too." She stood up, scuffled over, and kissed Gudrun. "Can I take you to brunch?" She squinched her nose. "I'm starving."

"Um—you go. I have stuff to do."

"You sure?"

"I need a minute."

WHEN KAT HAD LEFT, Gudrun turned to me with a troubled expression. "That girl drives me so fucking crazy sometimes."

"She's gone from a fifty-seven-year-old to a nineteen-year-old?"

"Well—" Gudrun sighed. "Kat and Finbarr? I'm kind of hoping it's not a thing. But it's a good step. It's a My Little Pony step. But at least it's a step." Gudrun began gathering empty beer bottles. "How much did people drink last night?"

"Wasn't me."

"Clifford," said Gudrun, staring into a cigarette-filled beer bottle, "you've been very good with Kat. And I know sometimes it's been hard—"

"She's your friend."

"But really"—Gudrun picked up another beer bottle—"it's time she got her own place."

"It's only been eight months."

"We're not the Unitarian Service Committee." But then, as if unable to continue, Gudrun dropped to the sofa. Her shoulders slumped, her strength dissolved, and one of the beer bottles slipped from her fingers and rolled along the floor.

"Clifford, are you okay?"

"No." Gudrun shut her eyes. "I'm not."

"What is it? Is it something you can tell me?"

"Not really." She reopened her eyes. "But I will." She lined up the beer bottles on the floor. "The publishing house is done, Aubrey. Walter Weir's going to declare bankruptcy. He's going to blame it on the Mike Harris government, but really it's his own incompetence."

"What happened?"

"There was a grievance." Gudrun placed her fists beneath her chin. "An intern's made a sexual harassment claim against Walter. Three other women have come forward. There's going to be an out-of-court settlement."

"What an *ass*hole—"

"But it's going to bankrupt the company."

"Oh, fuck. So—"

"The press is dead. 'Keening' is dead." She sniffed. "And I don't have a job."

21

Adderall®
TAKE AS NEEDED
Dextroamphetamine Saccharate, Amphetamine Aspartate,
Dextroamphetamine Sulfate and Amphetamine Sulfate Tablets
Mixed salts of a single entity amphetamine product 5MG
MAY CAUSE INSOMNIA

GUDRUN WAS CHANGED. Tribulation had changed her. The job to which she'd committed for four years was over. But she didn't despair. She went on unemployment and used the time to revise and resubmit her dissertation. In September, it came back with twelve pages of single-spaced notes from the advisory committee. She was on a second reading of these notes when she threw the pages to the floor.

"Fuck this," she said.

"Fuck what, my sweet?"

"Fuck these men," said Gudrun. "I can't pretend. I can't. I can't sit another day with a bunch of men who don't get it. They'll *never* get it. Fuck Folliot. Fuck Weir." She snatched up the pages. "I'm done. Because all these dudes who say they want to help me? They don't. Really they just want to fuck me. I'm not even going to say 'I guess I should've seen it coming' because what's the point? Their choices are clear. So fuck it. Fuck them all."

"Fuck them short and fuck them tall?"

"Clifford?" said Gudrun, lighting a match. "I'm done. This shit is all about fading male potency and I'd rather not get punished for it. They had their shot. They fucked it up. Now get out of the way." She lit the bottom corner of the first page and watched the others catch fire. "Look, I have a giant fear of failure. I do. But it's better to try and fail than not to try at all." She dropped the burning pages into the sink. "So I'm going to say yes to everything. I'm going to take that research position with Marie-Josette. I'm going to go after a million jobs. And if I don't get them? Fuck them if they don't like me. Because going forward is the answer." She stared into the flames. "From now on, I'm taking the pledge of achievement."

THAT PHRASE, the Pledge of Achievement, was never written on a Post-it Note and stuck to our bathroom mirror, daily affirmation–style, but it was sort of metaphorically stencilled into every mirror Gudrun happened to gaze into. She meant to advance. She was in it to win it. She wanted to prove the haters wrong.

I remember Gudrun looking at the Zoloft stockpiled on our dresser top and muttering, "I don't want to be on you little fuckers my whole life," and resolutely sweeping them into the garbage. She junked them all and spun to the other side of the alphabet, Adderall becoming her vitamin of choice.

I welcomed her new direction, but some of the changes I found worrisome. Her handwriting grew spiky. She was smoking all the time. Some mornings she threw up. And, although there were moods of elation and euphoria, there were just as often moods of impatience and causticity. To Gudrun, such side effects mattered little.

"I cannot *believe* how great I feel," she said. "I'm actually getting my brain chemistry back. It's like my real personality's returning."

A coffee meeting with Charlotte Lister led to a book reviewing gig. Then a restaurant review. Dalton Hickey introduced her
to the editor of *Flare*, a Canadian fashion magazine, for whom
Gudrun wrote "The Last Rock Star," a profile of Chrissie Hynde
that riffed on the experience of a Pretenders concert and the
ways in which a teenaged girl might construct a future identity.
"All I did was write what I felt," she said. "I wish I'd learned
that earlier."

That piece was wonderfully evocative, rightly nominated for
a National Magazine Award, and it brought Gudrun's name to
the attention of every editor in the city. Invitations resumed.
Offers arrived. Options proliferated. She was given a part-time
research position at Marie-Josette's production company and,
after finishing her duties there, stayed late to write her freelance work. She wrote fast. She wrote funny. She wrote
scathing. She became for six months a regular contributor to
the book section of the *Toronto Star* and there, in the modest
world of English-Canadian letters, a world only recently awakened from wood pendant necklaces, leisure suits, and early
colour photography, she found cause for criticism. She scorched
the earth with prairie poets, seared first novels, and burnt older
writers with happy derision. I recall her review of *The Collected
Poetry of Osborne Brown*, a Tennessee poet now living in Vancou-
ver, which closed with the line, "This book should come with
an ice pick because you'll want to lobotomize yourself rather
than read another Down-Goes-Brown wacka-do." Which *was*
sort of funny, but also sort of fucked-up, and the first time I
took issue with her aspersions.

"Oh, look," said Gudrun, "Osborne Brown is ninety-three
years old. No one cares about the Black Mountain Poets anymore. No one even knows who they are."

I remember the morning the managing editor of the *Globe
and Mail* called to offer her a weekly column. "Clifford," said

Gudrun, "do you know how much they pay? I can make in a week what I used to make in a month. I'm going to buy us a house, dude. I'm going to buy us a motherfucking house." That winter, Gudrun's column, "Peel in the City," debuted in the weekend arts section of the country's national newspaper. As I travelled far and near, I was thrilled-and-daunted to see her column, with its distinctive stipple portrait, when I noticed the newspaper being read by a family of four at the Senator Restaurant, say, or left behind in the food court at Sherway Gardens, or stuck in the webbed pocket of a GO Train seat. "Peel in the City" provoked many opinions, not all of them positive, and because Gudrun was young and attractive, she generated envy. In some sets she was respected, in others reviled, and a few folks began to publicly disparage her.

To all this noise, she remained indifferent. "As soon as you get a little famous, you become this random signifier that people can attach to any argument they want. Anyone trying to do something different is criticized, and a woman is criticized no matter what she does. Or how she does it. So I'm not going to worry what people think of me. What people think of me is none of my business."

True and not true. Gudrun was approaching the apex of her mystique and she was certainly aware of her impact on her society. She had in town assorted admirers and in their company often displayed an impetuous and exaggerated version of herself, a persona used to great effect in her television appearances. Her first segment, as part of a media panel on a noonday show, I recall in detail not only because it was the first time I saw Gudrun in a sheer blouse, miniskirt, and high heels, but because it was the first instance of The Trill. The Trill, and it was Sebastian Hickey who dubbed it that, was a soprano giggle of high delight. Gudrun's sexual interest sort of lived in this giggle, and if she then directed her gaze at you, her laughter seemed prelude to a deeper question, which was, "For the next few seconds, you have my attention. So, what are you going to do with it?"

WHAT WAS *I* doing with it? To be candid, I didn't know what I was doing. I was living with a woman who was becoming famous and I was confused by the fluctuations in our life and times. To walk up to a bartender and learn our bill had been paid by the owner, well, that wasn't because of me. And free books arriving at our house in the hope they'd be mentioned in the *Globe and Mail*, well, that wasn't because of me either. Nor were the upscale clothes sent over by designers keen to have their creations worn on-air.

All this abundance I found disorienting. I still remembered, in the impoverished early years of our relationship, when— mistaken for homeless people outside the Evergreen Centre for Street Youth—we were given twenty dollars. And we *kept* it. Most freebies and giveaways I could manage, but when Gudrun was offered the use of a Porsche 911, I didn't like it. The car belonged to Marie-Josette's mother, and because Madame Beaulieu was advancing in years—she was almost eighty—it was thought best by the family that she stick with the Volvo. Which freed up the Porsche. I understood the gesture to be tremendously generous, but the more I considered it, the weirder it seemed.

"Are you insane?" asked Gudrun. "We've never had a car. When was the last time we were even *in* a car?"

"It doesn't feel right to me."

"'It doesn't feel right to me'," she mimicked. She flicked her lips to make a bibble-bibble sound. "Are you a baby? This is a Porsche we're talking about. You want me to take the subway every day when I could be driving a motherfucking Porsche?"

It *all* seemed weird. Gudrun was ascending into the upper echelons of the city, what Otis Jones called the "the martini and bullshit crowd," and I knew how happy she was to move among the city's principal filmmakers, actors, and musicians. But about such molecular motion I was highly ambivalent. Why were we trying to get into these precious orbitals? Wasn't it better to pursue our own valence? And what happened to the people we used to know?

Everything was happening too fast for me. Gudrun, of course, was thriving on speed. She didn't want to slow down. She was too busy being Gudrun. She was too busy being a success.

But much of this came later. I'm jumping ahead in the chronology. Let me return to the weeks following the demise of Wyndham and Weir, the introduction of Finbarr Pinto, and the end of our interlude with Kathryn Culkin.

KAT WAS THERE and then she wasn't. I came home one day to find her gone. It was as if a fixer had come in the night and cleared away her lipsticks, parsnips, manuscripts. I was sad. I missed her. I often thought of Kat, I remembered her sudden giggles and rampant laughter, and, sure, I sensed an intimacy between us, but I really did admire her. She managed her life so differently from how I managed mine. Hers was a logic I hadn't yet learned. She was willing to make a performance of her life—to be the student in love with the art history professor, to be the chick who runs off with a musician—and to such situations she committed herself utterly. I understood why Gudrun liked Kat so much. And I'd been touched by Gudrun's concern for her. It was selfless. It was kind. Gudrun loved Kat absolutely. But she knew she'd have to tell Kat about the collapse of the publishing company. "Honestly," she said, "I don't have the heart to tell her right now." But *Keening* wasn't going to happen. And Kat needed to know.

WHY DO WE remember one day and not another? It was a Sunday afternoon in late September when Gudrun met with Kat near the sunken green space of Bickford Park. I was supposed to come by at five to say goodbye. The colours and smells of that afternoon, the soft pinks of the cirrus clouds, the green freshness of the wind off the park, went deep into my memory, and as I walked down Grace Street from Bloor, I remember seeing Gudrun and Kat far in front of me. I couldn't make out the dialogue, this last scene was silent, but, as Gudrun put her hand on Kat's shoulder, I realized she'd waited until this very moment to reveal what had happened. Kat stared at the sidewalk, morosely absorbing the news, and wiped at her eyelid. And then, rather savagely, she shoved Gudrun's hand off her shoulder. Twisting away, she hurried into the slopes of Bickford Park. She tried to keep her balance on its upper edge but slipped on the grass and, unable to right herself, was soon tumbling into Bickford's steepness, skidding out of view, and vanishing entirely from the CinemaScope of the afternoon.

22

THE TEMPLE AND THE CITY
Civilization from the Stone Age to the Present
By Dalton Hickey
Whitehead Publishing, 643 pp., $36

THAT DALTON HICKEY had influence at *Saturday Night, Flare, Toronto Life, Canadian Art, Canadian Business, Canadian Forum, Elle Canada, Books in Canada, Maclean's, The Idler, Lola, Shift,* and the *Globe and Mail* I'd learned to accept. The guy wrote an article every two weeks and seemed to publish a book every year. The first, *Guangdong Allegro,* was a memoir of his year teaching English in China. Next was *Interrogations,* a random miscellany of journalism that happened to be nominated for some non-fiction award. Those little one-offs I could abide, but when his third book became a bestseller in Canada, sold thirty thousand copies in Italy, and was featured on the front page of the *New York Times Book Review* with an accompanying author profile, I began having trouble with a world where such events were permitted to occur.

The Temple and the City was a work of cultural history beginning with the megaliths at Göbekli Tepe and proceeding to modern-day Singapore, and I'd already drunkenly frowned through its first chapter one snowy night at the Book City on Bloor Street. So I didn't need a review in the *Times* to help me decide if I'd like the book; I already knew I hated it. After skimming the review and scornfully reading aloud the first line of the profile, "Dalton Hickey has an air of deliberate expectancy," I shouted a swear word, tossed the section across the breakfast table, and said, "I want people to say stuff like that about *me*."

"Deliberate expectancy isn't really your thing, Cliffster." Gudrun picked up the section and began reading the review. "Just saying."

Our conversations about Dalton Hickey tended to involve gossip, anguish, and paranoia. I found them disturbing. My awareness of Gudrun was normally habitual—I always sought to locate my thinking with hers—but Something About Dalton didn't allow for our normal alignment. Those conversations risked morphing into quarrels, squabbles, and day-long arguments. Gudrun finished the review and speed-read the profile, looking briefly peeved by something at the end.

"What is it?" I asked.

"A list of Dalton's favourite books."

"What are they?"

"'The Consolation of Philosophy,' 'A Dance to the Music of Time,' 'At Swim Two-Birds,' 'The Odyssey,' and 'The Man without Qualities.'"

"I've only heard of one of them."

"Cute." Gudrun put down the *Book Review*. "All men."

"I don't think I'm ever going to like this guy."

"You may not like him"—Gudrun pulled out the *Times Magazine*—"but you have to respect him."

"Why's that?"

"His commitment to the truth."

"His commitment to himself, you mean. Because I don't think he's telling the truth. To who? The girlfriend he fucks around on? That guy's cheated on everyone he's ever *been* with. Why do girls like him?"

Looking up from a Chanel advertisement, Gudrun thought for a moment. "Dalton's educated," she said. "He's well-spoken. He's well-dressed. He listens to women—"

"Okay. Fine. I'm good."

"—and he says what everyone thinks but is afraid to say. And, like he says in the article, he's a brilliant journalist."

"He *said* that? What a tool."

"I don't know," said Gudrun. "Sometimes you have to say things like that. To protect yourself from the pricks."

"There are *worse* pricks?"

"It's called necessary arrogance, Aubrey. Otherwise you don't get anything done. And maybe Dalton can be a tool, but at least he has—" She looked at me as if her meaning were obvious.

"What?"

"Passion. At least he cares about something. He's not going to die without ever caring about something. The man has a point of view."

"Pretty pretentious point of view."

"Better to be pretentious than boring."

"Oh, *I'm* boring?"

"Really?" She sighed. "Look, Dalton has a book on the bestseller list. He's featured in 'Italian Vogue.' He's on the front page of the 'New York Times Book Review.' Do you really think he cares what we think?"

"He just seems," I said, "to take himself pretty seriously."

"And you don't?"

"Take him seriously? It's a bit much."

"No," she said coldly. "I mean do you take yourself seriously?"

The moment had shifted. So I asked, "Where are we going here?"

"Maybe Dalton's a bit much. Or at least you think he is. Maybe half the country does too. But so what? The important thing is, he's putting himself out there."

"And looking like a douchebag doing it."

"At least he risks being a douchebag."

"What is that supposed to mean?"

"He risks embarrassing himself. He risks getting it wrong. That's something."

"So you want me to risk being a douchebag? You want me to go around being embarrassing and wrong? What *is* this conversation?"

"Maybe a real conversation. Finally."

"Why are you fighting *me*, for fuck's sake? If your ex-boyfriend thinks he's a brilliant journalist, then great. Good going there, Ex-Boyfriend Guy. I just haven't been crazy about all the work."

"Different art form."

"What is?"

"Putting himself out there. Maybe he's creating a public life that people pay attention to and talk about."

"*That's* his art form?"

"Are we talking about it? It would appear that we are."

"Why doesn't he just let the work do the talking? Because at the end of the day it won't matter how pretentious he is or how passionate he is or how anything he is. There's just going to be the work."

"No," said Gudrun. "Because there will be people who have been changed by the example of his life. And if you think that's irrelevant, so be it."

IT WAS NOT EASY to win an argument with Gudrun Peel. I didn't win many. And when I did, I sort of felt I'd end up losing something later. After such spats, and there were starting to be a lot, I was often left alone in a room—vexed, confused, disordered. Moments *were* shifting. Our feelings for each other were mixed up in many different patterns and realities. And a looming reality was Gudrun's work with Vision Entertainment. The production company, one of the biggest in the country, and for whom Marie-Josette was now Senior Vice-President, Creative Affairs, came to Gudrun with a proposal for a series they wanted to pitch the Women's Television Network. Well, actually, they came to her with the *title* of a series. It was Gudrun's job to create the show and write the pitch document. The show was called *The Hot List* and, if you've seen the show recently, you'll know it's an extended infomercial aimed at advertising the very products it's meant to review. But it didn't start like that. At least not in Gudrun's mind. She saw it as a mix of *Vogue* and *Consumer Reports*—a lifestyle show that evaluated food trends, summer shoes, smudge-proof long-lash mascara—and the challenge, as ever, was to make it fabulous. And, because the deadline for WTN's Call for Submissions was two months away, it was a challenge she took seriously. Her response was to commit to an even more extreme conception of her working self. But I was worried for her. There were crying jags, screaming fits, and one day I asked why she needed to push herself like this.

"Because my dissertation? That was a disaster. And the anthology was its own kind of crushing shame. I can't have another failure. I can't. I really need this to happen."

"But you're also your own writer, Gudrun. You're a published poet. You're a columnist at the 'Globe and Mail—'"

"I don't feel much like a poet. And the 'Globe' could disappear any day. I'm not on staff. I'm only freelance. I can't get a mortgage as a freelancer. But if the show goes, they'll make me a producer."

After a month, she delivered a first draft. It came back with notes. So did the second. Things got worse when she discovered a rival production company was submitting a similar proposal. "I'm telling you," she said, blowing cigarette smoke out the bedroom window, "my reptile brain is going insane right now." After that, she cut herself off and withdrew to her desk with her blanched almonds and Diet Pepsis. She was smoking more, eating less, feeling sick. Mornings began with Gudrun vomiting in the bathroom and running the tap as a sound screen. At work, she kept a trash can beside her cubicle in case she had to throw up there too.

"I know the barfing's juvenile," she told me. "But when this proposal's done, our lives will get better, Clifford. I promise."

MY LIFE HAD *not* gotten better. Not recently. I was happy for her successes, they were important to her, but in this jumble of months and years I felt details were somehow getting lost. *I* was somehow getting lost. We'd been together six years, and even though the emotional schizophrenia of our relations sometimes mystified me, I knew my love for Gudrun had in it every other feeling too—respect, compassion, pride, lust, disgust, and wonder.

It was her feelings for me I began to question. With me she was irritable. She was sharp. My shaving cream gave her headaches. I left the bathroom floor wet. I made the vodka tonic too strong. I chose the wrong Bratmobile song. I left the overhead light on. I clomped my shoes on the floor. I sniffed too much. I snored. We lived in moods where I was too patient and she was impulsive. What she felt, I felt. And what I felt, she ignored.

This time was full of new-forming sadness for me. I understood relationships went through phases, but my sense of loss was sort of deadening me. And my thoughts weren't really my own. Driving Gudrun to work, I didn't think how a red light would slow me down, I anticipated how a red light would piss off Gudrun. And this was a process I began to internalize. I could be made anxious by a red light alone in that Porsche. This happened one morning after I'd dropped her at work, and I guiltily smiled—when I was *alone*—and as I glimpsed my reflection in the rear-view mirror, I saw I'd become some smiley, simpering twerp.

Such moments made me impatient I wasn't standing up for myself, and when she returned that afternoon, I said, "Listen, Gudrun, I'm not feeling so great. Like *really* not great. And I know you're in the middle of work stuff, but I kind of feel we have to talk."

"Of course!" said Gudrun, her eyes adazzle. "But Clifford? The proposal's done. It's submitted. Everyone's super happy with it and we're all going for dinner. Their treat. You're invited too. You want to come?"

LE SÉLECT BISTRO was one of the more modish French restaurants in the city, and to celebrate the completion of the *Hot List* proposal, Marie-Josette booked its entire backroom for a private function. Our table was elegant with creative types. The woman who directed the live broadcast of the MuchMusic Video Awards was there. So was the head of reality programming for WTN. Next to her was Jean-Luc Bilodeau, a champion skier turned talk show host, and Sylvain Cloutier, a recent National Theatre School grad already the lead of a Sundance film. Finally there was Delphine, Marie-Josette's sister, whom everyone crushed on because she was happily pregnant with her second child and happily drinking a second glass of Beaujolais. We were among Marie-Josette's intimates, and Gudrun, I felt, was acting for these intimates—charming the director of the video awards, chatting up the WTN exec, and delighting the French-Canadian men. It was another performance of her trilling persona and she wanted everyone to know how fabulous they were.

And yet towards me she was antsy. I felt she was embarrassed I wasn't better dressed—I wore a vintage curling sweater and jeans—or more accomplished. Yes, I'd contributed some material to Calvin's Fringe show, submitted a play to the

SummerWorks Festival, and could draw on a napkin the Lewis structure of benzene, but I hadn't won an Olympic medal or starred in a movie about a heroin-addicted biker gang. As I recall this moment, it must've seemed to the table that Gudrun was the impossibly glamorous supermodel and me her schleppy starter boyfriend. Which might be why, to prove these optics wrong, throughout the dinner Gudrun kept rubbing my shoulder and touching my hair, as if she thought these were the sort of things she *ought* to be doing. But it didn't feel real to me, it felt strained and fake to me, and the weirdness of her PDAs made me want to leave the table. So when Jean-Luc leaned over to praise Gudrun's current *Globe and Mail* column ("Seriously, chérie, you *nail* it!"), I asked if she wanted anything from the bar.

"I still have wine," she said, tapping her glass. "And remember, this is a work function for me. I have to see these people every day."

"Will do."

"So not too drunky tonight, right?"

"Uh-huh."

SOME MINUTES LATER, I was joined at the front bar by a young woman with a pageboy cut. She was neatly clad in black—in her look and movement she reminded me of Cat-woman—and, as she drank from her kir royale, she gazed at me as if we knew each other.

"You don't remember me, do you?" she asked.

"Sure," I said. "How do you pronounce your name again?"

"Sue."

"Right. So few syllables. So many mysteries. We met at the thing."

"The Cabaret Bam Bam fundraiser."

"Wait—" I put my pint of Guinness on the bar. "Wasn't that six *years* ago?"

"I was volunteering."

"You were on the door!" I said. "The cash box."

She studied me. "When we were talking that night, I don't know if you remember, you told me not to go to grad school and to do what I wanted to do."

"So what'd you do?"

"I work for Vision in development." She sipped her kir royale. "You were pretty funny that night."

"Couldn't've been me. I've never been funny."

"Hmm-mmm. So what're you working on these days?"

I pointed at my pint. "Extra Stout."

"Better than the wine that night."

"You remember the wine? Sue, this is spooky."

But Sue, I could tell, was enjoying her control over our exchange. I had a fleeting sense of scenes from a movie, *Good Sue, Bad Sue,* which Sue, still watching me, allowed me to have, but the moment was becoming a bit intense, so I raised my Guinness and said, "Nice to see you again."

"You as well." She clinked my glass. "So what *are* you working on?"

"I'm doing a SummerWorks show with Calvin Dover."

"I *love* Calvin Dover. I'm trying to do a pilot with him."

"Like a mile-high threesome? Cool."

"Yeah," Sue said. "Like a mile-high threesome." She finished her drink, set the glass on the bar, and picked up a Duvel beer coaster. "Send me the SummerWorks details." She wrote her email on the coaster and passed it to me. "And any writing samples you have."

"You sure?"

As she walked away, she glanced back at me. "You'll find out."

"Right." I put the beer coaster in my sweater pocket. "So many mysteries."

THE REMAINS OF *that* day, I remember in murky bursts and flashes. Jean-Luc showing us his six-pack abs. Delphine passing me her plate of frites and knocking over my Guinness. Gudrun borrowing my sweater as we looked on the street for a taxi. Me stumbling out of the taxi and, spoofing Jean-Luc, showing my stomach to the taxi driver.

"You're being a jerk," she said. "Jean-Luc's a sweet guy."

"He was certainly gushing all over your 'Globe' column."

"What did you think of it? Did you read it?"

"Not this week."

"Why? Do you just not care?"

"Of course I care. It's just—" I shrugged. "I may not read your column every week. I usually hear what you're ranting about long before it's in the column. So I don't really need to read it if I've heard it in person, you know?"

"Wait—" Gudrun lifted the sleeve of my sweater and smelled the spilled Guinness. "How many drinks did you have?"

As I moved towards the house, I threw a hand above my head to indicate a sky full of alcohol and said, "One million," then I missed the first step and stumbled into the banister.

Turning around, I saw Gudrun had taken the beer coaster from my sweater pocket.

"Why do you have Sue Sassoon's email in your pocket?" she asked, staring at me.

"Is that her name?"

"Jesus Christ," Gudrun said crossly. "Do you know how embarrassing it is that you're hitting on my co-workers?"

"She *asked* for my email."

Gudrun swung her jaw to one side. "If you make out with somebody, I better not find out about it. And no one else better either."

"I'm not making *out* with anyone, Gudrun. Check all my pockets if you want."

Gudrun took off my sweater and threw it at me. I made no move to catch it and it fell to the sidewalk. "You're being an asshole," she said, walking past me. "You know that, right?"

"Yup," I called after her. "I'm a blistering, puckering asshole. Finally, you've noticed. How long did *that* take?"

TWENTY MINUTES LATER and Gudrun was somewhere in our apartment, restless, troubled, seething. I opened a beer and sat by myself on the red velvet sofa. I felt abstracted and drunk and vulnerable to nine different frustrations. I knew I was being difficult, but I didn't understand why, and felt it wasn't entirely my doing. I sat stock-still on the sofa, as if confined by a spell.

I thought Gudrun might simply go to bed, but I soon saw her standing in the hallway, eating apple pieces off a plate.

"What are you doing sitting in the dark?" she asked.

"It would appear that I'm having a beer."

"Why'd you get this drunk?" Gudrun flipped on the over-head light. "And why were you talking to Delphine when you're this drunk?" She swallowed a piece of apple. "Why did you take french fries off her plate?"

"She *offered* them to me—"

"You don't take food off a pregnant woman's plate. At a restaurant? What are you—a hillbilly? You spilled them on the table."

"Gudrun—"

"And you don't need to help the waitress clear the table. It's what a person with low self-esteem would do."

"Gudrun, you're drunk."

"Not as drunk as you."

"Yes, I'm drunk."

"You're drunk all the time now."

"I'm drunk tonight. I might be drunk tomorrow. Maybe I'll have another beer right now. Who knows?"

"Well, it's just—" Holding the empty plate, Gudrun took a step into the hallway. "I don't want to be the girl whose date gets the most drunk all the time."

"Blah-de-bloo-de-blah."

She looked at me with gross annoyance. "What the fuck is *wrong* with you?"

"Hey, I thought you wanted me to be wrong. Isn't that an art form?"

With a quick sneer, Gudrun flung the plate at my head. It smashed into my eyebrow, shards falling to the floor. Then she switched off the overhead light, spun away, and went to the bedroom.

I SAT IN THE DARK, my forehead stinging. I was touching at the wetness of my eyebrow, focusing my thoughts on the pain of my wound, when Gudrun appeared like a spectre in the hallway.

"Come to bed," she said.

"I'm fine. Thanks."

"Just come to bed."

"That's going to be a no."

"Are you all right?"

I was silent.

"Aubrey," Gudrun whispered, "just come to bed. You know I can't sleep if you're not there."

"That's not my problem."

"Please don't sit in the dark. It's weird."

"No, it isn't. What's weird is you just threw a plate at my head. That's weird. Why'd you do it?"

"If you'd listened to me when I told you—"

I jumped up. "*Don't* you blame me for what you just did! I didn't throw a plate at anyone."

"Stop screaming—"

— 189 —

"Stop screaming? What about stop throwing plates at my head?"

"Why are you being like this? It reminds me of my—"

"Then go away." A few trickles of blood, set free by the swiftness of my standing, dribbled to the floor. "Leave me alone."

"You're bleeding," said Gudrun. "Let me wipe—"

"I said go away."

"Or you'll do what?"

"Go *away*. How many times do you need to hear it?"

Gudrun went to the kitchen. There was a short silence. Then she shrieked, "I don't—I don't *like* this!" and threw a stack of dinner plates on the floor.

Such antics, I felt, were intended to make me join her in the kitchen. But I stayed where I was. Still in the dark, I thought about my time tree planting in British Columbia and how happy I'd been walking the swamps of Kledo Creek, proud of my achievement of planting two thousand trees...and as Gudrun continued to smash dishes in the kitchen, I began to understand I was being defined by some severe dysfunction, that I'd become involved with a very troubled person, and I wondered if I was giving myself over to something that would sooner or later destroy me.

23

Gudrun Peel! So what's your deal? How do you stay so
fucking real?
— *Graffiti on the Queen and Dufferin overpass*

"WE SHOULD PROBABLY TALK."

The words were Gudrun's. It was the next day. She'd spent
the night in the bedroom. I'd passed out on the sofa. The mood
was shaky, sombre. Gudrun wore a blue kerchief in her hair
and was as pale as a ghost. She looked odd to me and I wondered if, after all this time, I still didn't really know her.

"Remember," said Gudrun in a frail voice, "when I told you
I went to Poland?"

"First night we met. I do. So you didn't go to Poland?"

"No, I did. But going to Poland, for me and Kat, it was also
code for ending a pregnancy."

"You mean you ended a pregnancy?"

Gudrun gently nodded. "I had an abortion, Aubrey, which
was why I was depressed out of my mind the six months I was
in Poland."

"I didn't know."

"And seeing Delphine last night, all glowing and pregnant,
sort of triggered me. It's not the easiest thing to go through.

— 191 —

It's not the easiest thing to talk about, either. I mean, Kat knows. And you know. But no one else knows."

"Does the father know?"

Gudrun absurdly shook her head. "It wasn't planned, if that's what you're thinking."

"Does your mother know?"

"God, no. I don't need my mother calling me a murderer on top of everything else."

"Gudrun, I'm so sorry that happened."

"Me, too. But it was the right decision. I wasn't in any kind of place to go through with a pregnancy. Emotionally. Financially."

"Right."

"Does this make you feel weird?"

"I don't know. I don't know how I feel. I think I'm glad you told me."

"Has that happened to you?"

"That someone I was with got pregnant? No."

"That's incredibly lucky. I mean, Kat's been to Poland four times." Gudrun made a feeble smile. "And what happened last night, look, that's not the way we should be. Mistakes were made. I don't know if the whole relationship should be judged by one night, but I think it's pretty clear there's stuff to work through."

"It's a lot to take in," I said. "Yeah."

All my earlier feelings of outrage and fury and self-righteousness had been made irrelevant by this news, which was serious, true, but it didn't seem quite right for the news to overtop *every*thing. And yet I knew if I spoke about my feelings, I would seem sanctimonious, self-serving, juvenile. So I sulked and blinked and said nothing.

Gudrun regarded me with some concern. Then she said, softly, "Aubrey, if I could say something?"

"Uh-huh?"

"I think you've been in a depression."

"*I've* been in a depression?"

"When I met you, you were the happiest, most supportive person. You really were. That's one of the reasons I wanted to *be* with you. But—I don't know—stuff piles up in a person's life. Like when I was depressed and couldn't get out of bed." She sniffled. "I think you're going through your version of that."

"Huh."

"Are you happy? Like when was the last time you were happy?"

"Me?"

"Have you ever seen a therapist?"

"No."

"I could pay for it if you want."

"Yeah? I think I have to think about all this. I'm not sure I understand it. It feels like there's a lot going on."

THERE WAS A *lot* going on. Believe me when I say I had very little idea what was happening. I am better placed now, many years later, but at the time, no, I was lost. I was conscious of misconstructions, but I could not, with any clarity, articulate what had happened or why everything felt off to me.

How did I cope? I went drinking with guy friends, sorted through their drunk advice, and pondered a dozen jangling proverbs. Communicate. Shit happens. Suck it up. Sometimes chicks are crazy. Relationships have ups and downs. Love isn't the same for everyone. This kind of stuff can happen sometimes. Good things are worth fighting for. Give the other person space. Put in some effort. Try to trust. Keep going. Persevere.

So I persevered. I sort of thought these events were normal, I knew relationships had fluxes, and they were certainly familiar enough to me. My own parents separated a number of times in my childhood and, after some years apart, reconciled and ended up together. And Gudrun's childhood, well, I think, rightly or wrongly, I was trying to give her the happy childhood she never had.

But I was truly sad. I'd been sad before, I'd been devastated at twenty-two when a close friend died, but it was nowhere near the desolation of self I was presently feeling.

"Did you ever think," said Otis Jones, "she might be an unhappy woman?"

Sure, I did. And there were days when our relations were miserable. But I'd seen her happy, I'd seen her *joyful,* so we could be happy again, couldn't we? My whole life was with Gudrun, I'd been closer to her than to anyone, and the possibility that we might break up spawned such feelings of failure... just this sense of panic replacing my personality, which made me feel helpless. No, I'd made a commitment to her and to the relationship and I wanted to honour that commitment. I wanted to be patient and supportive. I wanted to see it through.

I THINK IT WAS JULY, while I was proofing a new draft of the SummerWorks play, when Gudrun came through the door, her eyes busy with a dozen thoughts.

"Marie-Josette's family has a house in Prince Edward Island," she said. "Her family goes there every summer. But her mother's not well enough to travel this year, they're going to stay in Montreal, so she offered it to me."

"When you say they've offered it to *you*—"

"Yeah. I mean, you have your play in August."

"You want to go by yourself?"

"For a while." Gudrun touched her temple. "Except for Poland, I've never been anywhere on my own. Look, I know I've been a super perfectionist freak and I think I need time to decompress and sort stuff out. Maybe we both need time to sort stuff out."

"I have rehearsals till August twelfth. I could come after that."

"Let's talk on the phone. And after this, Clifford, why don't we go to Cuba or somewhere? We've never really gone on a vacation."

I asked how long she'd be away.

"Vision wants to get the first three 'Hot List' scripts to WTN by the end of August, so I have to be done everything by then."

"You're going there to work?"

"I have to! In September, WTN's submitting everything to Telefilm for production funding."

"So *that's* why you're going?"

"It's not that long! I love you, Clifford, you know that. I think it will be good for us. For both of us. I really do."

Three days later, Gudrun was driving east on the Trans-Canada and I was alone on Grace Street in our very empty, very dusty, and very silent second-storey apartment.

24

Aubrey McKee! Did I just see your name on a theatre poster? And did you just write a play? Aubrey McKee, are you an international man of mystery? So, good sir, I want to pick your brain about a new project. Maybe meet for a coffee? I'm around this week though I may pop out here and there. Wine's fine too! C ox

CHARLOTTE LISTER PERPLEXED me. I didn't know what I felt about her. I liked her. She was kind-hearted. Like the summer camp instructor who meets you out of session to help you finish your dream catcher. Or the friend who gives you the book she just read. Or the mother who, at her daughter's swimming lessons, loudly applauds *all* the kids' splash dives. And she was, as many have remarked, flagrantly pretty. She had wavy blonde hair, a youthful complexion, and a lushly proportioned figure. In certain sunbeams, her beauty was iconic, like the wholesome face and striding figure of a woman in a 1940s Buy Victory Bonds poster. But there were a few incongruities I found difficult to ignore. She was that person who laughs half a second *after* everyone else. And, complicating laughing matters, I think she'd been told she had a charming giggle, so she used it often, even if it cackled into stridency. Such quirks I generally put out of my mind. But her emails to me, which arrived every month or so, were not so easily disregarded. So I was glad when Calvin and I began rehearsals for the play and I had an excuse to defer any meet-for-coffees.

I was putting in long days at the theatre and, in Gudrun's absence, I was messy, unshaven, and wearing clothes picked off the floor. Most nights I went straight home to bed, but one Thursday, after a blunder-filled tech rehearsal, I went for drinks with the producer and stage manager to simplify lighting cues, sound effects, and song choices. I was at the Rivoli Pool Hall, ordering at the bar, when, from behind me, Charlotte Lister reached around to caress the whiskers of my cheek.

"Ooh," she said as I turned to face her, "I like the scruff." She wore a yellow polka-dot dress with a plunging neckline and visible between her breasts were a few bubbles of peeling sunburn. "I don't like it on everyone, but on you it works. Are you going to keep it?"

"I never know anything, Charlotte."

"Don't get me wrong, I like you clean-shaven."

"Right."

"Clean-shaven is the sign of a real lover."

"Oh?"

"Unless you like it rough around the edges—hmm?"

"What was that?"

"Did you say something?"

"I thought I was listening."

"I hope you were," said Charlotte. "Now I'm getting drinks. What're you having?"

So it went like that. We flirted with flirting, it was innocuous fun, until about the fourth drink. That's when, as she was bending over the pool table to size up her shot, I noticed she was choosing to rather freely exhibit her polka-dotted form. She sunk the eight ball, slid her cue into the wall rack, and leaned in to ask, "Where do you want to go now?"

SCENE: QUEEN WEST. TIME: LATER THAT NIGHT. Charlotte Lister and I walk towards Trinity Bellwoods Park. We have been drinking for hours. I am sloshed. She is tippled. I can tell from her enjoyment of our screwball scenes that she is sensing a romantic comedy in its entirety.

"What used to be here?" Charlotte asks, looking into a vacant storefront. "Was it a travel agency?"

"Hungarian diner? Schnitzel. I'm thinking schnitzel."

"Look how cute it is," Charlotte says forlornly. "I get sad when I see a place go out of business." She sighs. "In a hundred years there'll be two other people walking on this sidewalk. And it won't be us."

"Charlotte, we don't *know* that."

"Aubrey—" Reaching for my hand, she pulls me down the sidewalk. "Are you where you want to be?"

"I'll feel a little better when we get to the end of this block."

"I mean, are you guys going to have a baby?"

"We used to talk about having kids—"

"You'd make such a good father."

"—but I don't know."

"Well, I've never seen a man so devoted to his girlfriend. You've always been an angel to that woman."

"Oh, I don't know about that."

"What I'm saying is"—Charlotte swings my hand—"maybe you should be with someone you don't have to be an angel to."

"Oh?"

"I don't know. I don't understand why people don't tell the truth. I mean, Peter and I've been together twelve years. In that time, he's had two affairs, I've had two affairs. Marriages have highs and lows. And the idea of splitting up when you've seen each other every day for twelve years sort of becomes this weird, abstract proposition."

"You sure you want to talk about this stuff?"

"It's the truth! I don't fucking know."

As we cross towards Trinity Bellwoods, I brush a linden blossom out of her hair.

"You act very intimate with me," says Charlotte. "I like it. I could feel it when we met. Why is that?"

"Chemistry?"

"Did you feel it, though? What did you feel?" Charlotte rests her head on my shoulder. "Now I just want to make out. Do you want to go into the park and make out?"

I said it might not be the best idea.

"Why not? Be honest."

"Because it might break my heart a little."

"Why would it do that?"

"Because, if I am being honest, and we did make out, I'd feel I was kind of betraying Gudrun. And then I'd act weird around her and she'd notice and I'd probably end up telling her and maybe it would break up our relationship. But I don't think it really would. And Gudrun would be like, 'Well, fine, we'll stay together, but don't expect me to be Charlotte's friend.' And then we'd see you somewhere, and I'd feel awkward about talking to you, and gradually over time I probably wouldn't talk to you, or see you anymore, and then that *would* kind of break my heart, because I do like you."

"Oh my," said Charlotte, taking my face in her hands, "I *really* like you, Aubrey McKee." Then she brought my mouth to hers and French-kissed me.

AND WHAT HAPPENED? Did I make out with Charlotte Lister? Yes, I did. We went into Trinity Bellwoods and made out, and dry-humped, like college kids. Did I keep myself in my pants? Yes, I did. Did I ejaculate anyway? Very nearly. Did I walk home, bewildered, in underwear wet with pre-cum? Yes, I did. And did I call Gudrun in Prince Edward Island and tell her what happened? Are you out of your mind? No, I soaked stupefied in a bathtub, staring at the ceiling, grateful the encounter had gone no further but worried Charlotte would soon be emailing me. And, if I'm being completely honest about all this, I felt sorry for Charlotte Lister that she was unhappy in her marriage, that she'd had these two affairs, that she was drinking too much, that she had all these feelings she wished to direct towards *someone*. All this saddened me.

That summer, I was alone a lot, washing dishes, doing laundry, watching *The Larry Sanders Show*—imagine, if you will, that lonesome montage—and I was by turns saddened and listless. But I chose to be diligent. And I worked very keenly on the SummerWorks play.

25

The SummerWorks Theatre Festival is Ontario's largest
festival of independent theatre, dance, music, live art and
interdisciplinary forms. Since 1991, it has provided a
showcase for dynamic, cutting-edge, and fully-developed
performance.

I HAD BEGUN TO WRITE. I wrote anything. I scribbled skits.
I jotted scenes. My philosophy at the time was essentially "You
got a marker? You're a playwright!" I wrote on diner placemats
and used envelopes and paper plates from pizza shops. I contributed monologues to acting classes, spoofs to comedy
troupes, sketches to Fringe shows. Scenes I wrote piecemeal I
crammed into a play and gave to Calvin Dover. He promptly
rewrote it as a one-person show and this was the project invited
to the SummerWorks Festival. That festival is still going, and
still held the first two weeks in August, but back then it was
confined to the Factory Theatre. Downtime was spent in the
theatre's courtyard amid flower beds, park benches, and a
pop-up beer tent. All manner of summer folk materialized in
that courtyard, mingling, dallying, drinking beer from plastic
glasses, and one Saturday afternoon, three days into the run, I
was coming down the outside stairs when I saw Dalton Hickey
in the courtyard below.

He was reading a festival program with a certitude intensified by a change in his appearance. He'd cleanly shaved his head, and his baldness was offset by black-frame glasses and a Vandyke beard. I had a sudden aversion to him because I feared and disliked him, but, because we both came from the same province and because, in these years, I thought to support any and all Nova Scotians, I set aside my animosity and walked over.

"Hello," he said idly, looking up from the program. "We've met before, haven't we?"

I mentioned we'd seen each other most recently at his house on Borden Street.

"Of course. You came to one of our dinner parties."

I asked if he'd seen Charlotte Lister recently.

"Charlotte?" Dalton frowned. "She and Peter spend every weekend at the cottage."

"In Muskoka. Right."

"At least till Labour Day. Why do you ask?"

"She said she might swing by."

"I'm not sure you're going to see Charlotte Lister at a SummerWorks show." Dalton looked again at the program. "Why? Do you have some sort of play at the festival?"

"I do."

"And is it your hope to transfer to a legitimate theatre?"

"I'm not sure I'm very legitimate."

"No? I suppose you can't really produce a fifty-five-minute play at one of the mainstages. Inevitably, there isn't going to be the same sense of completeness." He regarded me. "And where is Gudrun Peel today? Out causing a revolution in the consciousness of our time?"

"She's in Prince Edward Island."

"In Prince Edward *Island?*" Dalton looked at me as if I said Gudrun had been air-dropped into the Atlantic. "Is there even a decent bookstore *in* Prince Edward Island?"

"I think there's a pretty good market for Stephen King."

"Is there?" said Dalton, raising an eyebrow. "You're a rather unassuming sort, aren't you, McKee? You like to think the best of people?" He yawned. "Keep doing that. I'll sleep better knowing you do."

Now Dalton Hickey was not only at the SummerWorks Festival to support independent theatre and interdisciplinary forms. He was also at the SummerWorks Festival to create independent acquaintance with actresses. More specifically, he was there to see Holly Yuen, whose career he'd been following since Spring Bust Up. Of course his interest in Holly Yuen did not by any means impair his appreciation of other talents. For he was keeping an eye on the courtyard crowd, and after some seconds of careful perusal, he gasped in reaction to a new arrival.

"Good Christ," he said. "Is that Kat Culkin?"

Indeed it *was* Kat Culkin. I had not seen her since her falling-out with Gudrun, and this year's Kat was a very different model. She was blonde, suntanned, curvy, and ambled towards us with easy grace, her loosely buttoned sundress offering a view of her bare breasts.

"Kat Culkin," Dalton said with real friendliness, "don't you look fetching? You're all aglow."

"I *know*," said Kat. "I think I'm the hottest babe here." She pushed her hair back. "It's a wonder what the pill can do."

"And how have you been?"

"Um—*good*." Kat snacked from a bag of blueberries. "I got blueberries. I got a new tattoo. And I saw 'Lost Highway' and that was amazing. Wait a minute—" She gazed over my shoulder. "Are those people drinking beer?"

I'd been given drink tickets by my producer and said I'd be happy to get Kat a pint. When I returned with a Guinness, however, I saw she'd acquired a Creemore.

"Here—" I offered the Guinness to Dalton. "Want this?"

"You don't have to do that," said Dalton.

"No worries."

"Are you sure?" he asked. "Will you let me get you back?"

"Sure. Get me next time."

"Will do," Dalton said, taking the Guinness.

"Mmm, beer," said Kat. "Hey, I meant to ask." She turned to me. "Am I too late for your thing?"

I was explaining there were three performances left when Kat, whose glance had been repeatedly flitting to a nearby driveway where she'd stored some stainless steel camera cases, screamed to see a tow truck reversing into the very same driveway. Shoving her Creemore at me, she sprinted to the sidewalk, ran around the outside of the courtyard, and started heaving the cases out of the way.

Dalton turned to me, reflectively, like a television panellist who had been waiting for his turn to speak. "You have a kindness for Kat Culkin, do you?" he asked. "I wasn't aware you knew her."

"Kat? She's great."

"You think she's great, do you? And how would you describe her mental health? To you, she seems a very steady, very sound sort of girl?" Dalton drank from the Guinness, a foamy residue showing on his upper lip. "I ask because McGill, when I was there, was haven to all manner of radicals and extremists. These were the sort of vaguely artistic, unbalanced women who might occasionally publish a poem or attempt suicide or fall seriously ill with lactose intolerance issues." Dalton made an enlightened smile. "Now, Luce Irigaray and Hélène Cixous are not names you will hear today, but not so long ago Royal Victoria College fairly reverberated with their daily allusion. And Gudrun Peel and Kat Culkin were prime casualties of this esoteric feminist mumbo-jumbo."

"Good to know."

"No, it isn't. Very dangerous to know. And I encourage you to continue to avoid it." Dalton sighed wistfully. "Oh, sometimes I *do* miss it. The screaming matches. The slamming doors. The friendships gone horribly wrong—"

"So you're saying you knew Kat at McGill?"

Dalton nodded. "My point is this. How *would* you characterize her mental health? Might the word 'unstable' come to mind? Well, it might more than come to mind. It might emerge out of the darkness with an incandescent brilliance to assume a rather unassailable position above the rooftops of the city. Sirens blaring. Klieg lights flashing." He pushed on his glasses. "Kat Culkin, in case you haven't put this together, is completely mad. And I don't mean a little dippy. I mean—" Dalton made a two-part whistle and waved at the horizon. "Crackers. Barking. She's a full-on screaming spastic wack job. I mean vegan enemas and blood art."

"I'm not sure I see your point."

"She's comple*te*ly off her bean. She's the sort of woman found naked in a phone booth in rubber boots."

"That's all she's wearing? Rubber boots?"

"No," said Dalton. "Perhaps there's a feather boa. And a recipe for chutney."

I laughed—it was the first time I'd laughed at anything Dalton Hickey said—but his routine had been so deadpan, so spontaneous, and so sustained, I couldn't help but admire it. It made me like him that he had such invention and I began to consider the possibility that one day we might be friends.

"My show's about to start," Dalton said, noticing the darkening sky. "McKee, you'd do well to remember what I said."

"No mumbo-jumbo."

"I'm doing you a favour," said Dalton, "whether you understand it or not."

"Right. I look forward to the Guinness."

"Quite so. Sois sage."

I watched Dalton Hickey stroll into the Factory Theatre. It began to spatter rain. I sighed. For various reasons, I was glum. It depressed me that Dalton Hickey's improvised remarks were as funny as anything in our play. It depressed me to think I'd be going home to an empty apartment. And it depressed me to be standing in the rain.

I was climbing up the outside stairs, fervently wishing for something new in my life, when I saw, far away on the sidewalk, Kat Culkin signalling for help.

"SO THIS IS a little embarrassing," said Kat. "I don't mean to embroil you—is that a word?—I don't mean to embroil you in my ongoing struggle and I understand if you have to sign the boobs of your adoring fans—"

"You met Kevin?"

"But I'm an idiot, because after I got the tattoo I only had enough money to take a cab here from Ryerson. And then I thought maybe I'd see your play. But now I have to get this stuff totally out of the rain."

"Because random driveways are not the safest place to leave expensive film equipment?"

Kat nodded, stepped into the street, and started frantically waving at taxis.

As she's doing that, let me take a moment to explain why Kat was travelling with twelve cases of camera equipment. She was newly enrolled in the film program at Ryerson University and her plan was to make a documentary of Coyote Head's first European tour. This was a venture, from my point of view, slightly problematic given the tour had begun in July, comprised only twelve more shows, and the equipment loan agreement with Ryerson prohibited students from taking materials out of the country. These complications had not so far deterred Kat. She planned to get everything back by the second week of classes, she'd found a director of photography in Germany, and she'd already bought a ticket to Frankfurt. Her flight left the next day at noon.

"Can you help me load this stuff?" she asked, pointing at a U-turning Beck Taxi.

"I'll help you, Culkin," I said, watching the taxi stop in front of her.

"Do you hate me?"

"I don't hate you, Culkin."

"And do you have any money?"

In the taxi, Kat sprawled in the back seat, her bag of blueberries on her lap. Much of her sundress had ridden up her thigh. But Kat simply lounged as she was, as though, at the moment, she hadn't the energy for much else. Stowed in the trunk, and piled between us in the back seat, were twelve camera cases. The vehicle was rickety, as if a cross-country ski were loose somewhere in its undercarriage, and as the driver clattered into every pothole on Queen Street, a bigger-than-normal bump upset the topmost camera case. It slid into Kat's shoulder and she happily elbowed it back into place.

"Can you believe Dalton Hickey?" she asked. "Holy Gestapo Boy." She ate a blueberry. "You should've seen what a dweeb he was at McGill. I heard he was in Toronto, but I had no idea he was doing the intense intellectual guy thing." Kat sniffed. "But do people change, though? Because it's like you talk to him and he looks at you with this really tolerant smile like he remembers some retarded thing you said six years ago and sadly you still *are* retarded, you know? To him, I'm still like—I don't know—Jemima Puddle-Duck." She offered me the bag of blueberries. "Blueberry?"

"So Kat," I said, taking one, "you're a filmmaker now?"

"Well, the boys booked this tour, I got into Ryerson, and I got a grant for something else, so things sort of totally came together."

"I guess so."

"It's called *logic*, Clifford." She tapped her temple. "Science. Philosophy."

"And where exactly are we going?"

"Didn't I say? Hey—" She leaned forward, another bump sending her off the back seat, and said to the driver, "Excuse me? We can turn right on Gladstone."

I asked which house it was.

"See that low-rise building?"

As I searched for the building, I felt something squish inside my ear, like a glow-worm in my auditory canal, and I made a sudden squeal.

"I'm sorry"— Kat giggled—"but it just looked like the perfect place for a blueberry."

"You put a blueberry in my *ear*?" I fingered out the squashed berry. "And you call me a freak?"

"Aw," Kat said in falsetto, "I *missed* you. You were like my favourite hominid."

A crash of thunder sounded above us.

"Uh-oh." Kat leaned out her window and checked the sky. "We should hurry."

When we arrived on Gladstone, I transferred all the camera cases to the sidewalk and paid the fare. Then I went to the back of the building. A cast-iron fire escape was bolted to the bricks, it looked like two giant Zs, and I decided an equipment load-in would work best here. The fire escape stairs were too narrow for both of us, so Kat lugged the cases from the sidewalk and I ran them up to the third floor.

As we were finishing, a downpour began. The rain fell in torrents, as if ten thousand swimming pools were dropping on the city, and the afternoon was soon soaked and dripping. I was inside the apartment, staring at the streaming windows, when Kat rushed in, her wet sundress sticking to her skin.

"You want a little hooch?" she asked, opening a cupboard.

"What do you got?"

She grabbed a bottle of Jack Daniel's and two plastic juice glasses, the sort you'd find in a preschool kitchen, and set these on the counter beside a blooming rosemary plant.

"Check out my rosemary, yo." Kat patted its needles. "It's humongous. You want ice?"

"Whatever you're having."

"Neat." She filled both glasses. "Thank you for helping me with the camera stuff." She passed a glass to me, her fingers fragrant with rosemary. "I really appreciate your chivalry." She bumped her glass into mine. "Cheers."

"Cheers, Culkin."

Kat knocked back her bourbon. "Crushed it." She put down her glass and stared at me, her eyes a vivid blue, and as she giggled, I felt a zing of connectivity between us. Of course, I had an awareness of much more between us, and my awareness of Kat, and her awareness of my awareness, was starting to imply all kinds of possibility.

But then, noting a stoppage in the rain, I finished my drink. "Have fun on this tour of Moldova or wherever," I said, putting down my glass. "You'll be in Germany tomorrow?"

Kat nodded. "I got some Deutsche Marks. Want to see?"

"Oh, I believe you." I went to the windows and looked at the sky. "I should go before it pours again. But thanks for the hooch."

"Thank *you* for coming. You sure you don't want anything else?"

"I'm good." I was pushing on the door when I remembered something. "But Kat?"

"Mmm?"

"Did you say you got a new tat?"

"A what?"

"A new tattoo?"

"Oh," Kat said demurely, "it's kind of dinky."

"What is it?"

Kat shrugged. "It's nothing."

"You don't want to show it?"

"Um," said Kat, "it's a bit tricky to see." She reached down and grabbed the hem of her sundress. "Could you maybe get down on one knee?"

I knelt on the floor.

As she walked over, Kat lifted up her sundress. She was not wearing any underwear, her pubic hair was cleanly shaven, and there was a pink heart tattooed above her labia. To make sure I could see it properly, she baby-stepped into my face.

After several seconds, I said it was a nice colour.

"Really?" She smoothed down her sundress. "Do you like it?"

"Has anyone else seen it?"

"Nope," said Kat. "Just you."

"Huh." I stood up. When I looked at the fire escape, I saw there was a last camera case on the stairs. "So, Culkin?"

"Mmm?"

"There's one more case outside. You want it inside?"

"Did you want to get it?"

"May be a good idea."

"Huh," said Kat. "Whatever works."

I went outside. The camera case was spotted with rain but still very much intact. I was not. I was in a very open and provoked state. I was with one of the liveliest women of the summer, but I didn't know what to do. To be with Kat was impossible. But *not* to be with Kat was impossible. I looked up. She was in the window, languidly staring at me, a sundress strap falling off her shoulder...

In the next moment, I'd jerked the case up the fire escape, dropped it inside, and before it settled on the floor, Kat was in my arms and kissing me. I kissed her back, opening my mouth to her roving tongue, her lips sucking mine as she made a soft sound, a murmur, which signalled a different way of being.

Pushing me against the wall, she leaned into my ear. "Did you like that tattoo?" she whispered. "I think you did. Because what's happening here? *Aw.* You want Kitty to take Daddy out of his pants? Would you like that? Let me unzip Daddy. There. Look at you. So big. Maybe I should give Daddy a kiss? Right here on the tip where he's leaking a little? Mmm. Daddy tastes so good. Now you grab my hair and pull it. That's right. *Harder.* You want me to suck Daddy and be a good girl? I bet you'd like that. Like this? All the way down my throat? But not too fast. Because Daddy's got to tie me up and fuck me later."

LATER THAT DAY, after the rain, in evening twilight, I lay in bed, staring at the ceiling, Kat sleeping now, her nose nuzzled into my neck, her slim body fitting faithful next to mine, and the moment filling me with such a sense of *her*—the fragrance of Pantene conditioner freed from sweat-damp hair, the scent of her underarm, the smell of her still-wet pussy—and just this gorgeous sense of femaleness and all the colours of the world it inspired, all of these relieved me, and I lazed there, feeling weirdly unashamed and wholly grateful, the details of the evening recurring in my mind—Kat on top of me, her hands on my chest, a feeling of my cock so deep within her, the wildness of her jiggling back and forth, and as she twisted her mouth to scream, she brought my fingers to her lips, suckling them, absently, spastically, lovingly—and as I looked at her dozing beside me, I knew I would want to feel again our intimacy in all its suddenness and collision and tenderness and renewal. For on this night, when I was behind her and came inside her,

I sensed my identity flooding back to me, infinitely returning to me, and I felt I was myself again, or more than myself, for the evening was showing me in shimmers who I might one day become and I thought now to rouse Kat, as she shifted a little, and kiss her awake, but with her head on my chest, her sleepy breathing in time with the rhythm of my heartbeat, I stayed as I was, staring at the ceiling, choosing, after some moments, to close my eyes and join her in the swoon of sleep.

26

———

seaglass

escaping from the city
we collect bits of sinful glass
your favourite: a soft green oval you call glacial
mine: ultramarine worn to smoothness
at thumb's touch
a sand spit darkened, a scattering of lupines
a copy of middlemarch stained with ketchup
from the fries at basin head
are all that remain of a day

at night I dream your body into mine
and splash into sanctity
only to dissolve in specks of lazurite
in my lagoon

and the young quebec family
to whose adored toddler
you gave your glacier—
look at him go! you cried as he ran off
eyes shining in sunlight

—*naufrage, pei*

LET ME TALK of those she loved. She loved Anna Akhmatova, Bella Akhmadulina, Cookie Mueller, Djuna Barnes, Emily Brontë, John Donne, Andrew Marvell, Jane Bowles, Annie Lennox, Pauline Kael, Jamaica Kincaid, Proust, Tolstoy, Turgenev, Daphne du Maurier, Patricia Highsmith, Hynde, Hanna, Hersh, Edmund White, Karen Finley, Zelda Fitzgerald, Ann Magnuson, Leigh Bowery, Christopher Isherwood, Christopher Marlowe, Ovid, Lady Miss Kier, Lorrie Moore, Lynne Tillman, Eileen Myles, Audre Lorde, Adrienne Rich, Arthur Rimbaud, Mary Shelley, Jean Rhys, Georges Bataille, Jean Baudrillard, Camille Paglia, Sandra Harding, Susan Sontag, Joan Didion, Joan Jett, Samuel Beckett, Madonna, Prince, Roseanne, Oscar Wilde, Dennis Cooper, Denis Johnson, William S. Burroughs, Mary Gaitskill, Vivienne Westwood, Toni Morrison, Emily Dickinson, Henry James, Gerard Manley Hopkins, Kathy Acker, Jeanette Winterson, Anne Sexton, Sylvia Plath, Louise Glück, Elizabeth Bishop, and so many more.

She was free-minded in her reading, she took up a book as if its writer were giving her an opportunity, and my first encounters with these spirits were through her thrilling introduction. I still think about Proust. I still think about Elizabeth Bishop. I still think about *Walking through Clear Water in a Pool Painted Black*. And Gudrun, wherever you are, if you happen to be reading this, not only did I grow up with you, not only did you teach me to be a grown-up in an adult relationship, to feel things I did not know I could feel, not only did you share your life with me, but this history's very words, locutions, and figurations have been influenced, and continue to be influenced, by the vocabulary of your fervours. *Gratias ago tibi valde.*

For me, a one-time chemist lost in spectra and field gradients, the shooting stars above were lead-ins to an extraordinary universe. And within that universe glimmered Gudrun's own talent for beauty, evident in the final lines of the poem above, a work that would become for me a favourite published product of hers, in part because it was written in tranquility, but mostly because there was a dew-like simplicity to the voice and scene. It would become Gudrun's second National Magazine

Award nomination and she had a tear sheet of the poem framed in our front room on Grace Street. As I'm typing this, I'm imagining the contents of that room, the red velvet sofa, the crammed bookshelf, as well as a mantelpiece of casual artifacts—a stack of *Sassy* magazines, a hockey puck, a VHS of *Jaws,* and a snapshot of Lake Winnipegosis precious to Gudrun because it featured a wafting beach ball and a hand-painted sign with the misspelled words "Unsuppervised Beach."

27

Top musical recording artists from Canada and around
the world are honored at this year's MuchMusic Video
Awards. Scheduled performers include David Bowie, the
Red Hot Chili Peppers, Britney Spears, The Moffatts, Len,
Barenaked Ladies, and Our Lady Peace.

BACK IN THESE YEARS, the MuchMusic Video Awards took
place in and around the ChumCity Building on Queen Street
West, and in September 1999, when Gudrun Peel was asked to
be a presenter, the show was having its biggest-ever moment.
Not only were random celebrities like Carol Alt and Geri Halli-
well in mingling circulation, but performing that night were
legitimate A-listers like Britney Spears, the Red Hot Chili Peppers, and David Bowie. The event had become an outdoor block
party—stage in the parking lot, audience in the street—and
the neighbourhood swarmed with thousands of fans, industry,
and media.

In the tumble of three years, Gudrun's star has steeply risen.
The Hot List has become a worldwide phenomenon, sold in
thirty-four countries, and just renewed for a third season.
Because broadcast lengths are slightly longer in Canada—fewer
commercials—the producers were forced to add a minute of
cheap content for domestic broadcast. It was Gudrun's idea to

create "Fab or Stab," a space-for-rant segment at the end of each show, and it was Marie-Josette's idea for Gudrun to perform it. "Fab or Stab" showcases Gudrun in a variety of outdoor settings raving to camera about things she loves and things she hates and the segment has become so popular that not only has it been added to *all* versions of the show but it has made Gudrun a recognizable media personality. She feels loyal to Vision Entertainment, *bien sûr*, but she has begun talks with other Toronto production companies who wish to pitch her as a lifestyle host to specialty channels in the US and Canada.

So today has been *busy*. She got up at six to revise and file her *Globe and Mail* column, she spent the morning finalizing the edit on the latest episode of *The Hot List*, and she met in the afternoon with Portland Street Productions, Jetliner Media, and Playmaker Films. In a moment she will be returning to our Grace Street apartment to get ready for the MuchMusic Video Awards, so let's join that scene in progress, shall we?

There I am, dressed in a black vintage suit and black shirt, sitting on the bed and, rather passively and methodically, tying my black oxford shoes. I, too, have had success in television, if on a decidedly more minor scale than Gudrun. In the whirlwind of a year, Calvin Dover was given a sketch comedy series, I was hired as a writer on that sketch comedy series, and, after a first season of exactly eight episodes, that sketch comedy series was cancelled. Since then, I've been unemployed and done very little in the way of productive work. I spend my time puttering, cooking, cleaning. Today, in case we have people over after the awards, I have scrubbed the kitchen and bathroom, neatened the bedroom, and bought fresh tulips for the front room. But such chores make me feel like a housebound drudge. So I am uneasy. It may be relevant to note that for several months I've been troubled by a gastrointestinal problem, chronic cramps and pains, which I do my best to ignore, though they spasmodically flare up. And, just mentionably, as I finish tying my shoes, I notice that Gudrun's father's wristwatch, left on the bedside table, seems to be slowing down. The second hand stutters on the thirty-seventh tick. I am winding this wristwatch, and idly listening for anything loose inside, when Gudrun rushes through the front door.

"WHAT A FUCKING week," she says, walking into the bedroom in a trench coat, black blazer, white blouse, grey skirt, and Chelsea boots. "If I make it till Saturday, I'll be happy."

I ask how the meetings went.

"Fine. Whatever. If you're ever in one of those pitch meetings, just pre-script what you're going to say so when you're asked a question, you just direct it to one of the five things you've prepared. That way, you don't flop-sweat all over the place." She hangs up the trench coat and blazer in the closet. "Having said that? I did perspire like a motherfucker." She unbuttons her blouse and sniffs her underarm. "Phew. Stinky pits." She glances at me. "Did we get any messages?"

"The phone rang a few times, but I only answered once. A publicist called to invite you to something at Holt Renfrew. After that, I just let the machine pick up."

Pulling off her blouse, Gudrun drops it in the wicker hamper in the closet. "I'm so bored of being a socialite." She sits on the bed and takes the cordless telephone from the bedside table. "I sort of don't want to see people for two years."

Listening to the first message, Gudrun makes a disdainful smirk.

"What is it?" I ask.

"Right," she says, deleting the message. "All the best in your future endeavours."

"Who was it?"

"Some lost soul on the chemin-de-douche." She shrugs. "Pip Berman. The literary agent. It's the third time he's called. He wants me to write a book."

"About what?"

"My whole life I've been misunderstood so it's not exactly new, but whatever. Pip Berman can suck a big toe."

As she listens to the next message, Gudrun's mouth tightens with a scowl. "I don't know what this chick's problem is."

"Which chick?"

"Charlotte Lister." Gudrun replaces the phone in its charger. "She calls me all the time."

"Why is she calling you?"

"To march in some protest."

"What's she protesting?"

"A pipeline in Alberta."

"In *Alberta*?"

"I don't know—" Gudrun frowns. "Charlotte Lister has this narcissism that doesn't really work for me. I mean, she's published one middle-of-the-road poetry collection with two good poems in it and instead of publishing another book, she's making a name for herself with all this political activism. So I'm supposed to take her seriously because she's aligned with all these causes? Fuck that." Gudrun pulls off her boots. "There's a difference between taking your work seriously and acting like you take your work seriously. It sounds bitchy, I know, but trust me. I'm right." Lying on the bed, she unbuttons her skirt, raises her pelvis, and pulls off her skirt. "To be honest, I don't really care for her politics. I care for her erotics. If I'm being really honest, I'd give her ass an A and her poetry a B."

"Whoa, Gudrun. That's a bit harsh."

"It's a bit true," says Gudrun, standing up. "Maybe I'm being hormonal, but I'll tell you what else bugs me." With both hands behind her back, she unfastens her bra and, moving to the closet, lets it fall into the wicker hamper. "Charlotte Lister loves you. She talks about you all the time. She's like, 'He's so wonderful and you're so lucky.' And I just think, 'I'm not lucky, bitch. I *chose* him.' Did we get any mail?"

"On your desk." As I watch Gudrun hang up her skirt, I have an impulse to change the subject. "What're you wearing tonight?"

"The black Donna Karan," says Gudrun. "The one Marie-Josette lent me." She scratches herself through her underwear. "Have you seen my Jimmy Choos?"

"Jimmy Choos shoes?"

"Seriously?" She grimaces, dismayed by my attempt at humour, then crosses to the dresser. "They're my black pointy pumps. Never mind." She searches the top drawer for available underclothes. Pulling out for analysis a beige camisole bra, a white lace bra, and a front-clasping black bra, Gudrun bites her lip. "How do I not have a decent strapless bra?" She sniffs each item. "How do I not have any *clean* bras? Fuck it, Clifford, I'm going commando. It's full boobies."

She turns to appraise my outfit. "And you're wearing that? Hmm. We need to get you some new clothes. You can't keep wearing the same suit to every awards show. And you need better shoes. I saw some suede loafers you'd look really cute in."

My expression must betray some despondency—I'd spent an *hour* getting ready—for now Gudrun makes a show of kindness.

"Aw, Clifford," she says, "don't be like that. Let me give you a kiss." She kisses my cheek, puts a hand on my crotch, and gives my cock a squeeze. "I may need you to fuck me up the ass later." She moves to the jewellery box on the dresser. "Honestly, if you did that once a month, my life would be *so* much better." Sorting through her earrings, she asks, "And how're you feeling today? How's the tum-tum?"

When Gudrun kisses me, I sense a blend of odours—pink vomit and Scope mouthwash—and I understand her bulimia has returned. Odd associations occur to me, Flintstones Chewables, Pepto-Bismol commercials, the word *krill*, and her bulimic breath provokes in me tannic tastes and stomach spasms.

"To be honest," I say, sitting on the bed, "I don't feel that great. I don't know if I should go out tonight."

"Oh, you'll be fine. You're so dramatic! I know it runs in the family, but sheesh."

She gazes into the mirror and holds to her earlobe a black feather earring.

"Oh, hey—" Finding my eyes in the mirror, she says, "Sue Sassoon really liked your kids pitch. And Marie-Josette's going to read it as soon as she gets back from Banff."

"Great, I guess."

"No, that's seriously great. She could take it to Kidscreen."

My stomach in the last few seconds has filled with gassy pain, so I roll over on my side and stare into the open closet. "I actually don't feel so amazing. Do you really need me to go?"

"You can't *not* go. I gave both our names for the red carpet."

"They don't need me. They've got David Bowie."

"Bowie's not doing red carpet."

Still gazing into the closet, I notice on the floor a flattened wrapper for Wint-O-Green Life Savers. Was it used once as a bookmark? I can't remember. I know it's from years ago, and it surprises me to see it, but I'm saddened I can't connect it to its earlier circumstances.

"Weren't we supposed to go to Cuba?" I say, staring at the Life Savers wrapper. "I kind of wish we were going to Cuba."

"Cuba will be around forever. When will we have another chance to meet David Bowie?"

"Yeah? Maybe I worry too much."

"Uh—*may*be?"

"And I'll take a pill for my stomach. They still in the bathroom?"

Trying on a pair of solitaire diamond earrings, Gudrun nods.

I ask if she is going to eat anything before we leave.

"No time. Run me a bath?"

"Sure." I get up and walk into the hallway.

"Hey," Gudrun says. "Did you hear about Kat?"

"Kat?" I pause to straighten Sebastian's painting. "What about Kat?"

"She got married."

"To who? The little drummer boy?"

"Finbarr?" Gudrun splutters. "He was four boyfriends ago. No, she married some film composer."

"When did that happen?"

"Last week in Spain. Can you believe it?"

"Not really."

"I know! What a little tramp. Clifford, can you call a cab to be here for five?"

A MAN CAN IMAGINE himself into many scenes and situations, but I don't think he will ever know what it is to be a strikingly beautiful woman. Such a creature rouses possibility, generates reaction, produces disjunction. When before she shied away from such complexity, Gudrun Peel now absolutely owns it, dazzling in evening wear any setting she graces, and as we walk the red carpet at the MuchMusic Video Awards, I realize I have witnessed her metamorphosis from scrappy grad student to glossy national celebrity. For this is Gudrun Peel in full career—smart, tart, and luminous to know—and she moves as if she is one of the more supreme achievements of the city. Which, very arguably, she is.

Indoors, moments are multiple, arrivals abundant, the canopies and hallways a spectrum of blondes—from caramel highlights to strawberry streaks to all-over platinum. With pitch-black hair and in black Donna Karan, Gudrun is instantly noticeable, like a raven among canaries, and I know she'll be pleased with her look and outfit. She checks in with the floor director, learns she's due backstage in an hour, then finds a female friend with whom to make a circuit of the floors. And does she want a vodka tonic?

"With lemon," she says. "And not too strong!"

In the drinks lineup, I am noticing that the young bartender has a compelling habit of leaning her bangs to one side when Dalton Hickey cuts in front of me.

His head and face are newly shaven, he wears black-frame glasses and a tailored tuxedo, and there is an expert gleam to him, as if he were the director of a merchant bank.

"Hello there," he says, after giving his drinks order. "It's McKee, isn't it?"

"Didn't know you liked music videos, Dalton."

"Might be much you don't know." He looks me over. "But how've you been?"

"Can't complain."

"No, I *know* that. But have you been ill? You don't look at all well."

"Little stomach issue. And yourself?"

"Tip-top," Dalton says. "Where's Miss Peel?"

I wave my hand in a vague circle. "Making her rounds."

"Do say hello." Dalton takes two flutes of champagne. "And for God's sake, man, get some rest."

I acquire drinks—a vodka tonic and two beer—and as I'm searching for Gudrun, two gents swagger up to the bar. They are both in suits and satin shirts, I will know them later as video directors Peebo Hassan and Huff Williams, and as Peebo orders two vodka martinis, Huff shares his assessment of the talent in the room. What he describes, in the next run of minutes, will have a direct bearing on me and my situation, as readers will provocatively imagine, but, because I'm about to get two fair-size scenes a little later, let's simply leave me listening—listening and drinking—a few moments more.

"Who do we have here?" Huff asks. "Hippie chick at three o'clock? Yeah, no. Hard pass. Hold on. Incoming redhead?" He makes a puckering frown. "That's going to be a no."

"Keep drinking." Peebo passes Huff a martini. "They get prettier."

"Dear God," Huff says, noticing movement at the stair-top, "who's this statuesque slut?"

It is, of course, Gudrun Peel, in all her fearful symmetry. She picks her way down the steps, holding her gown away from her shoes. She looks exquisite, like a figure out of John Singer Sargent, and many on the ground floor look up with interest.

"That's that chick from TV," says Peebo. "Gudrun Peel."

"Gudrun Peel?" Huff watches her. "You gorgeous little spit-fire."

"Dude, forget it. She's a bitch to everyone."

"I don't care if she *is* a bitch, I'm going to fuck her."

"Save some time and cut your balls off now. A chick like that, she's a box full of crazy."

"Buddy," says Huff, drinking from his martini, "I'm going to open that box and smash on that like a beast."

"I think she lives with her boyfriend."

"Puh." Huff shrugs. "I'm sure he's some pee-whipped ninny-boy. Because she looks like she hasn't been fucked right in years. My God, Gudrun Peel—" He stares at her reverentially. "You cocktease goddess."

GUDRUN ON THE STAIRS is aloof, preoccupied, and fierce with motive. In her heart is a kind of fighting she doesn't care if others see. I watch as a young man in a Raptors jersey approaches to offer her a business card. Shivering in revulsion, Gudrun descends the remaining steps and walks to me, the click of her high heels muffled on the red carpet of the mezzanine.

"I can't *begin* to express my contempt for these idiots," she says, swinging a middle finger over her head.

"Who? The guy on the stairs?"

"No—" Gudrun takes the vodka tonic. "That's some troll from the Comedy Network. He's like, 'Maybe you want to pitch me later?' Yeah and maybe I want to get gang-raped." She downs half the drink. "These television people, they're fucking wolves. They're coming at me from every corner. I mean it's stunning— *stunning*—the conversation I just had up there."

"What conversation?"

"Seaton McDaniel and Playmaker Films."

"One of the companies you met with today?"

She quickly nods. "Playmaker Films is a mess of overdetermined bro-dudes who've all swallowed the same loquacity pill full of dickness and douchery signifying nothing except the panic of their own irrelevance." She sucks an ice cube. "Get this. The pitch I wrote, that has *my* name on it, they just arbitrarily rewrote and sent to some buddy of theirs at the Life Network to get some off-the-record feedback. Can you believe that?"

"When did this happen?"

"And then, when I point out they have no right to alter my pitch, Seaton McDaniel starts disgorging the most phallocentric, bilious invective possible."

"What did he say?"

"He was trying to categorize me in this dismissive totalitarian way to justify his company's toxic relationship to misogyny so they can basically reinforce whatever dominance hierarchy available. And my aesthetic is supposed to fit into *their* narrative? Fuck that. I don't really have time to school Playmaker Films on the rather crucial implications of sexual misconduct, you know?

These fucks have no idea what's happening in the culture, or how it's changing, and they certainly haven't the faintest idea what I want to do." She bites the ice cube. "It's like, 'Dude, we get it. You're scary. You're charming. You have an important job. We *know*. If you don't like my series, fine. Just say so and get the fuck out of my face'." She spits into her glass. "He so much as *talks* to me again? I'll roast the little small-penis fuck."

"Gudrun," I say, holding up a hand, "do you hear what you're saying? Can you maybe calm down?"

"How can I calm down when I'm getting fisted from every direction? Do you understand I'm getting octofisted and you're telling me to calm down?" She shudders. "What is this telling me? It's telling me to get the fuck out of Toronto is what it's telling me."

She grabs a cocktail napkin from the bar, blots her lips, and glares at me. "I get that I'm being an impossible bitch right now. I just don't *care* I'm being an impossible bitch. You get it? Zero fucks to give at the moment. Zero." She closes her eyes, as if out of furious necessity, then stares into the remains of her vodka tonic. "I want another drink."

At this moment, Dalton Hickey reappears. I wave him over, hoping new interaction will help Gudrun to regulate her mood.

After a split-second hesitation, when he seems to pretend he hasn't seen us, Dalton turns to Gudrun. Opening his arms very wide, he asks, "Is that the gorgeous Gudrun Peel?"

Gudrun arranges her face into a smile, rises up on tiptoe, and kisses Dalton on both cheeks. As she takes her place again, her chin touches my nose and I smell for a moment the stales of her breath—a mix of lemon, Tic Tacs, and recent vomit.

"Gudrun, darling," says Dalton, briefly wincing, "don't you look mesmerizing? And did I see you on television this afternoon?"

"Very possibly. What was I talking about?"

"I think it was the grunge."

"Ah, yes," says Gudrun. "The Smashing Pumpkins have lost a bassist. What on earth will happen?"

"Shall we have a drink?" I say. "Gudrun, what would you like?"

Gudrun scans the bottles behind the bar. "Tequila," she says decisively.

"And Dalton?"

"Actually, McKee," Dalton says, smiling, "I believe I owe you a drink."

I'm not sure what Dalton means, but I have an immediate sense of adversity and my ass clenches in a sort of palpitation.

"Really?" says Gudrun, alert to my discomfort. "Why does Dalton owe you a drink?"

"Guinness, wasn't it?" Dalton asks, after placing his order. "You did say I could get you back."

"When the fuck," Gudrun says, intensely curious, "were you drinking Guinness with Dalton?"

"No idea. But I'll take the Guinness."

"At SummerWorks," says Dalton, passing out the new drinks. "I believe you were in Prince Edward Island."

"Oh, right," says Gudrun, picking up a salt shaker and sprinkling salt on her wrist. "I was in Prince Edward Island. Yippee." She licks the salt, tosses back the tequila, and bites through a lemon wedge. She steps to the bar to order another. "Anyone else?"

"I'm fine," says Dalton, taking two flutes of champagne. "And I'm sure the Smashing Pumpkins will find another bassist. It'll be an opportunity for another little monologue, I'm sure." Walking away, he adds brightly, "Enjoy the evening!"

Gudrun, I notice, is gazing dolorously at the floor.

"Jesus Christ," she says. "My life is shit. Because what am I doing? Why am I talking one day about the Smashing Pumpkins and the next about first dates?" She drinks from the second tequila. "I'm turning into one of those idiots. A talking head. A pundit. And say I do get a series? I'll just be some bitch in the bullshit media world. The commodification of female rage. The queen of snark. Where's the grace in that?"

"Oh, dude," I say snappishly, "would you just pick a side?"

Gudrun quivers. "Did you just call me *dude?*"

"You can be obsessed with your career or you can hate yourself. But you don't get to fucking do both."

"And did you just swear at me?" Gudrun steps back. "Aubrey, you've never sworn at me before. Why would you do that?"

"For fuck's sakes—" Three beer have made my stomach pains disappear. Three beer have freed me. Three beer have made me fearless and confident and sure of my rightness. "This is what you *chose*, Gudrun. At every turn, you chose the bullshit media world. So don't act like you have nothing to do with this when you fucking created it."

"Have you eaten?" asks Gudrun. "Because what is this *attitude* right now?"

"Tell me something—" I drink from my pint of Guinness. "How does it feel to be so wrong? And you heard that, right? Or did you hear? Or can you think? Or do you almost see?"

"Okay, look," says Gudrun, "I know I can be a cunt, but you're seriously picking now to do this? An hour before I go on national television? That's when you're choosing to have your hissy fit?"

"It won't matter when it happens. You get that, right?"

"Would you keep your voice down?" says Gudrun, walking through a doorway and into the empty studio for *Cityline*, a daytime talk show. "Lower your voice, please."

"Because"—I follow her into the studio—"when things are good, it's about you. When things are bad, it's about you. Everything's always, always, *always* about you."

"Don't you think I *know* that?" Gudrun says. "Don't you think I hate what's happening? It's like tasting puke all the time. Do you have any idea what that's like?"

"Actually, yeah, I do."

"Oh, you prick." Gudrun's voice falls. "You fucking prick. I can't help it if I feel sick all the time."

"Maybe not. But you choose to throw up. No one makes you."

"I can't believe you're—"

"Here's a question." I drink off the Guinness. "How do you expect me to feel? But wait. It can't *be* about me, can it?"

"I just hate what you're doing right now—"

"That's actually a question. I'd like you to answer it."

"This is your little cross-examination, is that it? This a trick you picked up from your father?" She sneers. "Stewart really did a job on you, didn't he? He really imprinted his fucked-up shit on your head."

"You should really keep talking about my father. See where that gets you."

"Or you'll do what?"

"I guarantee you will regret it more than anything else that happens tonight."

"Or you'll do what? Usually there's a threat. Just going by the Domestic Violence Handbook. Maybe you want to punch a wall to indicate it's going to be me you're going to punch next."

"Why are you *saying* that? I've never hit anyone in my life. So shut the fuck up about me hitting people."

"You're acting totally psycho right now. I need you not to do this."

"But this is what *you* do! This is what you taught me. You taught me how to hate! So thank you for that!" I pitch my pint glass so it shatters against a *Cityline* title treatment on the far wall. "What do you want to fuck up next?"

Gudrun flees the room. Having consumed four drinks in nineteen minutes, two of them tequila shots, she is not exactly on fleek. Although she intends to run through the crowded lobby, an unplanned lateral momentum takes her into a side table of cleared drinks and—crashing into this—she stumbles to her knees. She grabs the side table, saving it from toppling, and stands up. She picks up a half-filled rum-and-coke and guzzles it. Then she grabs a glass of red wine and chugs that too. Dropping the glass to the tray, she rushes past Carol Alt, Dalton Hickey, and Rick the Temp, hurries to an emergency exit, and totters out into a crowd of six thousand people.

IN CASE IT'S NOT EVIDENT, a flip has switched in my personality and my mood very finally has changed. I've passed into a very adrenalized and hyperreactive emotional state. My face is flushed, my shirt soaked with sweat, and surges of fury I've subdued for years have risen within me. Anger blazes in me like a fire and any errant detail—Carol Alt, Dalton Hickey, Rick the Temp—is a wood chip in that fire. Rather than stay inside another moment, for if I do, I feel I will smash a bar station into a wall, I stride towards the emergency exit, push open the door, and charge outside into the September evening—

Gudrun I find trembling in a Richmond Street parking lot.

"You were damaged when I met you," she says, "and you're still damaged now—"

"*I'm* damaged?"

"Because of all that Halifax stuff. That you can't get rid of. That you can't forget. I knew it was going to get me sooner or later." A sob escapes her throat. "But I have my own shit. Aubrey—" Gudrun tries to look at me. "I had an affair."

"What? When?"

"It started in PEI."

"It *started* in PEI?" I've never been in such a conversation and images—vivid, graphic, sudden—overfill my mind. "Who was it?"

Gudrun closes her eyes and shakes her head, as if unable to speak.

"What's his name?" I ask. "Do I know him? Did you suck his cock?"

"Oh, Aubrey—"

"*Did* you?"

"No," Gudrun says weakly, "she doesn't have a cock."

"It was a woman? Are you still seeing her?"

"No, it ended. She doesn't want me anymore."

"When did it end?"

"Please. I just—" She trembles slightly. "This isn't easy for me."

"This isn't easy for *you?*" I am in some new mood, a mood wholly unfamiliar to me. With sweat prickling on my back, my stomach juddering, and a feeling I might throw up, I glance at Gudrun. "I did too," I say. "I had an affair."

"I could tell something was weird," she says. "I could feel it with Dalton." Gudrun laughs hollowly, viciously, and asks, "Are you in love with her?"

"It was a one-night stand."

"Was it in our apartment?"

"No."

"Yeah, well," she says, "I'm surprised it didn't happen earlier." She puffs away a sigh. "Oh my fucking God. Everyone's so gutless and corrupt." Gudrun looks blearily into the street. "Who was it? Oh don't tell me. I already know."

"You do?"

"She told me."

"She *told* you?"

"She said she's in love with you."

"She did?"

"It's the same with Sue."

"When did she say that?"

"When did who say what?"

"When did Kat say she's in love with me?"

"When did Kat—" Gudrun looks at me in horror. "You mean— you fucked *Kat?*" She falters, bewildered, her world falling apart. "Are you telling me you fucked Kat?"

"I thought she—"

"Fucking Judas!"

Gudrun's first punch hits me square in the head, below my ear, and spins me to the side. The second lands below my eye, her thumbnail cutting my cheek. I am raising my arms to fend off further blows when she steps back to consider me.

"You fucking dis*gust* me," she says, spitting into my face.

She runs out of the parking lot and vanishes into the traffic of Richmond Street. I will hear a last scream, a jagged screech that seems to crack into the sky, and then she is gone.

28

mckee: you no longer have a place to live. i will call the
police if you attempt to enter this apartment. do not ever
call, write, or speak to me again. I hope that's clear.
gudrun.

PEOPLE WERE LEAVING. Streets were changing. Neighbour-
hoods were gentrifying. Toronto was a city emerging from a
continental recession. On College Street, an Italian shoe store
became an upscale organic grocery. The Portuguese laundry,
with its paint-peeling *Coin Lavandaria* sign, became a martini
bar called Bar Ultra. And that nameless place with all the
second-hand sewing machines in the front window, that
became a Baby Gap. As the years turned over, certain players
took the stage, others assembled in the wings, but many simply left for good. Calvin Dover went to Hollywood, Otis Jones
to Newfoundland. I didn't really blame them. We'd all been in
exile. It was exhausting. Everyone invented themselves. There
was no history. No one seemed to have a family.

Folks were breaking up or going home or moving on. I
knew, if I was to truly move on from Gudrun, I would have to
make myself forget everything we'd been together, and everything *I'd* been with her, the implications of which sort of
obliterated me. I didn't know how to start my life over. I felt

like Lois Lane in *Superman* when, after flying hand in hand in the clouds, she loses touch and falls to earth. My life with Gudrun became a movie once I saw. I didn't know what I was doing. Whole weeks passed with me sitting on some friend's couch, hungover, dumbfounded, bereft. I was a mess. I had no place to live. I didn't have a job. I knew I deserved what happened to me, I had no one to blame but myself, and I knew I'd failed Gudrun, as everyone seemed to fail Gudrun, but there seemed three dozen things to say and no way to say them. And complicating everything was I still loved her. I missed the shared details of our lives, me singing "Clifford, Clifford" to a dozing Gudrun, kissing her warm-from-sleeping face, the smell of her unwashed hair. I held on to these intimacies because I knew such moments of love gave back to us our lives and created for us our best meanings. But I was pretty destroyed. Learning that Gudrun's affair had been with Marie-Josette, that she'd rebounded with Huff Williams, these were story twists that affected me in variously confusing ways. I am not really confident enough to confess to you all the times, in some fucked-up perversity, I fantasized about her being with someone else, how she might return home, to the apartment we once shared, with her pussy full of another man's cum, I will just say that her smells and tastes I could not easily purge from my remembrance and imagining *anything* that might prompt her interest and excitement deranged me with desire.

I slept badly or not at all. I would wake before dawn from some new nightmare and try to wish myself back to sleep. I called her. No answer. I called again to find the number had been disconnected. I emailed to ask when I might get my stuff. No reply. A month later, an intern at Vision Entertainment contacted me to say I could collect my belongings on December 31.

By that time, Gudrun would be gone. I was to leave my keys on the kitchen counter for the landlord.

THE LAST DAY of the year was sunny and cold. Driving a borrowed minivan down the familiar-but-now-unfamiliar sweep of Grace Street, a neighbourhood I'd been lately avoiding, I had no idea what I would encounter in the apartment.

For some reason, Gudrun's red velvet sofa, with its sagging back and burst stuffing, was still in the front room, and there were coat hangers everywhere on the floors, but the only other evidence of her occupancy were scraps of packing tape and a Pixies sticker on the refrigerator. Of course, in my memory reminders were everywhere, and I could smell in the apartment traces of Gudrun's perfume, a provocation of citrus and vanilla, although competing with this was a musky fragrance, the sort that would be called a "uniquely masculine scent" by an eager copywriter, and it probably belonged to the guy who left the used Durex condom in the kitchen sink.

I packed my possessions in a miserable hurry, cramming clothes I'd forgotten I owned into garbage bags, rushing furniture down the stairs and out the door, and stashing everything in the minivan. I did all of this alone, as a kind of penance, and after three hours of zombielike movements, I finished by tossing loose ends—a bed pillow, five soup spoons, Adidas shorts—into the minivan's passenger side and slamming shut the door. Hobbling once more up the stairs, the winter sun flaming in from a southern window, I contemplated for a last time the rooms of my relationship, thinking on its scenes and stories, and then, briefly wondering if it was my responsibility to sweep and mop the floors, I chose to quit the place. I dropped my house keys on the kitchen counter and was limping down the hallway when I saw a man in a Ski-Doo jacket at the top of the stairs.

He was burly, faintly menacing, and frowning as if he had a dirty job to do.

"Hey," he said, jerking his chin up. "I'm Dwight."

"I'm DWIGHT," he repeated. "The uncle."

"Uncle Dwight," I said with a croaky voice, for it was the first I'd spoken that day. "Hey."

"Which one are you?"

"The ex-boyfriend."

"One of those, eh? You the easterner? Excuse me. The Maritimer?" Dwight smiled in the manner of someone who has a number of private jokes. "So where's this furniture she wants moved?"

I showed him the only piece in the apartment.

"Fuck me," said Dwight. "If it isn't my grandmother's chesterfield! That *is* my grandmother's chesterfield. What's it doing in Toronto? No, I'm serious. What the fuck is it doing here?" He pulled at its burst stuffing. "We weren't even supposed to sit on it and now look at it. And *that's* what she wants moved? Is this some recovery project or what?"

I said I thought the plan was to reupholster it.

"Rebuild it, more like. Or throw it the fuck out. I'd just as soon trash the fucking thing." Dwight wiped his runny nose. "Oh, I won't. I know when a woman gets something in her head. Jesus Christ, don't they have furniture stores in Toronto? Grab an end there, buddy. Let's take the feet off her first."

Dwight's pickup truck, a Ford F-150, was two years old and still in mint condition.

"Don't go flicking any shit on the vehicle," said Dwight as we arrived on the sidewalk. "Because it's not mine. I just stole it! I'm kidding. I kid everybody. But seriously, don't fuck up my enamel."

The truck bed was cluttered with discarded caulking tubes, crumpled cans of Kokanee beer, and three wooden pallets.

Dwight pulled down the tailgate, jumped up, kicked the caulking tubes and beer cans into a heap near the front panel, and spread out the pallets. Then we hoisted the sofa and placed it lengthwise on the pallets.

From the front cab, Dwight brought out two moving blankets, some medium-gauge plastic sheeting, a heavy vinyl tarp, and yellow polypropylene rope.

We covered the sofa with the two moving blankets and then wrapped it in three layers of plastic sheeting, securing each layer with duct tape. Over this, we placed the tarp and tied it with the polypropylene rope to the truck bed's cleating. When we'd finished, you couldn't tell if we'd secured a sofa or a snowmobile.

"And that's all she wrote," said Dwight. Wiping his nose again, he noticed five Bankers Boxes lined up on the sidewalk. Taped to the top of the middle box was a note, in Gudrun's printing, which said, *please take these!*

"I'm supposed to take those?" Dwight stared at the boxes resentfully. "The fuck I am. No one told me that. What the fuck's all this crap?" He walked over and kicked open the nearest box, revealing dozens of packed-in paperbacks. "Books? All tattered up?" He flipped open another box. "Sweet Jesus Murphy. Look at all these books." He pulled out a Penguin paperback and then, as if it were contaminated, quickly dropped it back into the box. "What am I? Some full-service junk removal technician? Fuck that. I'm not getting paid enough for this shit." He faced me. "What am I supposed to do with five boxes of books? Crate them off to the Goodwill? I don't have room for this. Whyn't she bag this shit and throw it in the trash?" He sniffed. "Just like her mother. *Just like her mother.*"

Dwight kicked open the middle Bankers Box, grabbed a paperback, and hurled it at the house. It whiffled through the air, bounced off the foundation, and slopped into a puddle.

I walked over to retrieve the paperback. It was *Swann's Way*. After a rather fraught, personal moment when I debated flinging *Swann's Way* at Dwight's head, I told him I'd take the books.

"All five boxes?"

"Sure."

"Put her there, buddy." Dwight strolled over and shook my hand. "I owe you one." He made a crooked smile, his breath sour with beer, his Ski-Doo jacket stinking of cigarettes. "This calls for a road pop." Moving to the front cab, Dwight extracted a six-pack of Michelob. He pulled a can from the plastic yoke, popped it open, and was about to raise it to his lips when he offered it to me. "Michelob?"

"Sure," I said, "I'll take a Michelob."

"Done." He passed it over. "Happy New Year." He pulled off another beer, opened it, and bumped it against mine. "Cheers, buddy."

I asked if he was staying in Toronto or driving right back.

"Hitting the road, Jack." He chugged the Michelob, crumpled the can, and tossed it into the truck bed. "I've been driving twenty hours. Might as well keep going." He reached for another Michelob. "But I'll tell you something. That Don Valley Parkway was the worst of the bunch. It's a fucking parking lot. Bumper to bumper for an hour and a half? Jesus. I seen this one woman in the car next to me? She *was* gorgeous, I'll give her that. Ukrainian or some such. I roll down the window to say hello, but fuck if she doesn't start talking Ukrainian?" Dwight hooted. "A lot of different people come to this country. Behind our backs, I might add. They're lucky we let them in." He opened the Michelob. "She was pretty sweet, though, and no wedding ring or nothing. But Ukrainian? Shit. I bet she'd suck the chrome off a bumper hitch."

For the last few minutes, Dwight's attention had been darting towards a black squirrel on the front lawn. As this squirrel chased away a pigeon, Dwight squinted with annoyance.

"I've been noticing that little fuckwad since I got here." He put the Michelob on the sidewalk. "He's a wiry little fucker." Dwight's voice dropped to a whisper. "Give me another one of them books. Something with a little heft. I'll tag the little fucker. Watch this."

I passed him a copy of *David Copperfield* and then, rather like a right-handed pitcher trying to pick off a baserunner, Dwight whirled around and threw the book at the squirrel. When he hit the squirrel in the spine, he crackled with laughter.

"See that—*boom*—I nailed the little fucker! Give it here. Give me another. I'm *liking* Toronto now, boys."

After throwing three more books, Dwight sighed, picked up his Michelob, and leaned against the truck. "My fuck, that was entertaining." He raised his chin at me. "So you seem like a good enough guy. Why'd you two break up? Ah, don't tell me. Didn't want the same things. Either works or it doesn't." Dwight burped. "My sister," he said. "My sister's not like other folks. You ever meet Cindy?"

"Once."

"Very religious. Goes to church every day. Every fucking day. Couldn't do it myself. And Mary-Rose?" He drank from the Michelob. "Jesus, when I think of Mary-Rose, I think of this little girl on the prairie—"

"Sorry," I said. "Who's Mary-Rose?"

"Gudrun. Excuse me. That's what her name used to be. She's christened Mary-Rose."

"I didn't know that. When did she change it?"

"Fucked if I know. I wasn't around for all this. I had my own shit to deal with."

"Right."

"But Mary-Rose, she came from nothing. The house she grew up in? You wouldn't want to be there. I didn't. Both parents alcoholic. Screaming and fighting." Dwight shook his head. "Mary-Rose lived three years in the laundry room. Didn't want to be upstairs with her parents. You'd carry her upstairs, she'd sneak back down again. Slept three years in the laundry room! That kid, she sure as hell wanted to grow up in a hurry. Birthdays couldn't come fast enough."

He crinkled the can of Michelob.

"After Johnny drinks himself to death, Cindy stops drinking, she finds God and all the rest, but that doesn't exactly pave the way for a little girl, now, does it? How many times she run away from home, I wonder?" Picking something out of his back teeth, Dwight spat it on the sidewalk. "I remember this one time, when Johnny was still alive, Mary-Rose calls me from the bus station, wanting to come live with me and my girls in Winnipeg. Couldn't've been more than nine years old. Sitting there in the Beaver Bus station in Selkirk with her nose in a book. That's all she had. Didn't even have pajamas. So I pick her up and drive her around. She's in the back seat, reading her book. She doesn't know I'm just driving her around. She doesn't know I'm taking her back to her parents. But when she seen where I'm taking her? The look on her face! She just sits there, tears coming down her cheek. What went through her head, you can only imagine." Dwight looked at me. "It's funny what you remember, ain't it?"

"Yeah," I said quietly, "sometimes."

Striding into the street, Dwight took a last look at the house. "She lived here with you, eh?"

"Yeah. Eight years."

Dwight smiled and bobbed his head at the surprising richness of it all. "She's come pretty far since that day at the bus station. Didn't she go to three universities? And she's all over TV and everything, ain't she? She's got the world by the balls,

I bet. Her mother doesn't hear too much from her, from what I understand, but such is life." Dwight got into the truck. "She's stayed true to herself. I guess you could say that. She's stayed true to herself."

29

"In her first book, Gudrun Peel proves herself a visionary.
A writer whose uncompromising intelligence perfectly
elides the evanescent quotidian."
　　—Walter Weir, author of *Beyond the Space Between*

"This slim book of forty-three poems is shot through with
brilliance and pain: comprehensive in its sparseness and
extraordinary in its confessionality and craft."
　　—Yasmin Hugo, author of *Haunting Matthew Worship*

"As brave as a kiss, as candid as an orgasm, and as intimate
as one of my own breakups."
　　—Dalton Hickey, author of *The Temple and the City*

SONGS INNOCENT AND MALIGNANT, poems by Gudrun Peel,
would be published two years later by Half Moon Editions, a
New York literary imprint. It was the author's debut collection,
the first of many books, and I saw it one day in Book City on
Bloor Street. A stack of copies was displayed on the New Arrivals table. It seemed a sort of thaumaturgy to see her name on
its glossy spine, to view again the Rivoli photograph on the
inside back flap. Scanning the table of contents, I recognized
all the titles except one, a last poem called "Myriad." Before
reading it, I skimmed the Advance Praise on the back cover.
When I read that last blurb, the commendation from Dalton
Hickey, I was filled with an anger so violent it made me want

to rip the book in two. Instead, I closed my eyes. Put the book down. Walked out of the store.

I WOULD NOT be able to bring myself to read it for some years. I don't know. I began to think that Gudrun would probably see our relationship as a detour from her real life, understanding me as some wonky diversion that held her back from her best purposes. And I wondered if, away from my influence, she would re-establish herself in all her moods and furies, in the genius of her tumult, and come into full possession of herself. I really don't know. She was choosing another way, she was structuring a different kind of life, she was going to flare through the world, demons be damned, for she had the fearlessness to become herself when many did not. That, to me, was a sort of magic. We were together nine years. At the time, I thought she was the bravest person I would ever know.

30

Myriad

How am I glutted with conceit of this!
Shall I make spirits fetch me what I please,
Resolve me of all ambiguities,
Perform what desperate enterprise I will?
I'll have them fly to India for gold,
Ransack the Ocean for orient pearl,
And search all corners of the new found world
                              —Christopher Marlowe

My pillow screams too
But so does my kitchen
And water and my shoes
And the road
I have a gun in my head
I'm invisible
I can't find the ice

                              —Throwing Muses

we started with a summer cake
you back from northern rivers
me free from dalton h

i had been magnificent in my brain
magisterially sane

yet you wanted me done
over again

the boy who played traveler
with a head full of molecules
searching for me under purple skies
white freesia sent from a too-shy you

and me a girl playing at poems
vexed in texts and haruspex
fulgurating in some desperate canton
so you followed me down one-way streets
my fish-feel and piquancy
teaching me who you were
we learned each other's words:
screef, obsidian, polyoblivion
you brought me baubles necromantic
you saw me flounce
in cunning verdigris
in my suit & white chemise

in bright meantimes
you made me gleeful
and wondered at my puissance
my poems unpleasant
my phosphorescence
but i was the cigarette losing its glow
and your kindness unshaped me
i was hooped, i was stooped
and i was sick with loathing

you will think me frangible
but i'm not made of glass

so why can't i forget
when i owned you with my ass?

o fundamentalize a devotion to me!
build me a steeple and a church
hold me down & kiss my neck
and i will needle your boy brain
till you spill your blessings
in this chapel between my thighs
teach me the secret to your lullabies
open the doors and praise me

you amazed me
when i was your fragment
when i was your spoor
but i didn't know who i was anymore
it was a voice that said i hate
my way was warped
when all was straight
and when i saw with your eyes
in every glance myself despised
it made me ill
and every day an omen
like a little yellow pill

i was bent, i was spent
in ways and means i never meant
while the damage in my heart
was sweetly seeping into yours
i forgot the girl i was before
on my way i slammed that door
in a rush to find a hall
of fits and wits and fake awards

was that the vision we explored?
tell me, darling, i implore

i've had so many men come shudder into me
that i would like one day to see
their million spermatozoa
and dozens would be my bibble-babble babies
all multihued, caressed, and candy-stained
assembled like little green soldiers
sun-bubbled, dew-sashed, igniting the earth
in a flurry of sparks

Capitalize a Devotion to me!
Eat me up with whispers
Murder me in dark meantimes
This smash of hands
And grope of greed
I wanted to raid you
Degrade you
Stab a blade through you
Why'd you do it?
Why put me through it?
Especially if you knew
It wasn't me

I found five years of us in the bathroom
Cleaned from combs and sinks our tangles
Lying in some shriven gloom
Forever writing stanzas
On the Death of Shannon Hoon
I coughed up my tacks, my Stygian stools
Drained my swamps of all their ghouls

And all were sluiced, all but one
For darling Kat you caught my tongue

Friend familiar, girl peculiar
When you loved with feints and lies
Did fancy keen within your eyes?
And underneath did further tell
Of fable, candle, book, and bell
Now I quash and crush, conclude and quell
O cherub Kit, so long, farewell
There's no more time in this ado
For what you want, can't have, won't do
For fractured, little, larval, you

I shall squeeze from pussy's willow
The very waning moment
And make myself a name
As the champion of nobodies
Let the cockled dead live thru me

O husband pup & boy unstuck
The fuck you know the hope I had
In my breast and sullen heart
Pine hope chest dwindle
Blood prick blaze kindle
You were fond of plays
In your way
Chasing strings of words
I'm not sure you really heard
But if you had years enough and time
You might have guessed
I was that rhyme

Hear it now O Beauteous Boy
After a hundred follies
And a thousand feeble lusts
Between the smudge and glitter
And the reddening of rusts
When all the peel is rotted
From ten thousand broken trusts
Please know I'm only grateful
For this myriad between the dusts

A Night *with* Quincy Tynes

Act One

_____

*It is the afternoon of Friday, January 26, 2007. We are in the
Parkdale neighbourhood of Toronto in the house of Quincy Tynes.
It's a bay-and-gables mansion built at the end of the Victorian era.
Following the construction of the nearby Gardiner Expressway, the
house, like the neighbourhood, tumbled into dereliction. But Toronto's
current prosperity has made Parkdale desirable again and Quincy Tynes,
into whose life has flowed a great deal of money, has just acquired
and refurbished a manor on Beaty Avenue.*

*The rooms are filled with taped-up moving-boxes—haphazard on the
front staircase, piled on the dining room table, stacked on the wide-
planked floors of the hallway—and only the kitchen has seen any real
unpacking. This newly renovated kitchen, home to a stainless steel
gas stove and refrigerator, marble-topped kitchen island, and copper
cookware, resembles the interior of an upscale French restaurant.
Which is apt because the homeowner is a restaurateur, entrepreneur,
and among the more successful chefs in the city.*

*Some will remember him as Sneaky Tynes, friend of my drug-dealing
youth, and when last we saw him, Sneaky Tynes was walking off
with sixty-three joints, stolen from me, on the Wanderers Grounds in*

Halifax in 1979. Vagaries have been manifold since that day and I will fill them in as we move along, but let's get now to the present dramatics.

Because there, at the front door, wearing a hoodie and sweatpants, and searching in a box for a birchwood cutting board, is the man of the hour. QUINCY TYNES *is Black Nova Scotian, 48 years old, with an open face and broad shoulders, and if there is a hero in this period of my education, that hero is Quincy Tynes.*

He is not without imperfection. He can be neurotic, cranky, and judgmental and often walks around with an expression of obscure annoyance as if Something Isn't Quite Right. This might be the hiss on a Miles Davis record, an incompetent preparation of a mirepoix, or a newly noticed crack in a newly purchased baseball bat—a baseball bat that, after finding his birchwood cutting board, he has been inspecting for a while now.

QUINCY How the fuck does this shit happen? Didn't I just *buy* this baseball bat? Oh, I don't know how I feel about anything anymore. What about you? Where you at?

QUINCY *takes the cutting board and joins* AUBREY MCKEE (43) *in the serving pantry. And* AUBREY, *as I'll be called going forward, now shifts his attention from several bottles of olive oil to a box of vinyl LPs. He wears a dark suit starting to show wear and tear, appears wan and tired, but is still full of smarts.*

AUBREY Okay, superstar. Why do you need fourteen boxes of records?

QUINCY Those records, son, have been lovingly collected over a fucking lifetime.

AUBREY   Boney M.? The Hues Corporation?

QUINCY   You're kidding, right? "Rock the Boat" is widely
considered the first disco hit. Although some
people—

AUBREY   "Love's Theme." Yeah. You told me.

QUINCY   Masterpiece. Out-and-out masterpiece.

AUBREY *lifts up a record protected in a Mylar sleeve.*

AUBREY   The Three Degrees?

QUINCY   "When Will I See You Again" is probably the best
example of Philly Soul and one of the greatest songs
ever recorded. Did you wash your hands? You wash
your hands before you touch that shit.

QUINCY *moves to the kitchen. He places the cutting board on the
kitchen island beside several vidalia onions. At the stove, he turns a
burner to low and places on it a copper stockpot. Into this, he drops
half a pound of salted butter.*

QUINCY   One thing about "When Will I See You Again,"
and you like little fucked-up bits of information,
McKee, every lyric in that song is a question.

AUBREY   What're you making, anyway? Weren't you
supposed to be meeting someone?

QUINCY *grabs a knife and begins fine-chopping the vidalia onions.*

QUINCY   I'm supposed to be doing a pre-interview. Did I tell
         you they want me back on *Breakfast Television?*

AUBREY   You may have mentioned it thirty-two times, yes.

QUINCY   My new cookbook's out and my publisher wants
         me to do media. But I don't know.

AUBREY   You're being forced to go on TV? Tough break.

QUINCY   I mean, I can wing it, but the segment producer,
         she wants to go over what we're talking about.
         Fucking media people.

AUBREY *joins* QUINCY *in the kitchen.*

AUBREY   Hey, *I'm* a fucking media people.

QUINCY   These are people who use words like "liaise."
         As in, "I'll liaise with the production team and
         be back in touch." You ain't going to liaise my
         ass, motherfucker. What do you want to drink?
         Wine, beer?

AUBREY   I brought beer.

QUINCY   You didn't have to do that. What'd you bring?

AUBREY *opens the refrigerator, pulls out a tall can of Labatt 50,*
and shows it to QUINCY.

QUINCY   Labatt 50? That's old-man beer. *Cinquante.* You're a
         strange dude, you know that?

AUBREY   Says the guy with sixteen types of olive oil. Who
          needs sixteen types of olive oil?

QUINCY   Who needs sixteen types of wine? Same thing,
          motherfucker. Same thing. (*He yawns.*) God, I'm
          tired. What'd I have? Three hours' sleep? Too much
          work. Not enough sleep. So here it is, playboy.

QUINCY *trowels the onions into the stockpot with his knife.*

QUINCY   I was given tickets to the Raptors. Platinum seats.
          Which is actually a fucked-up way to see a game.
          Too close. But it's the Celtics and if you haven't seen
          Paul Pierce play, you should. I mean, Paul Pierce?

AUBREY *sits down at the kitchen island.*

AUBREY   Who's Paul Pierce?

QUINCY   He's the motherfucking truth.

QUINCY *grabs a wooden spoon and stirs the onions.*

QUINCY   If he was white, he'd be the biggest deal in New
          England. But that's Boston for you. They go
          apeshit for any white dude. Bobby Orr. Tom Brady.
          Or who's that fucker on first base?

AUBREY   Wade Boggs?

QUINCY   Wade fucking Boggs.

AUBREY   And he played third.

QUINCY   What a motherfucker.

AUBREY   Why is Wade Boggs a motherfucker?

QUINCY   Didn't a *Playboy* centrefold sue him?

AUBREY   Penthouse Pet.

QUINCY   How much she get?

AUBREY   Settled out of court.

QUINCY   That's Boston for you. Keep it hidden.

AUBREY   Look, if you're going to the game and meeting
          the Raptors at the Westin—

QUINCY   Try Sotto Sotto. Players won't be at the Westin. But
          I ain't getting blinged up and do that downtown
          shit. That's for the young men. The single guys.

AUBREY   Quincy, *you're* a single guy.

QUINCY   Yeah, I might not be single.

QUINCY *sprinkles some kosher salt into the stockpot.*

QUINCY   So you know what we're making here?

AUBREY   I'm not your fucking sous-chef.

QUINCY   Damn right you're not. You burned the only red
          wine reduction I ever gave you.

AUBREY   Quincy, that was eight *years* ago—

QUINCY   Took me months to get that pot clean. I had to
          get some stainless steel cleanser shit from
          Germany. How you directed a fucking movie, I
          have no idea. I'm surprised you can find your
          own shoes.

Chopping up two more onions, QUINCY *adds them to the stockpot.*

QUINCY   Put in some more of these cocksuckers right here.
          That's what I'm about. Fresh vidalias. Come here
          and smell these.

AUBREY   I'm good. I don't need to smell your cocksuckers.

QUINCY   This is going to be a serious French onion soup,
          son. We got butter, vidalias, quarter of a cup of
          cognac—

AUBREY   In a soup?

QUINCY   Everybody does it different. I do it right.

AUBREY   Then what do you use? Water?

QUINCY   You *can* use water. I use beef stock. Do you make
          your own beef stock?

AUBREY   Who am I? Martha Stewart?

From the refrigerator, QUINCY *takes a Mason jar of homemade
beef stock.*

QUINCY   I use this for beef noodle pho. Stews. Tourtière. But you can also just drink it. This is *very* fucking good for you. For your joints. For digestion. And homemade is a fuck-load better than the shit you get in a store. That has thickeners, preservatives, additives. You don't need that crap.

AUBREY   Got it.

QUINCY   If I can teach you one thing, McKee, it's make your own beef stock. When you ready, you let me know.

QUINCY *returns the stock to the refrigerator. Then he picks up the wooden spoon and moves to the stove.*

QUINCY   We caramelize the onions very fucking slowly. This will be an intense soup, son.

AUBREY   You make tourtière? And you could show me how to make it? But do you think we could actually cook something together?

QUINCY   You and me?

A cordless phone on the counter rings. QUINCY *looks at the call display and answers it.*

QUINCY   Hey, Momma. What's up? (*He listens.*) Just a minute. I'll check.

QUINCY *crosses to the basement door, opens it, and calls down the stairs.*

QUINCY Lydia, it's your grandmother!

QUINCY *sniffs the air and frowns.*

QUINCY Do you smell weed? She better not be smoking
weed down there.

AUBREY Quincy, you smoke weed up here.

QUINCY Never did. Once. Twice, maybe.

QUINCY *calls down the stairs again.*

QUINCY Lydia!

He speaks into the cordless phone.

QUINCY She's not here. Do you want to call back and leave
a message? She'll call in to get her messages. (*He
listens.*) Hell no, I'm not writing it down. Just call
back and leave a message. Yeah, bye.

QUINCY *puts the phone back in its base.*

QUINCY Did I tell you? She's a vegan. Lydia.

AUBREY Since when?

QUINCY She won't eat meat. She eats these chickpea
falafels. I've got three fucking restaurants and she
won't eat in any of them. She comes in and has
breadsticks.

AUBREY   If that works for her.

QUINCY   I suppose.

QUINCY *crosses to a fully stocked liquor cabinet and searches through it.*

QUINCY   Okay. Cognac. But what the fuck?

Wrinkling his nose, QUINCY *pulls out a colourful bottle.*

QUINCY   What the fuck is this? (*He reads the label.*) Mango-flavoured rum? Get this abomination out of my house.

Holding the bottle, QUINCY *moves again to the top of the basement stairs.*

QUINCY   Lydia! Is this your shit?

He leans down the basement stairs and bellows.

QUINCY   LYDIA!

Shaking his head, QUINCY *looks at* AUBREY.

QUINCY   Lydia brings this shit into the house—

AUBREY   If it's Lydia's, isn't she allowed to have what she wants?

QUINCY   Tell her to get her own fucking liquor cabinet!

AUBREY   Isn't she seventeen?

QUINCY God *damn* this stuff.

QUINCY *returns to the liquor cabinet, puts back the mango rum, and pulls out a bottle of El Dorado rum.*

QUINCY But this? (*He shows it to* AUBREY.) This mother-fucker's delicious. Aged fifteen years. You have to try this.

AUBREY You try it.

QUINCY I've had two drinks in six months and I intend to keep it that way. But this shit? Here. Let me give you a taste.

QUINCY *takes a snifter from a cupboard, fills it halfway, and passes it to* AUBREY.

QUINCY What do you think?

AUBREY *takes a small sip, swishes it around his mouth, and swallows.*

AUBREY Smoky. Oaky. Might benefit from mango sweetener. It's also fucking potent. What's the alcohol? (*He reads the label.*) Forty-three percent?

QUINCY *takes the snifter, brings it to his nose, and smells it.*

QUINCY Jesus, that's good. That's some top-shelf shit.

He sets it down on the kitchen island.

QUINCY   Back when your people were fucking sheep in the
Highlands of Scotland, mine were inventing rum in
Barbados. So who wins?

AUBREY *reaches for the snifter.*

AUBREY   Probably not the sheep.

QUINCY   (*Laughing*) You are a sarcastic little wise-ass, you
know that?

AUBREY   I'll take it under advisement. (*He finishes the snifter
of rum.*) Yeah, I don't know from rum. I tend to
drink beer.

QUINCY   Too much of it. That shit'll kill you. My brother, he
died from drinking.

AUBREY *shakes his empty can.*

AUBREY   Didn't you used to cook drunk?

QUINCY   The fuck I did.

AUBREY   That's what you told me.

QUINCY   Why would you say that? Wait, I know why. It's
because you're racist.

AUBREY   This isn't a Black people white people thing, Quincy.

QUINCY   It's because you're a racist motherfucker.

AUBREY It's because you used to cook sloshed to the tits on
Hennessy.

QUINCY Never did.

AUBREY The fuck you didn't. You're making some flambé
and three Hennessys later—

QUINCY Woodford. Not Hennessy. See? That's exactly what
I'm talking about. Racism.

The cordless phone rings again.

AUBREY So it's a different kind of cognac. Whatever.

QUINCY Bourbon, motherfucker. Bourbon. (*He picks up the
cordless phone.*) Momma, can you hold on? I'm just
dealing with some racist bullshit right here. (*He
listens to a burbling hysteria.*) Well, I *forgot* you were
calling back! Jesus. Call back and this time I promise
I won't pick up. Yeah, bye.

QUINCY *ends the call.*

QUINCY Fuck me.

From an iPhone in QUINCY'S *sweatpants, there is the sound of an
incoming text.*

AUBREY Popular guy.

QUINCY *pulls out his iPhone and looks at the text.*

QUINCY   Who's this? *Breakfast Television? (He reads the text.)*
         She's bailing on the pre-interview. Rescheduling. I
         knew it.

AUBREY   The segment producer?

QUINCY   Crisis averted. Looks like you're going to the Raptors.

QUINCY *is about to put his iPhone in his pocket when he scrolls
to another text.*

QUINCY   This segment producer, she sent me a photo of
         herself. You want to see?

AUBREY   She sent you a selfie?

QUINCY *passes the iPhone to* AUBREY, *who examines the image.*

AUBREY   She's totally cute. And she knows you're single?

QUINCY *picks up the wooden spoon and stirs the onions.*

QUINCY   This woman, now she *is* Korean, but she actually
         has a serious ass. And you do not see that very
         often. You just don't.

AUBREY   What's her name?

QUINCY   Sang-mi. *(Pause.)* God, I'm getting hard just saying
         the name.

AUBREY   Sang-mi?

QUINCY   Hang me. Put me in your bed and bang me. (*He stares into the stockpot.*) That's not appropriate.

AUBREY   What's she say? (*He finds the text message.*) "Can't do tonight. See you tomorrow—exclamation mark." Dude. Sang-mi likes you.

QUINCY   She had lunch at Tynes Downtown today. She sent me a photo of her having the porchetta sandwich.

AUBREY   She sent you *two* selfies? (*He finds the earlier text and reads it aloud.*) "Are all your snacks this tasty—happy face?" Dude! Sang-mi *likes* you.

QUINCY   Nah. I'm sure she's like that with everybody.

AUBREY   Um, no. She could've been all business, but she's being flirty.

QUINCY   Whatever. I'll see her tomorrow. Or not. I don't know. (*Pause.*) We sort of had a drink the other night.

AUBREY   You went on a date? Quincy, you're on fire!

QUINCY   (*Somewhat dramatically*) Why, why, *why* do I keep going back? Asian women, I know the whole story. I can feel it already.

AUBREY   What do you feel?

QUINCY   What the fuck you think? Gorgeous Korean woman with an emotionally distant father and a mother you

can never tell *what* the fuck she's thinking. (*Pause.*)
Her mother's not going to like me.

AUBREY   Why are you thinking this?

QUINCY   Because! First-generation Asian mothers, they
want their daughter to date an Asian guy. Or a
white guy. Not a Black guy. It's ingrained. They see
a Black guy and it's warning bells. Not wedding
bells. Meanwhile, girls just want to have fun, I get
it, but— (*He shivers.*) That's danger, Will Robinson.

AUBREY   You went on one date. I don't know if you have to
start worrying about this. Have you actually *met* the
mother?

QUINCY   Of course not!

AUBREY   Well, I don't know, instead of worrying if Sang-mi's
mother's going to like you—

QUINCY   This shit's important!

AUBREY   —why don't you worry if you like Sang-mi?

QUINCY   Hmm. I suppose.

As AUBREY *moves to the refrigerator, he reads two new texts on
his cellphone. Whether* QUINCY *notices this, we can't tell. His
attention seems focused on the onions in the stockpot.*

AUBREY *puts his cellphone in his pocket. After taking another beer
from the refrigerator, he reads an invitation stuck to its door.*

AUBREY What's this? Susheel? He's opening a restaurant?

QUINCY Hmm-mmm.

AUBREY Isn't he your garde-manger guy?

QUINCY Was. Now he's one of the dudes on the come-up.

AUBREY Nice he invited you.

QUINCY Is it?

QUINCY *takes the invitation from the refrigerator and looks it over.*

QUINCY He calls himself a "culinarian"? Ta? That is such a
        Eurotrash thing to do.

QUINCY *drops the invitation on the kitchen island and returns to
stirring his onions.*

AUBREY Let's see.

AUBREY *stands over the invitation and reads out a phrase from the
bottom of the card.*

AUBREY "Come Meet Us. Come Make Us." Not sure about
        that tag line.

QUINCY That's a faggot-ass tag line.

AUBREY And it's tonight?

QUINCY Soft opening. For friends and media.

AUBREY *studies an image on the invitation.*

AUBREY I like the cherrywood and mahogany.

QUINCY They put two hundred grand into the reno.

AUBREY He saved that kind of dough working for you?

QUINCY I think he's got Bay Street money.

AUBREY 1180 Queen West? That's just up the street.

QUINCY You want to go?

AUBREY What kind of food is it?

QUINCY Samosas. Pakoras. Susheel does a nice sautéed mushroom with cardamon. He's all the way in with that fusion shit.

AUBREY Maybe have your soup and go over?

QUINCY Soup won't be ready for two hours.

AUBREY You want to go?

QUINCY For like twenty minutes? We could walk over. After I add the stock, I can leave it to simmer. Come back, jar it, go to the game.

QUINCY *turns up the heat on the gas stove.*

AUBREY *is watching him.*

AUBREY   And you're going to go like that?

QUINCY   Like what?

AUBREY   Sweatpants that smell like onions? What about
          wearing a suit?

QUINCY   Which suit?

AUBREY   The bespoke pinstripe.

QUINCY   Doesn't fit me anymore.

AUBREY   What about the charcoal suit?

QUINCY   You want me to wear a suit and get all swagged up?
          Fuck that shit.

AUBREY   It's a restaurant opening, Quincy. What's the invite
          say? (*He refers to it again.*) Attire is "Creative Cocktail."

QUINCY   You want me to wear a suit? Fucking Susheel. (*He
          sets the wooden spoon on the stockpot.*) All right. Let's
          do this quick.

QUINCY *walks to the front stairs. As he picks his way between the
moving-boxes on the staircase, he notices* AUBREY *behind him,
looking at his cellphone.*

QUINCY   Why do you keep checking that fucking thing? You
          get a text?

AUBREY   I might've got a text.

QUINCY   I thought you broke up.

AUBREY   That was last week.

QUINCY   And didn't she break up with you? Why is she
texting you?

AUBREY   Going out with a younger woman, Quincy, it's not
all pantyhose and vodka hangovers. There's also a
negative side.

QUINCY   Too nice, son. You're too nice. And your girlfriend?
What's her name again? It's a name like Krista.

AUBREY   Her name *is* Krista.

QUINCY   No. It's a name like Krista.

AUBREY   Dude, I've gone out with her for three years.
You've met her a million times. It's Krista.

QUINCY   It's one of those fucked-up names like Kirsten. Or
Kristin. I mean, she *looks* like a Kristin.

AUBREY   Okay, it's Kristin. I'm in love with Kristin. I just
got a text from Kristin.

QUINCY   Nice. (*He smiles warmly.*) So how's it going with
you two? Is it back on?

AUBREY   Just a second.

AUBREY *reads through a few more texts . . .*

Which is all the answer QUINCY *needs.*

QUINCY   You don't know, do you? Well, you obviously love
              the woman. No other man would put up with the
              shit you do. (*He watches* AUBREY *text a reply.*) She
              breaks up with you but won't stop texting? Fuck.
              What's it say? Let's see.

QUINCY *takes the cellphone from* AUBREY.

AUBREY   I don't think you want to read that.

QUINCY   (*He reads aloud*) "Mama needs some D."

QUINCY *returns the cellphone.*

QUINCY   Your generation's fucked.

AUBREY   She's in a weird space at the moment.

QUINCY   Another fucking astronaut? Move on. You didn't
              get married. No one got pregnant. It's win-win.

QUINCY *nudges a moving-box with his socked foot.*

QUINCY   I mean, if you're back together in a week, I'll say
              good luck. Because this shit happens. I got back
              with Lydia's mother six times and she was the only
              woman who actually tried to kill me. I ended up in
              Emergency with a boning knife in my chest. Shit
              don't get more symbolic than that.

QUINCY *glances behind him to see* AUBREY *reading more texts.*

QUINCY   I mean with this shit, son? It's like what
         Gandhi said.

AUBREY   What did Gandhi say?

QUINCY   Don't stick your dick in crazy.

AUBREY   Gandhi said that? I thought it was Wade Boggs.

QUINCY   I just don't want to see your balls get nailed to the
         wall and your head set on fire, you know?

AUBREY   Sweet of you to say, Quince. Means a lot.

QUINCY   I mean, this girl, she's cute. But I don't know if a
         committed relationship is what she needs right
         now. How old's she?

AUBREY   Twenty-eight.

QUINCY   Twenty-eight! She could be anywhere next year.
         New York. Machu Pichu. She's figuring things out.
         She's trying on clothes.

AUBREY   So I'm a dress?

QUINCY   You're totally a dress.

AUBREY   I'm a mid-length frock with an empire waist and
         delicate yellow piping on the inseam?

Reaching the top of the stars, QUINCY *shakes his head.*

QUINCY   Want my advice? Don't call her. Don't text her. And stop drinking.

AUBREY   What was the third thing?

QUINCY   Fuck this shit and make another movie. You'll be out of your prime, son. You'll be done. Then where you at?

AUBREY   Alone?

QUINCY   I'm sure she can survive one night. (*He moves to the master bedroom.*) You and me? We'll see Sushecl then hit up the Raptors.

Inside the master bedroom, QUINCY *slides open a walk-in closet. Hanging inside on wooden hangers are shirts, suits, and neckties.*

QUINCY *takes out a blue dress shirt.*

QUINCY   Which shirt you like? You like the blue?

AUBREY   With my skin tone, I can't wear it.

QUINCY   You don't like the blue?

AUBREY   The blue's okay, but it's fighting your eye colour. (*He slips into a* Goodfellas *voice.*) With your complexion, you can wear purple. You can wear mulberry. You can wear pink.

QUINCY   I'm not wearing pink!

AUBREY Whoa, whoa, whoa. No one's forcing pink on you, guy.

QUINCY Damn straight they're not.

AUBREY But it does bring out a certain glow.

QUINCY What about a tie?

AUBREY The lavender works with the mulberry. Or the yellow.

QUINCY The yellow?

AUBREY Susheel's place, it's dark. Oak and mahogany. You wear yellow or pink, you're going to pop out of the background. If you want to blend in, wear the blue. Your call.

Pause.

QUINCY You're messing with me! (*He points at Aubrey.*) You're messing with me. You're trying to fuck up my night.

AUBREY Do what you feel is right. (*He speaks under his breath.*) Just don't wear the blue.

QUINCY The—what?

AUBREY Hmm?

QUINCY You said something.

AUBREY   No, I didn't.

QUINCY   You fucking said something, so what was it?

AUBREY   Nope.

Pause.

QUINCY   All right, I'll wear the fucking mulberry.

AUBREY   (*quietly*) With the yellow tie.

QUINCY   What?

AUBREY   Your call. Like I said.

QUINCY   You want me to wear a yellow fucking tie? You're still fucking gay.

AUBREY   You'll look like that Ralph Lauren guy. Tyson Beckford.

QUINCY *brings out a charcoal-grey suit.*

QUINCY   Except the pants to this suit, I don't know why I got them. They don't have back pockets. They're faggot pants.

AUBREY   They're not faggot pants. They're just pants without back pockets.

QUINCY   Sends the wrong message.

AUBREY So wear the shirt untucked if you're so concerned about your butt.

QUINCY Where do I put my wallet?

AUBREY Front pocket.

QUINCY That's where I put my keys. It's going to look fucked-up.

AUBREY So give me your wallet.

QUINCY Yeah, motherfucker, like I'm going to give you my wallet.

AUBREY Put the wallet in the inside pocket of the suit and your keys in a side pocket.

QUINCY Ruins the line of the suit.

AUBREY For fuck's sakes. Give me the keys. *I'll* carry the keys.

QUINCY *takes his house keys from his sweatpants and raises them above his head.*

QUINCY You lose them and I will end you.

The downstairs smoke alarm makes a shrill beep-beep sound.

QUINCY Motherfucker!

QUINCY *throws the house keys at* AUBREY'*s head.*

He hustles downstairs, turns off the gas burner, and stares miserably into the stockpot.

QUINCY Fucking hell. You burnt the onions.

AUBREY *comes into the kitchen.*

AUBREY I burnt nothing.

QUINCY You burnt the fucking onions.

AUBREY This is on you, pal. I offered to help. But you were all— (*high-pitched voice*) "Ooh, look at me. I'm on *Breakfast Television*. I have a wooden spoon." (*He looks in the stockpot.*) Hmm. Tasty, delicious blackened onions.

Pause.

QUINCY All right, then. You want to go to this?

AUBREY Susheel's opening?

QUINCY We can get a samosa.

AUBREY Done.

QUINCY And I'll get dressed. Just remember, I'm doing this for you, motherfucker. I'm doing this for you. You can come as my Plus One.

AUBREY I'm not anybody's Plus One.

QUINCY   You can come as my friend, then.

AUBREY   Yeah? I don't know if a man can really be friends
with another man.

QUINCY   Why not?

As the cordless phone rings again, AUBREY *puts his arm around*
QUINCY *and fondly smiles at him.*

AUBREY   Because the sex part always gets in the way.

Curtain

Act Two

Later that day. We are now at Khush, an Indian fusion restaurant. It's a medium-sized space with swooping mahogany curves, cherry-wood trim, dozens of mirrors, and a central bar. Because Aubrey and Quincy are still some blocks away, strolling coatless on this mild evening, let's add a few biographical details for Quincy Tynes.

After his drug-dealing teens, and following a college football career cut short by a blown knee, Quincy began employment with Canadian Pacific Hotels. He worked as a dishwasher at Château Halifax, a prep cook at Château Laurier in Ottawa, and a line cook at the Royal York in Toronto. It was while at the Royal York that he purchased a bankrupt flower shop on Dundas Street West, acquired a liquor licence, and opened a bar called Slade.

And it was at Slade where Aubrey McKee drank the night away after breaking up with Gudrun Peel. That night, Quincy decided to help Aubrey, covering his bill and offering his dormant truck as a place for Aubrey to sleep, and as AUBREY *and* QUINCY *arrive at Khush, you should know that an awareness of this generosity is never far from Aubrey's mind.*

Outside the front door is a STAFFER *in a headset. She holds a clipboard and smiles at* QUINCY, *who wears a charcoal suit, mulberry shirt, and yellow tie.*

QUINCY Hey. I'm Quincy Tynes and—

STAFFER We know who you are, Mr. Tynes! (*She puts a plastic wristband on his wrist.*) And this is—

QUINCY My Plus One.

AUBREY I'm his friend.

STAFFER Uh-huh? (*She puts a plastic wristband on* AUBREY's *wrist.*) Enjoy!

QUINCY *and* AUBREY *move into a room of diversely fashionable people.*

QUINCY So you know how to do this?

AUBREY Do I know how to be at a party?

QUINCY Every social event you go to, you go with a goal.

AUBREY Who are you? Ayn Rand?

QUINCY So what's your goal?

AUBREY Ignore your advice and drink. What's yours?

QUINCY Congratulate Susheel. Try not to get sucked into any bullshit. And avoid my enemies.

AUBREY   What was the third thing? (*He looks at* QUINCY.)
         What enemies? You don't have any enemies.

QUINCY   Well, avoid idiots, then.

AUBREY   Good luck with that.

People at the bar recognize QUINCY. *They beckon him over with greetings like, "The Mighty Quin!" "Tynes-ee!" "Hey there, Playa."*

QUINCY   All right. I'm going over.

AUBREY   All right. I'm having a cigarette.

QUINCY   (*startled*) You're still smoking?

AUBREY *strolls along the sidewalk, lights a cigarette, and reads his recent texts. He sighs and stares at the sunset over the Gladstone Hotel.*

Into this reverie walks ZOË FONSECA (22), *a young woman in hoop earrings, double-breasted overcoat, and high heels. She talks rapidly into her smartphone.*

ZOË   Amber—*Amber*—listen. Would you listen? That's
      sweet he sent flowers but I still think he's being a
      douche. (*She listens.*) Because he's always checking
      up on you! He thinks you're automatically going to
      tell him everything you do three weeks after you
      break up? Ah, no. You're not. You said you need
      space but does he respect that? (*She listens.*) But you
      have been solid with him. Like, girl, seriously, what
      the fuck? Because Brayden keeps showing up
      wherever you are like three out of the last six

nights? And why would he ask if you hooked up with that bartender? That's just some random guy you barely even know on Facebook from your birthday two weeks ago. Like so what? Case closed. Point blank period. But Brayden's all like, Did you fuck him and da-da-da-da-duh? He doesn't get to do that. He doesn't. (*She listens.*) Because *he's* the one with issues. And he hates it when you call him on his shit but he's been like this since day one. I mean, I feel bad for him? But getting back together is not going to happen. He's *so* not the guy. He's not. Because Amber? It's called boundaries. So you have to seriously rethink what—(*She listens.*) He's calling you? Okay. Call me back.

ZOË *checks her texts, replies to two of them, and then looks at* AUBREY.

ZOË   You have another cigarette?

Opening his pack of cigarettes, AUBREY *offers it to her.*

ZOË *picks out a cigarette.*

ZOË   Thanks. I'm Zoë.

Pulling a lighter from his pocket, AUBREY *lights her cigarette.*

AUBREY Hi, Zoë.

ZOË   So what party is this?

AUBREY It's a restaurant opening.

AUBREY *finishes his cigarette, stuffs it into a litter bin's cigarette receptacle, and glances inside where* QUINCY, *staring at him, wildly signals for Aubrey to stop smoking.*

ZOË *looks inside and is impressed to see Quincy Tynes.*

ZOË   You're friends with Quincy Tynes?

AUBREY He's got a lot of friends.

ZOË   I love his suit.

AUBREY Totally.

ZOË   I like a man who knows how to look good.

AUBREY I know, right? Isn't it just one less thing to worry about?

ZOË   And he's a chef?

AUBREY Not a lot missing from that package.

ZOË *smiles and drags on her cigarette.*

ZOË   What about you? What's your package? Are you a chef too?

AUBREY Me? No. I can barely open a window.

ZOË   But I've seen you before. What do you do?

QUINCY *comes to the door as* ZOË'S *smartphone begins to ring.*

ZOË   (*checking the call display*) Oh, I have to take this. (*She talks into phone*) Amber? What'd he say? Everything chill? Because I have an idea.

QUINCY   Okay, motherfucker, riddle me this—

ZOË   (*into phone*) Wai-wai-wait. I have to go where it's quiet. (*to* AUBREY) Be right back, you guys!

She walks away in her high heels, her smartphone held tightly to her ear.

AUBREY   Sure thing, Zoë. Keep it real.

AUBREY *joins* QUINCY *inside. The room is crowded and busy.*

AUBREY   What's up?

QUINCY   She's here.

AUBREY   Who's here?

QUINCY   Sang-mi.

AUBREY   Sweet. Can I meet her?

QUINCY   No. Not sweet. Messed.

AUBREY   Why?

QUINCY   She fucking lied. She didn't tell me she was coming. I caught her in a lie.

AUBREY   You didn't catch her in a lie, you drama queen freak
           show. She said she had to reschedule. Which she
           did when she texted you.

QUINCY   I shouldn't've come. I should've trusted my own
           instincts. She's playing angles.

AUBREY   She's not playing angles. I don't see what she did
           wrong.

QUINCY   She didn't tell me she was meeting Susheel.

AUBREY   She's not meeting Susheel. She's covering this event
           for *Breakfast Television* or *Entertainment Toronto* or
           whatever it is. This is a gig. She's here for work.

QUINCY   Then that's how I'm going to play it. Like work.

AUBREY   Play it however you want, but Sang-mi did nothing
           wrong.

QUINCY   Shit always comes to me from somewhere. First
           this Sang-mi bullshit. Then—

AUBREY   This is *not* a problem, Quincy. Look, one of your
           friends is opening his own place. You're supporting
           him. You look great. Aren't you glad you're not in
           sweatpants?

QUINCY   No, because I shouldn't've come.

A server approaches with a tray full of glasses of champagne.

QUINCY   And now I feel like fucking drinking.

QUINCY *grabs two glasses of champagne from the tray.*

QUINCY   I blame you for this, motherfucker. I blame you.

AUBREY *reaches for one of the glasses in* QUINCY's *hands.*

QUINCY   Not a chance, son. (*He holds the two glasses close to his chest.*) They're both mine.

Before the server moves away, AUBREY *grabs the last glass from the tray.*

QUINCY   What're you doing? I told you not to drink. Didn't I tell you not to drink? Stop drinking!

AUBREY   Stop drinking? It's one of the few things I'm still good at.

QUINCY   Drinking's your way of dealing with people's bullshit. But drinking's becoming *your* bullshit. You get that, right?

AUBREY   Cute theory.

QUINCY *picks up a menu from a table.*

QUINCY   I'm going to find you in a dumpster down by the lake. I'm going to have to fish your ass out of a motherfucking dumpster.

AUBREY *gestures with his glass towards the people at the bar.*

AUBREY   So how's it going with your enemies?

QUINCY   (*starts to study the menu*) I don't like these Bay
         Street boys.

AUBREY   What Bay Street boys?

QUINCY   Brian Bristol and his whiteboy brigade.

AUBREY   You know Brian Bristol?

QUINCY   Give me somebody from Sri Lanka. Panama.
         Philippines. Them dudes I can trust. I don't trust
         these Richie Rich motherfuckers.

AUBREY   How do you know him?

QUINCY   I met with him. He wanted to franchise my
         restaurants to Vegas. Or maybe he pump-faked me
         to get Susheel onside. I don't know. But Brian
         Bristol? Creepy as a motherfucker.

AUBREY   You didn't like his proposal or you didn't like him?

QUINCY   And he's investing in this place? Hmm. These
         Rosedale boys—

AUBREY   He's from Forest Hill.

QUINCY   I have no time for those Gucci suit motherfuckers.

ZOË *appears in the doorway. Waving at* AUBREY *and* QUINCY,
she breezes past the STAFFER *in the headset.*

ZOË   Hey you!

AUBREY   Zoë, you made it! I was totally freaking. Quincy,
           you remember Zoë, right?

QUINCY   I do?

AUBREY   Zoë, this is Quincy. He's been saving you a
           champagne.

QUINCY   I have?

ZOË   For real?

QUINCY   Sure.

QUINCY *passes* ZOË *his other glass of champagne.*

ZOË   Sick!

AUBREY   Sweet, isn't he?

ZOË   You guys are both totally sweet. So I'm just texting
           my friend to come? Like, how late does this go?

AUBREY   Well, Quincy's on his way to see the Raptors.

ZOË   Shut up! (*She smacks* QUINCY *in the chest.*) Are you
           even serious right now? I would *love* to see the
           Raptors. But should I still text my friend though?

AUBREY   It's a dilemma, Zoë.

ZOË   Hey, can I get a picture?

Positioning herself between the two men, ZOË *holds up her smartphone, makes a duck face, and snaps a selfie. She is showing the image to* QUINCY *when* SANG-MI YENG, *a very assured Korean woman, walks up.*

SANG-MI I don't mean to interrupt anyone's moment, but I
          have to bounce...

She smiles at QUINCY.

SANG-MI . . . as the kids say.

She leans in to touch QUINCY's *elbow.*

SANG-MI See you tomorrow, Q.T.

QUINCY, AUBREY, *and* ZOË *watch* SANG-MI *walk out the front door. She is followed by a cameraman from Citytv.*

After a pause, ZOË *turns to* QUINCY.

ZOË   Is that your girlfriend?

AUBREY That's what I'm talking about, Zoë. Hey, could I
          get your advice on something? If, hypothetically,
          someone breaks up with you—

ZOË's *smartphone rings. After reading the call display, she simultaneously answers the call and holds a hand in front of* AUBREY's *face.*

ZOË   (*Into phone*) What's up? (*She listens.*) He's there?
           Brayden's *with* you? Hold on. I'm on my way. Tell
           him I'm coming over to kick his ass.

ZOË *exits the restaurant.*

QUINCY *watches* ZOË *run off as* AUBREY *goes to the bar for drinks.*

QUINCY   I wonder about this world.

QUINCY *resumes reading the menu.*

After several seconds, AUBREY *returns from the bar with an opened
bottle of Kingfisher beer for himself and a glass of champagne for*
QUINCY.

QUINCY   Okay. Had enough?

AUBREY *offers the champagne to* QUINCY, *who shakes his head.*
AUBREY *downs the champagne and sets the glass on a nearby
table. Then he turns to* QUINCY.

AUBREY   Dude. Sang-mi likes you.

QUINCY   Nah.

AUBREY   I was standing right there. She called you cutie.

QUINCY   Q.T. Initials.

AUBREY   Oh.

QUINCY   Yeah. Whatever. Women.

AUBREY   Did you see how she smiled at you?

QUINCY   Aubrey, I'm forty-eight. She's thirty-two. What the
         fuck am I going to do with her interest in me? Am
         I going to satisfy that fantasy? That shit gets weird.
         And I don't want those problems.

AUBREY   Never know till you try.

QUINCY   Hey, I've been to Georgia and California. I think of
         Sang-mi like someone who's in Lydia's class. She's
         like four years older than Lydia. That shit ain't
         right.

AUBREY   I think she's fifteen years older, but okay.

QUINCY   Still not right.

AUBREY   Sometimes these things are about a connection.

QUINCY   Says the man who has gone out with the most
         *dys*functional, *fucked*-up women on the planet.

AUBREY   I'm just saying I don't know if I'd shut that door.

QUINCY   Yeah? I've got three restaurants. I don't have time
         to be in a relationship. We going?

Frowning, QUINCY *puts the menu back on the table where he
found it.*

AUBREY, *in preparation for departure, hides the bottle of
Kingfisher beer in the inside pocket of his suit jacket.*

— 293 —

QUINCY   They won't let you take that in the Air Canada Centre.

AUBREY   It'll be gone by then.

Waving goodbye to their hosts, QUINCY *and* AUBREY *leave the restaurant and walk east on Queen Street.*

AUBREY   So what'd you think?

QUINCY   Nice look. Sexy vibe. But seriously? Amateur Hour at the O.K. Corral.

AUBREY   Why?

QUINCY   Too many fucking things on the menu. A restaurant only has to do eight dishes right. And do them better than anyone else in the city. You have thirty-three things on the menu? It's impossible to do them right.

AUBREY   Why?

QUINCY   Too much choice for the customer. Too much inventory for the kitchen. Too many burners being used for too many different things. Keep it simple. But people complicate shit. I mean, Susheel? Fuck, son. He could lose all his money.

AUBREY   Or lose all Brian Bristol's money.

QUINCY   Or maybe it blows up and Bristol franchises this culinarian shit to Vegas. I don't know. Road is long, motherfuckers. Road is long.

AUBREY's *cellphone jingles with a text. Then another. And another. He pulls his cellphone from his suit jacket and begins reading them.*

QUINCY She text you again?

AUBREY Yep.

QUINCY Do not respond to this shit. These are mind games, son. You won't win.

AUBREY *reads through the texts.*

QUINCY You sure you know what you're doing? Because this woman sure as fuck don't. She doesn't know what she's doing or why she's doing it.

AUBREY Relationships have ups and downs.

QUINCY Ups and downs? This is a woman who tried to run you over with your own car! What the fuck is that?

AUBREY (*as he reads a long text*) Vehicular homicide.

QUINCY That is fucked-up is what that is.

AUBREY Manslaughter on a good day.

QUINCY She would've run you over, thrown you the keys, left you to die, and, here's the thing, you would've thanked her for the keys.

AUBREY Small steps, Quincy.

QUINCY Small steps nothing. When you going to decide
        you're not putting up with this shit? I have *never* seen
        you so fucked-up about a woman. Want my advice?

AUBREY I'm trying to ignore your advice, remember?

QUINCY Two words. Move on. Three more. Too fucking
        crazy.

But AUBREY *does not appear to hear, so absorbed is he in a new
text.*

AUBREY Oh, Jesus.

QUINCY What is it?

AUBREY I don't know about the Raptors, dude.

QUINCY Get the fuck out of here!

AUBREY Krista's in the hospital. She just got admitted.

QUINCY *begins nodding as his face, somewhat gradually, reverts
to his Something Isn't Quite Right expression.*

QUINCY Mmm.

AUBREY She's alone in Emergency. So look—

AUBREY *is taking the Kingfisher beer from his suit jacket and
raising it to his mouth when* QUINCY *stays* AUBREY's *hand.*

QUINCY Don't do this. I need you not to do this.

AUBREY *You* need me?

QUINCY Why she in the hospital? She drunk?

AUBREY That's not the point.

QUINCY Yes, it is.

AUBREY No, it isn't.

QUINCY Yes, it is. Did you put her there?

AUBREY What kind of question is that?

QUINCY Then why you going?

AUBREY I shouldn't help her?

QUINCY You don't know what you're talking about when it
comes to this shit! You got to stop spoiling this girl.

AUBREY Quincy—

QUINCY She *dumped* your ass! Why you doing this?

AUBREY Because I care about her. No one's ever mattered
more. Krista and me—I mean, I'm *in*.

Pause.

QUINCY You talk like a girl.

AUBREY Excuse me?

QUINCY   You talk like a girl. When you going to act like a man?

A severe look starts in AUBREY'*s eyes.*

QUINCY   I have to explain something to you.

AUBREY   No, you don't.

QUINCY   Yes, I do. Because you seeing her—

AUBREY   I don't need—

QUINCY   Listen to me!

AUBREY   —your advice.

QUINCY   Because this isn't—

AUBREY   She doesn't *have* anybody else! Her mother's
         alcoholic. Her father's a wastrel.

QUINCY   Would you fucking *listen* to me?

QUINCY *slaps* AUBREY *full in the face.*

QUINCY   It's not helping!

AUBREY *stiffens.*

QUINCY   You seeing her is not helping!

AUBREY   You want to knock a man down? Hit me again.

QUINCY (*He knows he went too far.*) All right. All right. Okay.

AUBREY What's the matter? Need a reason?

AUBREY *jerks the Kingfisher beer at* QUINCY, *spraying his face.*

AUBREY There. Go for it.

QUINCY *closes his eyes as the beer drips off his chin.*

AUBREY Have a great night.

AUBREY *walks into the street.*

Puckering his lips, and controlling great emotion, QUINCY *opens his eyes and stares at the sidewalk.*

QUINCY McKee?

But AUBREY, *in the middle of Queen Street, keeps on walking.*

QUINCY McKee!

AUBREY *starts sprinting down the street.*

QUINCY AUBREY!

AUBREY *keeps running, staring straight ahead.*

Curtain

Act Three

Two hours later. We are back at Quincy's house on Beaty Avenue. QUINCY *approaches down the sidewalk to see his front door open. Coming closer, he notices splotches of fresh blood on the hallway floor. Instantly on guard,* QUINCY *removes his shoes, grabs the baseball bat from inside the front door, and follows the blood towards the kitchen.*

Hearing movement in the kitchen, QUINCY *stops to listen. He tightens his grip on the baseball bat and creeps closer. As he comes into the doorway, he sees* AUBREY *standing over the sink and washing the burnt stockpot with baking soda and vinegar.* AUBREY *is drunk, he is bleeding from two deep scratches on his face, and his shirt and suit jacket are stained with blood.*

QUINCY *begins laughing, his laughter high-pitched at first, but as he takes in more details—the baking soda on* AUBREY's *nose, the blood dripping from* AUBREY's *cheek, as well as the seriousness with which* AUBREY *scrubs at the stockpot—*QUINCY *is sent into gruff hysterics.*

QUINCY   Time out, time out. Time the fuck out. You want to
         tell me—

Laughing helplessly, QUINCY *drops the baseball bat on the floor.*

QUINCY —what the fuck you doing?

AUBREY *(straight-faced)* Oh. Hey. Well, I was remembering what you said. That you have to have goals. So I remembered one of my goals.

QUINCY What's that?

AUBREY Beer. But I finished it. So I was sad. But then I remembered—

AUBREY *lifts up a tall can of Labatt 50.*

AUBREY —I had more in your fridge. So I was happy. And I drank it. But then it was empty. So I was sad again. But then I remembered—

AUBREY *points to the bottle of El Dorado rum.*

AUBREY —you had rum. So I drank that too. But mostly I remembered—

AUBREY *pulls something from his pants pocket.*

AUBREY —I had your fucking keys!

AUBREY *throws the keys at* QUINCY. *They hit the wall and slide to the floor.*

AUBREY Believe me, I almost threw them in the sewer.

QUINCY *looks at the fallen keys, stares at the blood-splattered* AUBREY, *and bends over with new laughter.*

QUINCY   This is some magnificent fucked-up shit right here. (*He makes a delighted sigh.*) All right, motherfucker. Give me the rum.

QUINCY *takes the El Dorado rum, pulls out a glass, and pours himself a very stiff drink.*

AUBREY   Where were you?

QUINCY   Where you think? I was at three different hospitals looking for your ass. Toronto Western. Mount Sinai. Women's College.

QUINCY *drinks from the rum and sits down at the kitchen island.*

QUINCY   Let me tell you. There were some strange motherfuckers in those Emergencies. Car crash fuckers. A lady with a spike in her head. Homeless dude who wanted to sell me a trumpet.

AUBREY   How much he want for it?

QUINCY   I kept waiting for the paramedics to wheel you in dead.

QUINCY *drinks again from the rum.*

QUINCY   All right, motherfucker. What happened? She all right?

AUBREY *slowly nods.*

QUINCY   Glad you went?

AUBREY *slowly shakes his head.*

QUINCY   You want to tell me why you're bleeding?

AUBREY *thinks about that . . . and slowly shakes his head again.*

QUINCY   Is that your blood?

AUBREY *takes some paper towel, wets it under the faucet, and wipes his bloody face.*

AUBREY   I don't feel at this interval a pressing need to talk about it.

QUINCY   Anything you *do* want to talk about?

Pause.

AUBREY   I will say I did not deserve to be treated the way I was just treated. (*He shivers.*) And it's not right what happened.

QUINCY   Doesn't matter.

AUBREY   It's not fair, either.

QUINCY   Doesn't matter.

AUBREY   It does to me.

QUINCY Doesn't matter who's right or what's fair. That's not where she at right now.

QUINCY *watches* AUBREY *for a few seconds.*

QUINCY So what happened?

AUBREY Well—

AUBREY *jiggles his glass of rum in an ironic sort of toast.*

AUBREY Krista has a little problem with raging at me for ridiculously inconsequential reasons—

QUINCY Sounds familiar.

AUBREY —which does not seem justified and which I find highly fucking frustrating. And I'm trying not to take out my frustration on her even though I am totally justified—

QUINCY Sounds *very* familiar.

AUBREY —and instead I'm trying to validate her feelings. But halfway into it I'm like, "Why should I validate her feelings when they're the *wrong* fucking feelings?"

QUINCY For you.

AUBREY For—what?

QUINCY For you they're wrong. For her they're not.

AUBREY   Whose side are you on?

QUINCY   It's how she deals with her shit, how you deal with
         your shit, and how you as a couple deal with shit
         together.

AUBREY   What was the third thing?

QUINCY   It's that third thing, motherfucker. That third thing.
         And the way I see it? You as a couple ain't working.
         Krista and McKee? Ain't fucking working. You got
         to let her be. Because, motherfucker? The more
         you put into it, the less it matters. You don't get
         that yet?

AUBREY   And you don't get I'm in love with her?

QUINCY   And how's that working out? Seriously. How's that
         working out for you? You think love conquers all?
         Love don't conquer shit. Not without respect. For
         three years, you been walking on eggshells—

AUBREY   I've been walking in a minefield—

QUINCY   Yeah, and you keep getting blown up! Look at
         yourself. Covered in your own blood. Bleeding all
         over my kitchen. This is what love looks like?
         Why do you do this? Why do you *keep* doing this?
         You may want to ask yourself that.

AUBREY   There aren't a lot of people in the world who
         care about her. She needs to know someone cares
         about her.

QUINCY   She know already. That's why she fucked-up.
          It's like I said, you're not helping.

AUBREY   It's not helping that someone *cares* about her?
          She's lived her whole life without anyone caring
          about her. This bright, brilliant woman. The
          injustice of that is ridiculous.

QUINCY   Hmm-mmm.

AUBREY   Her parents are writeoffs. She was sexually assaulted
          at her last job. It's not always easy being a woman—

QUINCY   Oh, it ain't easy being green, motherfucker.

AUBREY   Quincy, what the fuck? Are you listening to me?
          What happened to her was not her fault.

QUINCY   But neither is it—look at me now—but neither is it
          your responsibility. The problem with you is you
          think you're fucking Rumpelstiltskin.

AUBREY   She's a lot cuter than Rumpelstiltskin.

QUINCY   You want to spin this shit into gold, and it ain't
          happening.

AUBREY   She doesn't have anyone else in the world.

QUINCY   She has herself. That's more important than you
          right now. She's the only one who can save herself
          or change herself or whatever-the-fuck herself.

Psychiatrists say this shit for a reason,
motherfucker. Because it's true. She is her own way
and the truth and the life. Maybe take a moment to
reflect on this shit.

AUBREY *pours himself some more rum.*

AUBREY Quincy, I thought I was the luckiest man in the
world. I thought I'd won the lottery. I didn't care
where I was. I was happy just walking across a
parking lot with Krista. Because I knew if I was
with her, I'd be happy.

QUINCY Hmm-mmm. But where you putting your energy,
son? And how much longer you want to do this?
How much longer *can* you do this? Plates thrown
at your head. Punched in the face. And this shit is
still making sense to you?

QUINCY *takes the rum and liberally refills his glass.*

QUINCY This is social work. Figure this shit out. Because,
let me tell you something, this is fucking you up.

AUBREY So what am I supposed to do?

QUINCY Send her goodwill. Rub a crystal. Do your little
butterfly dance. But let Krista be Krista. Get out of
her way. Don't mess with the bitch no more.

AUBREY You understand this is somewhat
counterintuitive—

QUINCY   I *know* it's counterintuitive.

AUBREY   —given that I've been with this woman every
              day—

QUINCY   That's why someone got to tell you.

AUBREY   —and there's no one else I care about.

QUINCY   Hmm-mmm.

There is a small silence. Then, with a sudden gasp, tears come to
AUBREY's *eyes, tears that he immediately clears away.*

AUBREY   This is fucking me up so hard.

QUINCY *is about to say something when he decides to stay quiet.*

AUBREY *swirls his glass then sets it on the table. He wipes at his eyes.*

AUBREY   But it's not working. I hate that it's not working.
              But it's not.

QUINCY   I'll tell you what does work. Calling her on her
              fucked-up shit and getting her to be accountable
              for her fucked-up choices. That's what works. And
              if she can't do that—

AUBREY   I don't think she can do that. Not right now.

QUINCY   Then you got to book. Because this shit's not
              sustainable. Guaranteed. One hundred percent.

A drop of blood trickles off AUBREY's *face. He wipes this off the kitchen island and then, sensing another drop about to fall, he positions his glass to catch it. When the drop falls inside the glass, he watches it diffuse within the rum.*

AUBREY   I hate that I'm bleeding. It's fucking embarrassing.

QUINCY   Yeah, motherfucker? If you took my advice when I said—

AUBREY   *(interrupting)* Really, Tynes? I've been listening to you for three fucking hours. I'm done listening. And you don't get to say that to me.

AUBREY *angrily shakes his head. He rubs his face then looks to* QUINCY *as if to say, "How do you not know this?"*

QUINCY   It's all right. I forgive you.

AUBREY   You forgive *me*? How the fuck do you get to forgive me? What'd I do wrong? You forgive me? You don't even *listen* to me. All you do is tell people what to do.

QUINCY *reaches for the rum and tops up his glass.*

QUINCY   Can I help it if I know this shit?

AUBREY   Can I help it if I don't? Your problem is you keep telling everybody what *their* problem is. Look, Quincy. No one's been kinder to me in times of trouble and strife than you. You took me in when I didn't have a place to live. And the meals and drinks I owe you are fucking countless. And I thank you for that. I do. But, motherfucker, just listen once in a while. That's all you have to do. Sometimes people are idiots. But you don't have to fix them. Or tell them what to do. Or what dishes to have on the menu. All you have to do is listen. I've been listening to you for eight years and just once—*once*—in eight years I'm asking you to hold off with the advice and give me a fucking break. Is that asking too much?

There is from QUINCY *a long and somewhat studied pause.*

QUINCY I'm listening.

AUBREY Go *easy* on me, motherfucker. For fuck's sake, I'm barely holding on. I've got a movie studio who fucked me over. A girlfriend who tried to run me over. I don't need my friends smacking me in the face too.

QUINCY *pushes out his lower lip.*

QUINCY I did...I didn't...What I did didn't help.

AUBREY I have been trying to do everything right and everything wrong is happening to me. Can you understand why I might feel fucked-up?

QUINCY *slowly nods.*

AUBREY   And that I can't see Krista anymore, and I have to
          change my whole fucking *life*, is going to mess me
          up. Because now I'm thinking about all the moments
          of the last three years and where do they go?

QUINCY   Into the junkyard of fucked-up relationships.

AUBREY   That's a big junkyard.

QUINCY   That's a *very* big junkyard.

AUBREY   I didn't want them to go into a junkyard. I didn't
          get into this for that.

QUINCY   Nobody does.

Pause.

QUINCY   She was raped?

AUBREY *nods*.

QUINCY   The poor girl. I feel sorry for her.

AUBREY   I feel terrible for her.

QUINCY   This is not good. Oh, this is not good.

QUINCY *gets up and gazes into the serving pantry. Noticing the
album from earlier,* The Three Degrees, *he walks over to it. He is
about to put it back in the box when he takes out the record and*

places it on the turntable. He switches on the turntable, picks up the needle, and drops it on the second track, "Can't You See What You're Doing to Me."

As this music begins, QUINCY *returns to the kitchen, grabs his glass of rum, and sits down. He listens for half a minute, the song sending him to another place in his mind.*

QUINCY Do you remember Lydia's mother?

AUBREY She looked like Diahann Carroll.

QUINCY She's prettier than Diahann Carroll. Diahann Carrol's a fine-looking woman, but she doesn't have shit on Zab. Zab stop a room cold. Zab give men wet dreams for weeks. Men lost their motherfucking minds. I know I did. Damn near lost my life.

QUINCY *downs his rum and reaches for the bottle.*

QUINCY Not a day goes by I don't think of her. And most of the time? Wouldn't change a thing. But six days a year were a disaster. And three were worse than that.

He pours himself another full glass of rum.

QUINCY I remember, I think Lydia was a year old, I was so broke, I was so down. Zabby and I split. No job. I couldn't see a way forward. But I had to find a way. I remember it was raining, I was on Duke Street in Halifax and went into Scotia Square to dry off in the department store. Was it a Zellers?

AUBREY   Woolco.

QUINCY   Woolco. And what did they have? Red tag sales?

AUBREY   Dollar forty-four day.

QUINCY   Dollar forty-four day! (*He smiles at the memory.*)
Fucking hell. I haven't thought of that in years.
How do you remember this shit? That fucking
amazes me. What else you remember?

AUBREY   In Scotia Square? Petsville.

QUINCY   Hmm.

AUBREY   Hobby Shoppe.

QUINCY   Hmm-mmm.

AUBREY   Cinema Scotia Square.

QUINCY   Cinema Scotia Square! That's where I saw
Apocalypse Now with my father. He ain't never
seen no shit like that. What does Duvall say?
Smells like destiny?

AUBREY   Smells like victory.

QUINCY   Who the fuck else is going to remember this?
Cinema Scotia Square. Do you remember the
Lobster Trap?

AUBREY   The Fabulous Lobster Trap Cabaret.

QUINCY   It was a strip club called the Lobster Trap. You
         can't make this shit up! Who else remembers this
         shit? Nobody remembers this shit but you, McKee.
         You have a good memory. That's worth something.
         Crazy fucking kid. Twelve years old and following
         Howard Fudge into the Halifax dockyards.

Pause.

QUINCY   I'm rooting for you, son. You are a crazy-ass
         motherfucker and you pick the craziest women I
         have *ever* seen, but I'm rooting for you. Whatever it
         is you want to do. And you can tell me to go to hell
         if you want, I just don't want to see you dead from
         drinking at forty-six. My brother, Maurice—
         Reeso—he died from drinking. Shit.

QUINCY *pours himself some more rum.*

QUINCY   Killing yourself is no way to live.

"A Woman Needs a Good Man" begins on the stereo and QUINCY
goes silent.

AUBREY *stands, lurches to the sink behind Quincy, and resumes
scrubbing the stockpot.*

After a while, QUINCY *speaks again.*

QUINCY   God put us on this earth for a reason, McKee. And
         that rainy day in Woolco, I understood something
         about mistakes. And if I can teach you one—

He looks for but can't find AUBREY.

QUINCY The fuck you at?

AUBREY *continues to scrub the stockpot.*

QUINCY Because there's going to come a day when you
        beyond this shit. But you got to work to get there.
        If you ain't working, it ain't happening. You sit
        around drinking, ain't no one going to find you.

AUBREY *rinses the pot under the faucet.*

QUINCY This shit's tough. Life ain't fair. But you can work
        to make things better. Just don't let no bullshit
        distract you.

AUBREY *raises the clean stockpot.*

AUBREY There.

AUBREY *drops the stockpot in front of* QUINCY.

AUBREY Finished.

AUBREY *staggers around to the other side of the kitchen island.*

QUINCY So where you at now?

AUBREY *sits down and picks up his glass of rum.*

AUBREY I'm drunk. I'm fucked-up...

QUINCY Hmm.

AUBREY And I need to heal. I just don't know how.

AUBREY *burps and picks up his cellphone. He struggles to read a text then puts it down.*

QUINCY Everybody makes mistakes.

AUBREY Pfft.

AUBREY *slumps forward, his head hovering above the kitchen island.*

QUINCY But it's not your mistakes that make you—

AUBREY*'s head hits the kitchen island with an audible thunk. From the sound of it, that would have hurt. But* AUBREY *doesn't move.*

QUINCY It's how you come back from your mistakes, that's
         what makes you.

QUINCY *sees* AUBREY *is out cold.*

QUINCY Hmm.

AUBREY*'s cellphone jingles with a new text. After another moment, it begins to ring.* QUINCY *is staring at this cellphone when the album's final song, "When Will I See You Again," begins on the turntable in the other room.*

QUINCY God fucking damn it.

QUINCY *listens, humming along to the song, his eyes tearing up, and pours himself what is left in the bottle of El Dorado rum.*

QUINCY   When I hear this song, I think of Zabby. And Zabby wasn't always so—

He scratches at the scar below his collarbone.

QUINCY   But when Zabby was…she was…she was…

His head droops.

QUINCY   She was everything…She was everything.

He stares into the bottle of rum.

QUINCY   I'll tell you what I miss. I miss the beginning of her laugh. I miss her warmth in bed. I miss her sleeping beside me. The smell of her shoulder. The smoothness of her thighs. The *thighs* of this woman.

He pauses as a tear slips down his cheek.

QUINCY   So I'm *still* in love with her?

He closes his eyes.

QUINCY   How is this shit possible?

A tear dribbles off his chin.

QUINCY When does it stop? When does it fucking stop?

*He tilts forward. He is falling into a drunken sleep, and the song
beginning to fade, when* LYDIA TYNES (17) *walks into the
kitchen carrying her backpack.*

Putting down her backpack, she takes in the scene: AUBREY
unconscious and bleeding, and QUINCY *passed out, his hand
clenching a glass of rum.*

As a skip in the record sends the song back to the chorus, LYDIA *asks
her own question, which, although spoken in a prolonged falsetto, is
actually quite simple.*

LYDIA   What the *fuck?*

Curtain

END BOOK TWO